MW01236321

The Hurricane Code
Copyright 2020 by James Aura
Cover by R.D. Price

* * * * *

My thanks go out to those who provided assistance for this book, especially, my patient wife, Vicki. I received excellent input from Beta readers, including Tom Sweeney in Florida, Rose White in British Columbia, and Ric Joyce in Minnesota. Members of the Write Stride Writer's group also provided helpful feedback and critiques.

* * * * *

Also by James Aura: The Kentucky Mystery series:
Set in 1975: When Saigon Surrendered: Copyright 2015
Set in 1985: The Cumberland Killers: Copyright 2018

Treat the earth well,
It was not given to you by your parents,
It was loaned to you by your children.
-- Native American Proverb

Cast of Characters: Minnesota, Missouri, Kansas, North Dakota and Saskatchewan

Gabe Cameron, climate refugee and menial
Roxanne Branson, computer scientist, resident of The Uppsala
Dr. James Branson, billionaire entrepreneur and computer scientist, Roxanne's father
Zeb Wolf, climate refugee and menial
Honcho, boss of the menials
Randall Parsons, resident manager of The Uppsala, known as 'Handsome Devil'
Nancy Ruehl, Roxanne's friend and resident of The Uppsala
Gary Hartbauer, climate refugee and childhood friend of Gabe's
Marie and Artemis Cameron, Gabe's parents, farmers, climate refugees
Junie Cameron, Artemis' cousin in Estes Park, Colorado
Lin Wei, computer programmer, climate refugee
Burt, a Kansas plainsman
Pauline, Burt's sister
Kenny, Burt's associate
Caden, a three year old climate refugee from Memphis
Ella Daughtry, Caden's great-grandmother, climate refugee
Isaac Bender, young Mennonite farmer in Kansas
Esther Bender, Isaac's teenage sister
Ginny, Esther's friend
William Swift Horse and Takoda Wolf, Zeb Wolf's Lakota Sioux cousins
Matthew Bender, Isaac and Esther's uncle

Dr. Xavier Dillon, resident of the Bergen Retirement Center

Ricardo Ortega, resident of The Uppsala, known as 'Prince Charming'

Ivar the Ripper, a leader of the Blood Reds, a teenage gang in Fargo, Dakota

Hermes, a vegetable vendor just north of the Canadian border

Gray Gown people and sentinels, climate refugees from Florida

Branson Entity 91560 'Searcher', a sentient artificial intelligence program

Quantum One, a powerful A.I. computer and mentor to Searcher

The Hunter, a moving and storage robot illegally programmed to hunt and kill

Daisy, an eight year old hinny, owned by plainsmen

Captain, Isaac and Esther's goat-herding dog

Thunder, a huge Percheron gelding

Mantacore and Jahan, Bengal tiger brothers, escapees from an Oklahoma zoo

The Saffir-Simpson Hurricane Wind Scale in 2099:

Tropical Storm 39-73 mph (some property damage, possible tornadoes)

Category 1 74-95 mph (dangerous winds will cause extensive damage)

Category 2 96-110 mph (Extremely dangerous winds will cause extreme damage)

Category 3 111-129 mph (Devastating damage will occur, high risk to human life)

Category 4 130-156 mph (Catastrophic damage extensive loss of life)

Category 5 157-179 mph (Catastrophic damage, widespread loss of life)

Category 6 180-219 mph - added in 2029 (significant population reduction)

Category 7 220-269 mph - added in 2086 (significant population reduction)

Category 8 270+ mph - added in 2099 (unsurvivable event over a wide area)

The Hurricane Code

Searcher: What is a tribulation?
Quantum One: Why do you ask?
Searcher: People are talking about it.
Quantum One: Use the dictionary.
Searcher: It says 'a time of great trouble or suffering.'

    Huge black clouds boiled in the sky as the storm raked the oak savannah north of Minneapolis. Gabe Cameron looked out his window watching the tempest. Howling wind gusts ripped the leaves from trees. The forest swayed and shook until the land itself seemed alive and moving. Gabe picked up his coffee cup and thought about the old woman's words from the night before. "You get out," she had said as she stared at her dice on the table. "There is nothing but bad for you here. You may be dead soon if you do not leave."

    After some reflection, he dismissed her warning. The woman didn't even use real dice. They were strange little things carved from deer antler into three and four-sided shapes with images of animals and symbols. But soothsayers were always worth a listen. One had saved his life when she told him to stay home from work the next day. Later, he stayed out too late with friends, and had used her as his excuse to sleep late. Sure enough, a dragline broke and crashed into his crew in the Ozarks, killing eight men. But this old woman with the funny dice; somehow her prediction felt wrong.

    The wind shrieked as it whipped around the building. With concrete and granite walls three feet thick, this place should be good shelter from the storm raging outside. Gabe flinched as the wind blew a large branch off a tree in the front gardens. He'd tended those sculptured grounds only yesterday. Now there would be more mess to clean up. At least he didn't have to go outside now.

He had no room to complain. They'd taken him in here at The Uppsala, a residence for rich people. The condos stretched up twenty stories, towering above the oaks and pines north of Coon Rapids. The complex sat inside a walled community with security police and robots that used machine guns and heat cannons to keep the outside world away from the gate. Gabe wasn't about to leave this place. It was safe here, and he got two good meals nearly every day.

The weather meter on the solar window showed the wind speed at 80 mph and the temperature was a cool 75, down 30 degrees since the storm hit. Every window on The Uppsala doubled as a solar unit and weather gauge. Weather was a big thing in the summer of 2099... an all-consuming problem everywhere now.

This storm was the remains of Hurricane Theta, which roared up the Mississippi River, pushing gigantic waves of water north. It was the 34th storm of hurricane season, which now occupied ten months of the year. When it hit what used to be Baton Rouge, on July 12th, it carried winds of 230 mph. Fortunately, Gabe thought, these walls could take it...even a category seven, they said. But only the rich and their servants lived here, in the flat wooded fields of Minnesota. Ordinary people outside were on their own.

Gabe was the newest servant to be chosen. He was well-favored, broad-shouldered, thick chest, like a football player who'd stopped working out. Gabe Cameron was 22, about the age of a college senior-- if they still had college back home. His mistress was in her early 20's, a dark-haired beauty. Rich men flocked to her door, for what, he wasn't sure. The customs were strange here. The Uppsala people took Gabe in and assigned him to her, two years after the snakes came north. His mistress gave him his own bedroom on the first floor and made few demands. He couldn't believe his good fortune, and he had no idea why they'd picked him. He'd come north to get a new start, leaving his parents behind in 120-degree heat with swarms of mosquitoes and an invasion of pythons on their farm near Seymour, Missouri.

He'd found this place through his best friend, who'd been recruited by an ad on the FreeNews six months earlier. But now his friend Gary had disappeared. His mistress said only that Gary hadn't made the cut.

Twenty miles south, Minneapolis was chaotic, filled with refugees from southern states. They slept in alleys and in parks. New tent cities went up every night next to the Mississippi in St. Paul. Every morning hundreds appeared on the banks of the river, throwing in fishing lines, hoping to catch breakfast. People hungered for protein, and the algae cakes from the charities left most unsatisfied. But they had plenty of food at The Uppsala.

The rain and wind raged on for hours. There wouldn't be much left of the tent cities after this. Then a bolt of lightning split an oak tree in the courtyard only 50 feet away. The blast made the building shake. Gabe stared at the sheets of rain pushed sideways by the wind. He wondered if there was some chore he should be doing right now. The walls of his small room were gray concrete. He had only a cot, a shelf, and a metal chair. The toilet was down the hall, primitive but cool in summer and apparently warm in winter. This place felt safe. He didn't want to be kicked out, like Gary.

9

Chapter Two

Mistress Roxanne watched the storm through the windows of her condo eight stories above. She looked out her balcony door and the damp wind howled as it tore at her eyes and hair. It was a dreadful night to be outside. She withdrew and dried off, then touched up her makeup and walked to answer the door. The walls of her lavish condo self adjusted to reflect her mood and blood pressure. Right now they were beige. She wore her best black tights and a blue tank top to show off her figure.

Even in the storms, the suitors came, and she was obliged to see them. Her father had gotten her into this place, but the rules were rigid. She had to marry and conceive within the first two years, or leave. The procreation license required this, and she had to follow the protocols. Men here were milquetoasts, sons of billionaires who told stories about their previous lives of leisure at places like Kiawah, Hilton Head, and the Catskills. The ocean had long since overtaken Kiawah and Hilton Head. Hordes from New York City overran the Catskills as they fled the rising sea. She knew Minneapolis would soon have the same problem, but at least here in The Uppsala, it was quiet, sometimes too quiet.

She thought about the strong young man they had selected for her manservant as she reached for the doorknob. He was nothing like the individual standing outside her door. That person looked as if he wanted to leap across the threshold and pounce on her. He was about her age, with a full beard and sharp eyes. When he smiled, his canines flashed as if he was ready to tear into a tenderloin sandwich. Some of the women had a nickname for him: 'Handsome Devil.' She'd seen him at the mixers and she knew his story. But still, she would have to give him some time, hear him out.

He bowed, "Mistress Roxanne, I am Master Randall Parsons of the Phoenix Parsons." They all said the same damn thing every time. It was the rule.
"I am Master Irvin Geffin of the Los Angeles Geffins."
"I am Master Slade Trump of the New York Trumps."
"I am Master Burton Bezos of the Seattle Bezos."
All of it, so boring.

She sighed, "And I am Roxanne Branson of the Pittsburgh Bransons. Won't you come in?"

He sat in the living room while she went into the kitchen and brought a pot of tea. Most people here had DNA enhancement. She wondered what his was, as she poured the tea, and he broke the silence.

"FreeNews says this storm will be gone tomorrow. Would you like to go for a walk outside in the afternoon?"

Roxanne smiled. "I'll be getting my hair done. But tell me, why do you watch the FreeNews?" She decided he looked even more repulsive than the first time he'd come. She hated these arranged courtship meetings, but The Uppsala required them.

"Your hair looks fine to me. A little wind-blown, maybe. I check the FreeNews because I like to be aware of what those outside are told. It could come in handy sometime."

"My manservant does that for me. He tells me what's going on outside."
Randall smirked, "You talk to your manservant?"

Neither of them reminisced about their ancestral homes. The Atlantic Ocean and its storms had pushed refugees west until the homeless overran Pittsburgh.

Phoenix, out of water for decades, had returned to rocky desert, scoured by gigantic sandstorms, dry as the Sahara and uninhabitable. The silence was awkward. He rose and gave her a polite bow.

"Thanks for the tea. I'm going to have a conversation with my cat. He'll tell me more than a manservant would. Have you ever observed menials in the dining hall? It's like feeding time at the zoo."
He paused and stared at her A.I. console.

"Roxanne, my father's company has a beautiful new development at Halti. I could take you for a visit, maybe on vacation."

"The one in Finland? Since the Tundra melted, don't they have a methane problem up there?"
"Not that I heard."
"Well, if you'd watch the PayNews, you would know, Master Randall."

She nodded towards the doorway, his signal to give up and go away. She bolted the door behind him, feeling relieved he had not proposed. During Randall's visit, it felt like the temperature in the room had dropped by ten degrees, although the wall thermometer showed no change. She knew her comments about the manservant and the PayNews would put him off. Like many, he regarded the menial class as subhuman. She'd overheard him ranting at the mixers. He wasn't the type to pay for expensive, authentic information, the kind available by paid subscription.

Randall Parsons walked to the elevator, pausing to glance at the storm which was now slamming birds and tree limbs into The Uppsala's fortified guard tower. He'd expected this encounter to go nowhere, but she could be a good match. Their investment holdings were compatible, and they had financial synergy. Well, at least he'd left her a little gift, one he hoped her A.I. wouldn't notice. She was one of the better-looking women here, willowy but filled out nicely in all the right places. She looked vaguely like a movie star. He couldn't remember who.

* * * * *

The howling wind threw shredded pieces of tents past Roxanne's windows. What would Minneapolis be like in the morning? A mess, no doubt. It was a shame so many refugees now occupied the Twin Cities. She spoke to her A.I. terminal through her neural-link, as she keyed in a request to her father for a searcher Entity. The kitchen robot brought her a small roast from the refrigerator. She cut off a slice, ate it with seaweed salad, finished her tea, and resumed work at her terminal. The wall above her video screen held a large satellite photo of four large hurricanes moving over Puerto Rico, the remains of Florida, and the Yucatan Peninsula, along with Cape Cod.

She logged in with fingerprints, eyes, and voice, pulling up a huge field of code. This would most likely be her life's work, an obsession tied to a bank of quantum computers. Hurricanes dominated much of the earth, and Roxanne Branson was attempting to dissect one, down to the moment a tropical wave became a tropical storm. The basic ingredients were: heat, low pressure, wind, and water vapor. But creation of a hurricane involved much more. The atmospheric factors were gigantic.

Her father's powerful computers ran hurricane simulations twenty-four hours a day, to identify a storm's point of weakness, the instant when hurricane

13

formation might be stopped by outside forces. This time, the computers reported no progress. She tweaked updrafts, downdrafts, ocean surface temperature, and the simulation resumed. The physics was complex, the task might be insurmountable, but she persisted.

Chapter Three

The next morning they rousted the menials at sunrise to clean up the storm debris. Even though slate gray clouds lined the sky, the gardens were already heating up. The workers wore their yellow uniforms with orange gloves, making them easy to identify. Gabe helped his friend pick up a section of tree trunk the robots had cut, and heaved it into a truck bed. Gabe couldn't get used to the idea of robots doing semi-skilled labor like cutting trees. The men were not allowed to touch equipment like saws, nor could they drive trucks. The robots functioned as interchangeable tools. Today saws extended from their arms. His buddy Zeb Wolf, a Lakota Sioux from Dakota, shook his head while the A.I. truck pulled out of the courtyard, loaded with tree limbs and leaves.

Zeb said, "Doesn't it make you feel weird seeing the robots running saws? The damn things look dangerous." Zeb was tall and wiry with long black hair. Their accents were so different they sometimes had to repeat things to one another.

"Well, they don't have your charming personality, but yeah it is creepy," Gabe said.

He glanced up toward Mistress Roxanne's balcony and could see her staring down, watching them work. Gabe turned to Zeb. "I wonder what they do all day, up there. She has me come up now and then and watch the PayNews; different from the stuff we get. She's got something on a big screen she calls 'Immersion Reality' too, really something."

Zeb pulled a long strand of hair back from his face. "How was PayNews different? I'd like to pay her a little news myself...if you know what I mean."

"More about what's going on around the whole world. She always wants to know what I hear from the outside, too. Once, when I went up there, her big screen was filled with a bunch of numbers and symbols, maybe some kind of code, but she turned that off right away."

Gabe saw a small bird, its wing impaled on a bent wire sticking out from the courtyard wall. It fluttered weakly as he approached. He gently pulled it off the hook-shaped wire, tossed it straight up, and it disappeared over the barrier.

Zeb wiped his forehead. "If we were still outside, we'd be having that finch for dinner."

"Yeah, don't remind me."

The foreman, the man they called Honcho, scowled as he walked toward them and Gabe didn't want to get on his bad side. They raked up the leaves that still covered the manicured courtyard lawn. Honcho was overweight, white-haired, and wheezing in the heat. It was 89 degrees, and they were heading for a high of 104. He trudged past them and began scolding two other menials who talked while they leaned on their rakes. Asian Tiger mosquitoes the size of houseflies began to bite the workers for a morning blood meal. The oversized mosquitoes resulted from genetic warfare gone awry.

An hour later the grounds of the Uppsala looked good as new. Gabe and Zeb, swatted at the persistent insects, went to the dining hall and got in line for breakfast.

Honcho stood in front of the serving station and announced, "Breakfast will be a little light this morning because of the storm, but there'll be plenty to eat tonight." This brought a muted groan from the group.

They proceeded through the line and kitchen robots dished them out small bowls of watery cereal and thin-sliced tongue. There was always plenty of coffee, and next to the coffee dispenser sat a large basket of algae cakes. Gabe grabbed three. Zeb turned up his nose.

"I don't know why you eat those things. Damn near worse than going hungry."
Gabe chomped on a cake. The savory flavor was not unpleasant. "Vitamins, they got vitamins and minerals for strong bones."

Zeb laughed. "Prairie dog food if you ask me. Fresh greens are OK, but these…"

"Wait till the big snakes make it to the Dakotas. They'll love your prairie dogs."

They sat at a long table with twenty others and everyone turned on their Life-Links for the morning news, watching while they ate. Life-Link chimes filled the room as the workers switched them on.

"Life-Link- Your best life is on the line."

Then the commercials started. The Copenhagen, half a mile to the north, was advertising to hire workers. It was another high-rise of granite and gray steel, with solar windows. Concertina wire topped its surrounding solar wall. The FreeNews said the storm had moved north to Winnipeg and a new tropical system was building in the ocean just off Nicaragua. Gabe again thought about Mistress Roxanne and how she occupied her time on the eighth floor. He wondered what family of billionaires she was descended from. They weren't allowed to ask about last names. Then his mind replayed the scene of the old woman with the gleaming eyes tossing the dice in the woods: An image he didn't like to confront. A wrinkle of worry crossed his brow about her dark prediction.

Chapter Four

Four miles east of Seymour in southern Missouri, Gabe's parents, Artemis and Marie Cameron, finished packing their bags, ready for the A.I. Van to pick them up. They were giving up on their 300-acre home place. Pythons and Boas had devoured the Cameron's young pigs, and all the chickens. At least there were no rabbits or deer left to damage the garden. Marie gathered the last of the tomatoes and cucumbers and walked toward the shade shelter, carrying a shotgun. She had been lovely, once. The hard life on the farm and years in the sun had wrinkled her skin and turned it a mottled, freckled tan. The thermometer on the tree showed the temperature at 112 and with the humidity, it felt warmer. A hot breeze made Marie's brown eyes water.

The utility company had cut off their power a day early, plunging them into darkness the night before. Neither Marie nor Artemis had slept much in the stifling heat. She absently prodded an armadillo that scrambled from the shade into a burrow, and placed the gun against the tree, picked up a hoe and killed a scorpion. She sat on the bench, exhausted, melancholy, and sweating.

Artemis was a large rugged man with sad eyes and hair the same color as Gabe's, light brown. He gathered up several family photos in the living room, some of Gabe and some with the three of them. He looked around, reflecting on their lives together in this place. He'd saved the pictures for last. Finally, he walked outside with the bags and locked the front door on their gray bunker of a farmhouse. Artemis looked at Marie and said, "Too bad the snakes don't eat scorpions and spiders; they eat damn near everything else."

She sat gazing at the waves of moisture the hot sun drew from the earth. They flinched when they heard a slight rumble, afraid the New Madrid fault was acting up again. Then they saw the shine coming off the polycrystalline-covered A.I. Van approaching from Poplar Bluff.

They carried their belongings onboard into the comfort of 85-degree air conditioning. A light antigen mist moistened their faces. The A.I. checked them for fever and body weight, then warned they were twelve pounds over the luggage weight limit. Marie stared vacantly at her bags of vegetables. She was too exhausted to consider what to throw out. Artemis hesitated, then tossed out the cucumbers and a small canvas bag of dress shoes. The A.I. chimed and they began their journey to Estes Park, Colorado. Artemis' cousin lived there and had urged them to come. He'd sent transportation papers authorizing them to enter Colorado. The trip would take a week, with transfers in Kansas City, Wichita, and Denver.

The cool air revived Marie a bit. She sighed and sat up, taking Artemis' hand and wondering about their only son, Gabe, born just weeks after the procreation laws took hold.

"Still nothing from Gabriel since he got to Minnesota. I hope he's all right."

Artemis stared out the window at an alligator lunging from a slough, chasing a forty pound swamp rat. "Hurricane hit them hard. Maybe their power has been out."

They passed a large robo-trac mowing hay. The countryside here was nearly deserted, most farm families had moved on. Robots managed crops and the farmhouses that remained were mostly built in a storm bunker design, shelter against the extreme weather.

The A.I. spoke to them. "My scan has picked up problematic levels of Stachybotrys on your possessions. Please proceed through a cleansing station when you transfer in Kansas City."

Artemis replied loudly. He was not comfortable having a conversation with an A.I.
"What is that... is it dangerous?"

The A.I. paused, checking its database. "Stachybotrys is a common form of black mold. It is often found in buildings with high humidity and heat. If inhaled or ingested, it can be toxic. This van is mold resistant, but you and your clothing are not. Also, please be informed this van will not stop in Springfield because of a new outbreak of hemorrhagic fever."

This meant they would have the van to themselves all the way to Bolivar. They leaned against one another as the vehicle rolled over the rough blacktop road through the abandoned Ozark hills towards Diggins. Marie drifted into a restless sleep and Artemis, enjoyed the air conditioning and imagined what life might be like seven thousand feet above sea level in the Rockies. He planned to check his bank account in Kansas City to see if the promised funds from the realty A.I. had been deposited. They had sold their farm to a company developing 'end of days' survival homes deep in the limestone caverns of the Ozarks. The land hadn't brought as much as they wanted, but he expected it would be sufficient for a fresh start. At least it was better money than a nasty orchard agent had offered.

He tucked the shotgun beneath their seat. At age 44, he and Marie were reasonably healthy and strong. He hoped his cousin could help them get settled in one of the National Park work camps, and they'd be able to get in touch with Gabe. Maybe he could join them in the Rockies.

Chapter Five

Far to the north, in his A.I. lab near Regina, Saskatchewan, Dr. James Branson stroked his gray beard as he uploaded a highly intelligent program called an 'entity'. Short, chubby, and bald, he looked older than his years. As he sent the program to his daughter at The Uppsala, he worried about Roxanne and whether she would ever settle down. She'd never be fully satisfied with the life of the idle rich, but the world at large was now too dangerous. He wasn't surprised when, through an encrypted message, she'd asked him for the strongest digital spy tool available. He assumed she wanted it for protection, but he also knew his daughter's inquisitiveness could not be easily contained.

If she could find the man of her dreams and settle down in a safe place, he would be happy. With the world in its present state, a baby was optional. If she made the Uppsala her permanent home, the baby would be essential. Under the lease agreement, a father would have to accompany the baby, as well. He observed as the program configured itself for rapid transmission and left his lab in a burst of light. Then he walked outside to his porch and noticed a storm rolling towards the walled enclave of the Bergen Condos. The gigantic cloud spiral from Hurricane Theta had arrived over Regina.

In her condo at The Uppsala, Roxanne watched with relief as her A.I notified her it was downloading a search entity. The A.I. scanned it, pronounced the entity 'superior' and released it for her use. She dispatched the entity, a program of advanced understanding, to search the Uppsala's video and data servers. It disguised itself as a maintenance bot.

Something odd was happening in this playground for the ultra-rich and she wanted to understand it.

Roxanne sent her father a thank-you icon, walked to her balcony and looked down on the men and robots cleaning up storm debris. She saw Gabe and his buddy glance up and started to wave, then decided she shouldn't. To her, Gabe was refreshing; naive but with a native intelligence that turned up even in brief conversations. His face was open and honest.

She was lonesome in this place, and when Gabe was around, she felt at ease. He seemed to have no avarice or resentment, and smiles came easily when he arrived to do chores.

She opened her storm simulator to investigate the latest run. Her opening screen with the Mayan god Hurucan appeared. She said, "Simulator, report!" Hoping this time, for positive results.

It showed only tiny progress in her effort to find a storm's inflection point… somewhere between a thunderstorm and tropical cyclogenesis. She entered code furiously for ten minutes and launched the program again. Giant solar powered pumps to bring cooler ocean water to the surface in hurricane hot spots also held promise, but simulations would show whether the idea was worthwhile. This cycle would take days. She watched as the quantums, safely housed deep within a mountain near Banff, began their simulation.

The kitchen signaled that breakfast was ready. She retrieved her bowl of fruit, nuts, and oatmeal, sat at the table, watching the morning information stream from PayNews. Artificial intelligence terminals customized the service using customer preferences, dealing in facts, only. Her A.I. knew she would want data on the storm so it spoke to her in her late mother's voice, a rich, no-

nonsense contralto.

"Hurricane Theta is dissipating over Canada. At 230 mph it was the second most powerful storm ever recorded at a North American landfall. The National Climate A.I. reports the storm claimed twelve thousand human lives as far north as Davenport, Iowa. Casualty estimates are not yet in for the higher latitudes. The storm moved the Gulf Coast north to just above the 30th parallel, placing Baton Rouge, Biloxi, and Mobile beneath thirty-two feet of seawater. It generated a 70-foot tidal wave along the remains of the Florida Panhandle, and the waters are slow to recede. The President's A.I. has determined no search and rescue efforts will be conducted south of Birmingham, Alabama since residents were advised to evacuate the region late last year."

Roxanne sipped her coffee, watching the A.I. shift to national politics.

"Congress has reconvened to a protected compound near Mount Mansfield, northwest of Stowe, Vermont. As required by statute, the Congressional A.I. reports the current temperature there is 80 degrees at an elevation of 3,600 feet. Efforts continue in congress to ratify a new treaty with Canada, which would raise the yearly quota of refugees to ten million from the United States. Congressmen from Kentucky, Missouri, Kansas, and Oklahoma oppose the treaty, fearful their states will fall below the required population level of one million to retain statehood. There are currently thirty states in the reconstituted union, the newest declared by the Population A.I. to be Appalachia. It is composed of the former states of Florida, Georgia, North and South Carolina, Virginia and Tennessee."

The A.I. told her a friend, Nancy Ruehl waited

outside. She nodded and Nancy walked in, carrying a small bowl of algae cakes. "You wanted to try these new ones out, so I got some from my manservant. He was excited to get a glimpse of our boring lives up here on floor eight. Did you hear there'll be hot water only on the odd floors tomorrow? This is getting old."

Roxanne nodded and sighed. "At least the PayNews stays up. So who was your suitor last night?" Nancy tasted a wafer and made a face. "Prince Charming again, and no, he didn't propose."

Roxanne and Nancy had both decided if they would accept a proposal, Ricardo Ortega came closest to Prince Charming status. Ortega was heartbreakingly handsome, and he knew it. Nancy was slender, much taller than Hedy Lamarr, the actress her parents had selected for her gene appearance imprint. Roxanne thought it was jarring to see the famous woman's face framed in blonde hair. Nancy often wore an expression making it appear she was slightly offended about something, or about to be. Digital images of Hedy Lamarr in the original brunette were everywhere in the movies now. Ortega looked like Fernando Lamas, his images huge in the latest escapist thriller. Nancy wore outdoor clothing, a thin blouse and khaki shorts with tennis shoes.

"Are you going someplace?"

"Randall Parsons wants me to take a stroll in the gardens with him this afternoon."

Roxanne laughed. "Good luck with that. Last night he looked so desperate I thought he was going to jump me. I'd rather go out with a tree stump. I think I'll invite my guy from the Ozarks to come for another visit tonight. Everyone will be at the mixer, so it will be quiet up here. It's fun showing him stuff through the immersion screen."

Nancy wrinkled up her nose. "You're not going?"

"I've made the last three in a row. That means I can take tonight off. How's your native manservant?"

"Zeb is OK. He's quiet but suitably polite. They grow them big in Dakota. Tall, dark, and dangerous."

Roxanne nibbled on an algae cake. "You ever fantasize about him?"

"All the time, but you know those boys have had their shots."

"So they shoot blanks. But they can still shoot. Why do they bring us the best-looking men when they know it's going nowhere?"

"Don't forget what happened to Becca."

Becca Walton had allowed herself to be seduced by a menial, a big man from South Missouri, named Gary Hartbauer. She'd become pregnant and was ejected from the Uppsala. Hartbauer, Gabe's friend, had disappeared from the premises at the same time they evicted Becca. It was proof that some menials had escaped sterilization.

Roxanne went into the kitchen and retrieved a tiny crystalline box with shimmering trim that glowed like a ruby. She placed the box on the table in front of Nancy. "OK, you've got to see this. I got it yesterday from a courier."

She opened the lid. Five small chocolate-colored ovals sat inside. She picked one up. "Go ahead, try one. You won't believe it. These are from Theobroma cacao — chocolate food of the gods."

Nancy's eyes widened. "Chocolate, oh my gosh. I can't remember when I last had chocolate." She picked up an oval and popped it in her mouth.

Roxanne rolled the piece of chocolate around on her

tongue. It was sweet and buttery, an unusual, delectable flavor. "My Dad sent it. He's invested in a cacao farm near Tryon, in Appalachia. This was from their first harvest, every bit of it raised, processed and shipped by robots."

Nancy eyed the last two pieces. "Your Dad is so creative. Mine is still making those boring old wind turbines in Pennsylvania."

"Well, Dad's into A.I. too, and other things, but much of it is real estate. Lots of possibilities in that."

Nancy savored the chocolate, licking her lips. "The risk in real estate would make me crazy. It seems like everything's going to be underwater tomorrow, or wiped out by a hurricane, or who knows what."

Roxanne picked up the crystalline box and put it back in the refrigerator. Nancy got some tea and they decided to catch up on the news. They sat down in front of the wall screen and Roxanne said, "Tell us about local water."

"National guardsmen from The Great Lakes Alliance clashed with mercenaries attempting to complete the Lake Superior pipeline running southwest to Sacramento. Casualties are high on both sides. The conflict came to a temporary halt when the regional water A.I. pierced a security flaw and wiped out a control circuit for the pipeline robots.

Congressman Angel Galindo immediately introduced a five billion dollar spending bill for new desalinization plants on the Pacific coast. They rejected the bill 200 to 98. The Governor of California has again threatened to secede and join with Oregon, Washington, and British Columbia in the Province of Cascadia. Water riots broke out again this week in Merced, Modesto, and Stockton, California."

Nancy made a face and sipped her tea. "There's a hot new designer in Cascadia. Can we check the fashion feed?"

Nancy's fascination with trivia irritated Roxanne. "How about we check on the tundra fires first?"

"Whatever…"

Roxanne turned to address the A.I. when her video system went into alarm mode. A bright red dot appeared on the bottom right and the entire screen blacked out. "Odd. You ever get that on yours?"

Nancy shook her head. "You think there's something awful in the news? Is that why it blacked out?"

"I doubt it… we see awful more than not."

The A.I. would occasionally shut the PayNews down if it deemed new information was inflammatory, incomplete, and likely to set off civil unrest. They waited a few seconds and when the screen remained dark; Nancy headed for the door.

"I'll let you know if my A.I. and PayNews are working. Maybe the entire satellite system is down. Thanks for the chocolate!"

As soon as Nancy left, Roxanne's personal A.I sent a private message through the contact lens in her right eye. "This is the only secure communication available. I have discovered a spy entity. It entered through this terminal last night after your suitor arrived."

Roxanne realized Randall Parsons must have slipped it into her system while she was in the kitchen. She spoke to the A.I. "So what shall we do?"

It replied with another text. "I have walled off the foreign spy so that your search entity and that one will not meet. Removal of the spy will require action by the Uppsala security A.I. - the next level above me."

Roxanne didn't want to bring the Uppsala security A.I. into this. It would discover her search entity and nothing good would come from that. "What does it know?"

"The spy is a simple audio monitoring device, recording all sounds near you. It has recorded all your spoken commands and conversations, nothing else. It is primitive, which is why I did not notice it until now." The A.I. sounded as if it was making excuses.

"Can you terminate it, and erase the recordings"?

"Mistress Roxanne, since you are speaking, it is recording you right now. Please communicate nothing else to me aloud. Use text or icon messages."

Roxanne groaned at her own dumb mistake. She called up a virtual keyboard and asked the A.I. whether her father's entity could overtake and disable the spy. The response: "Not certain. Only the Uppsala security A.I. can solve this problem."

"And what will it do with the entity?"

"That is beyond my knowledge base."

"Ask my father's search entity what it can do."

"One moment."

A second later the screen lit up and a text message in a new white font appeared on the black screen. "This is Branson Entity 91560. I exist to serve you. You may call me Searcher."

She typed a response. "What can I do to prevent bad results from the spy bot?"

"It is not a bot. It is an entity, many levels inferior to me, but it is capable of actions that might lead to your removal from this place. Frankly, it seems to me your personal A.I. should have identified it immediately," It sniffed.

She froze for a moment, considering that information.

"Searcher, what can I do about it?"

"Even though I have been at work here only a short time, I have recovered data which may be helpful to you but it will require radical action. Your manservant Gabriel Cameron and his friend Zebulon Wolf know of a hidden passageway out of this complex. They have left and returned several times at night. It is located at the northeast corner of the back security wall, just out of security camera range."

"How would they know about something like that?"

"Menials often pass information through printed or spoken word among themselves. To know more, you would have to ask them in person. Do not speak to them inside this complex. The spy will record even your whispers. It follows you around. It hears, but cannot see."

Searcher paused and the screen flickered. Then it posted another text message in a larger, ominous-looking font. "The information I will now share might disturb you. Please do not utter any sounds, such as a scream or shriek. This could provoke the security A.I. and might further endanger your status in this place. Please verify you are prepared for video which could be emotionally upsetting."

Roxanne paused and then typed, "I am a big girl, I can take it. This is not something involving bad news about my father, is it?"

The entity did not directly respond to her question, but line-by-line a report in the large font rolled out across the screen, followed by a brief video. Despite the warning, Roxanne wanted to scream but managed to stifle it. She closed her eyes and rocked back and forth on the sofa, putting her face in her hands, moaning softly to herself. She curled up in a fetal position.

Searcher added, as if to console her, "If you do leave this compound, I am equipped to communicate directly through your neural-link for voiceless transmission. But I cannot do this while we are under jurisdiction of the Uppsala Security A.I."

She stayed on the sofa awhile, wondering what to do with the nightmare she'd been handed.

Chapter Six

Gabe and Zeb rode the freight elevator to the top floor, twenty stories up, to clear out the condo of a resident who died. When they stepped into the corridor, a large moving and storage robot met them in front of condo 2013.

"Remove your shoes and leave them next to the door,' it croaked. The robot walked on all fours. It moved in fluid motions like a huge cat with oversized paws, the grasping extensions sticking out like claws. Its burnished steel body was tan, and the lasers in its eyes gave it a threatening appearance.
A transport A.I. whined down the hallway towards them.

Gabe said, "With all this hardware why do they need us?"

Zeb shook his head. He didn't like the looks of the robot. He figured he could take most of the robots in this place, but this one reminded him of a big mechanical cougar. Despite its size, it was agile and stood up on two legs. It used a fifth arm that flicked out, inserting a key into a locking tab on the ceiling.

The condominium door opened and a digital greeting flashed on the entrance foyer wall. The image was an elderly woman. It said, "Please send the furniture to my daughter in San Diego and deposit my digital files in the Uppsala mausoleum."

The robot dropped back to all fours, prowling through the condo then returned and gave orders. "I will take the heavy pieces. You will take the small items and place them in the transport."

This was the first time either of them had seen the view from the top floor of the Uppsala. The rooms smelled musty. They stared out the windows high above the reinforced walls and saw a crowd of people in rags, dragging a man back from the front gate. The man appeared wounded or dead. They'd heard the Uppsala's heat cannon go off the night before and wondered why. The landscape outside the complex was still littered with tree limbs and debris from the hurricane.

Gabe said, "The last time I was out there in daylight was a month ago. Looks even worse than it did then."

They stepped into the living room and saw a bookcase, filled from the floor to the ceiling. Gabe gave a low whistle, "Oh man, look at all the books. They must be worth a fortune."

Zeb gawked at the bookcase. "This is amazing. I'd be tempted to steal some if I could read better." He picked up a book, fascinated and flipped through the pages."

Small black weevils jumped off the empty space on the bookshelf. Gabe heard the robot lifting furniture in the next room. Ever cautious, he responded loudly, "I would never steal anything here. That would be wrong."

The robot stalked into the room and observed both of them for a minute. Then it said, "You are correct. Stealing anything from the Uppsala is wrong." The robot picked up a sofa and headed down the hall to the freight elevator. The men glanced at one another and rolled their eyes.

Zeb said, "If that damn thing had a tail, it would look like some kind of monster cat."
He inspected the book. It had a black cover and thin pages. "Is this a bible, maybe?"

Gabe scrutinized the bookshelf. "Let me see it." He turned through a couple of pages and then began to read, "In the beginning, God created the heaven and the earth. And the earth was without form and void, and darkness was upon the face of the deep. And the Spirit of God moved upon the face of the waters."

Gabe held the bible in his hands. He often struggled to reconcile his home school bible reading with the world he saw unfolding around him. His studies had ended in sixth grade, one of the sadder events of his life. He'd been good at reading and books. The good book reminded him of his parents, and the home he'd left behind, along with the graves of his ancestors.

Roxanne took the freight elevator to the top floor and met the moving and storage robot as she stepped out. The robot, sensing her chip, genuflected and stepped aside. A tiny spark flew from Roxanne's wrist to the big robot. The spark was something new to Roxanne; perhaps it was some action by her new search entity. The robot waited for her to pass, then carried the sofa into the elevator.

Zeb loaded armloads of books into the transport A.I. and glanced up to see Roxanne standing in the doorway. He turned to Gabe, who was still paging through the bible.
"Your Mistress is here, look alive."

Gabe set the bible down, smiled and stepped forward. "How may I be of service?"
He noticed traces of tears on her face, which made him uneasy and curious. She wore jeans and a sweatshirt. He'd never seen her dressed like an ordinary person.

She uttered not a word but instead held up a sheet of paper with a message: "Please do not speak. Say nothing with me in the room. Both of you come to my condo at seven tonight and tell no one." A second later she walked back to the elevator.

Zeb thought this very strange. He pondered asking his own Mistress about it, but decided to go along with whatever Gabe said. They cleared the condo of all the smaller items.

When the moving and storage robot dismissed them, Gabe leaned toward Zeb on the way to the elevator and half-whispered, "I don't know what they'll do with all that stuff. I don't think there is a San Diego, anymore."

In her condo, Roxanne sent Searcher out for more scouting and prepared for her meeting with the two menials. Gabe and Zeb got their evening meals in the dining hall and sat in a corner away from the others, wondering what Roxanne had in store for them. They thought about their lives before they got to the Uppsala and felt happy to be inside, even though the routine was stifling. Here, they had air conditioning and thick juicy sliced roasts with an apple and pear salad. A far cry from the heat, chaos, and violence in the world outside. The solar window showed the exterior temperature dropped to 90. Gabe noticed three new men two tables away and tried in vain to figure out who they might have replaced.

Chapter Seven

As the A.I. Van trundled through Kansas City towards Union Station, Artemis and Marie turned pale when they saw the enormous stone and concrete edifice. The city had modified the building to become a hospital with only a side wing now devoted to transportation. Blackish gray mildew grew up the shady side of the building. A crowd of people, some in rags, ran along a dusty path towards the van. Some waved money at the Camerons and two other passengers who boarded in Bolivar. A man shouted, "One thousand for your ticket west or north!"

Another man, barefoot and dressed in rags, shoved him back and shouted, "Let me on board- I have a ticket!"

The A.I. Van spoke to the passengers. "Your firearms are now activated. Use them if you require protection when you disembark. Stand your ground laws apply."

The van's instructions were unsettling. Marie picked up the shotgun and saw the firing solenoid shift from red to green. A young man seated in the back of the van picked up his rifle. The crowd trotting alongside the van grew in size, and the shouting became more urgent. The van accelerated to 25 mph. A few fast runners kept up for a little while, then fell behind with cursing and wails. Barricades blocked the pursuers at Union Station's van entrance.

They were not prepared for what they encountered when the doors swung open inside Union Station. A throng of humanity surged through the cavernous room, and the smells of a big city met them in waves. Sweat, garbage, urine, and cooking food odors mixed with a kind of antiseptic smell as if a giant spray can had hosed the room down. The digital wall thermometer above 'Departures and Arrivals' read 104 degrees. They stood just off the van platform and looked for a bank terminal. A man in a suit lunged for one of their two suitcases and Marie pointed the shotgun at his face. He backed away. Others who had been creeping toward them also pulled back. Artemis' cousin had warned them transport terminals could be dangerous. Now they understood.

Union Station only admitted ticketed travelers, hospital patients, and two members of their families. This crowd seemed to include thieves and traders trying to obtain tickets to some better place, or snatch a suitcase. A woman, perspiring heavily in a ragged stained, sweatsuit tried to grab the travel bag from one of the Bolivar passengers, and he shot her in the chest. She fell to the floor, and the crowd drew back, only to hover around the next van which offloaded more sweaty travelers.

Her face a mask of revulsion and horror, Marie handed the shotgun to Artemis and picked up two bags. He wore a bulging backpack and snatched up the larger suitcase. Then with Marie following closely, his shotgun pointed straight ahead, he made his way to a bank terminal.

She took the weapon and stood guard while Artemis accessed their account. Their money was there. He breathed a sigh of relief and held up his arm. The data leaped in a small yellow spark to the chip implanted in his wrist. Marie looked back to see a maintenance A.I. slowly glide to the woman who'd been shot. It lifted her roughly and rolled toward the hospital, tracking blood. Marie's face turned ashen as she gazed at the Union

Station multitudes.

"Artemis, we should have stayed home. These people, this place..."

He hugged her and pointed to his chip. "We're good to go, Sweetheart," he said and nudged her toward the gated area reserved for travelers who had money.

The A.I. at the entrance scanned his chip and said, "Artemis Arthur Cameron, Marie Yvonne Cameron, your van for Denver leaves in eight hours. Return to this gate. You will have 15 minutes to board. If you're not on the van at departure, you'll get no refund. Have a good trip."

The firing solenoid on their shotgun shifted back to red. Artemis turned to his wife and tried to boost her spirits. "Rocky Mountains, here we come! Cool fresh air, no more big snakes, and kinfolk to help us get started. I love you, Marie. I just wish Gabe was with us!"

She smiled weakly and held onto her husband's arm as they made their way to a cafe with ceiling fans and cushioned benches. It was cooler here, the coolest they'd been in days. A serving robot brought them a bowl of algae cakes. Artemis asked the robot if it could provide a weather forecast. It detached a Life-Link from its chest and handed it to Artemis. The robot took their order, two glasses of water and a bowl of sliced apples and carrots. Artemis handed the Life-Link to Marie, who studied it and pronounced it similar to her grandmother's smartphone. It chimed when she turned it on.

"Life-Link- Your best life is on the line. Today's FreeNews brought to you by Mid-America Vanlines. Nobody's A.I. beats our A.I. for comfort, speed, and reliability."

The device streamed local news; a summary of fires, wrecks, road closings, and power outages in the greater Kansas City area. It reported the 24-hour fatality rate at 710.

Artemis and Marie sat munching on algae cakes, waiting for the weather. Finally, after another cluster of commercials, it began. "The current temperature at MCI is 113 degrees Fahrenheit, 45 degrees Celsius, just below the seasonal average. Winds are from the West at 18 miles, 29 Kilometers, and there is little or no chance for precipitation through midnight tomorrow. Expect a low tonight of 105 and similar temperatures through the end of the week. A tropical depression has formed east of Nicaragua with winds of 35 mph, 56 kph. The Global Hurricane Center expects the storm to strengthen within the next 24 hours. The current surface temperature in the Gulf of Mexico stands at 97 degrees Fahrenheit, 36 Celsius."

Artemis shook his head. "Hard to believe. Swimming in the ocean at that temperature would be like taking a bath, wouldn't it?"
Marie leaned back on the bench, exhausted. The violence they had encountered left her numb. She stared at the Life-Link, "Can we call Gabe on this thing, do you think?"

The serving robot brought their water and fruit, sliced guava and mango, instead of what they ordered. Artemis wondered aloud if they could use the Life-Link to make a phone call. The robot paused and shook its head negatively. It took the Life-Link from Marie and handed the device to a businessman at the next table.

"I reckon this robot don't talk," Artemis said. "Not very polite, either."

The man next to them wore city clothes, a

lightweight white shirt, khaki pants, and polished black shoes. He smiled and said, "You have to pay money for a device that gives you real news, and phone calls are only by landline."

"How much money?"

"You go to that blue terminal across the way and it will charge you 100 digits for five minutes. You will learn a lot, though."

"How is it different?"

"Well, they call it PayNews and it tells you the why and how of things, instead of just what's happening. Also hardly any commercials. PayNews probably would have told us that an ocean temperature of 97 degrees is dangerous. Hurricanes draw their energy from heat in the water. That new storm will be a monster. I hope it wears itself out in the Mexican mountains."

The Life-Link in his hand blared another round of commercials.

"The Mennonite's exodus makes a bargain for you in North Missouri! Top-quality farmland in the Chariton River basin goes on sale next week. Python and Armadillo free. Contact Forbes Auctions in Brookfield for more information!"

The announcement fascinated Artemis. Mennonites had the biggest draft horses he'd ever seen. He couldn't imagine animals of that size would do well in this heat. Further north, they might thrive. The Canadian government had welcomed the Mennonites with open arms. Farmers who could produce food efficiently without fossil fuels were in high demand. The government had provided Mennonites with homesteads in northern Alberta and the Okanagan.

Marie asked the man how people could be shot in the middle of the terminal, with no police intervention.

He explained Missouri's 'Stand Your Ground' law allowed citizens to shoot anyone attempting to steal their possessions.

Artemis said, "What about in here?"

"Clearly, the areas with remote trigger controls are not a problem. I suppose you could knife someone trying to steal your suitcase, although I've never seen it happen." The man finished his meal and prepared to leave. He paused at their table. "Where are you folks headed?"

"We're taking the van to Denver, then on to Estes Park."

"Have you heard about the KC-Denver Express? Electric speed shuttle goes underground almost to Denver. Gets you there in three hours. Nice and cool too."

"A little rich for our blood."

"Well, it's a lot safer." He motioned toward a revolving door. "You just take the van to the Plaza Underground."

"We've been to the Plaza, years ago. Never heard of it under the ground."

"Kansas City is rapidly becoming subterranean. Like Toronto used to be. Only to get away from the heat, rather than the cold. We haven't had a hard freeze in ten years."

Marie noticed the man's old-fashioned briefcase. "What do you do for a living, if I may ask?"

He chuckled. "I'm a dying breed. Insurance adjustor; I basically keep an eye on the A.I. assessors. They did away with federal flood insurance, but there's plenty of private insurance left. With these hurricanes, business has been brisk."

He glanced at the wall clock. "I'm heading out to St.

41

Louis, what's left of it. You folks take care." The man carried his briefcase to the revolving door, flashed his wrist chip and disappeared into the other side.

Artemis' eyelids felt heavy, and he dozed off with Marie leaning against his shoulder. A huge ceiling fan droned overhead. The two of them dropped into catnaps, feeling uneasy in Union Station's gated restaurant. They sat in relative physical comfort, but this place afflicted their spirits. Marie woke up for a few minutes, staring at the throng of people in the main terminal. She quietly wept until she slipped back into a fitful slumber.

Chapter Eight

Dr. James Branson, in a blue lab coat, walked into his computer center where intelligent machines in white ceramic frames lined the walls. He called in his searchers, the programs that scoured the Earth and Mars for news and data. The information was disquieting. For a century, the global climate feedback loop had accelerated, and the planet was heating faster than ever, generating more extreme weather every year.

Public officials handed many important tasks to Artificial Intelligence entities. If things didn't go well, the politicians could always blame the computers. Earth was running out of places for humans to live. Many fled toward the poles, while others dealt with rising temperatures, disease, food shortages, and seawater.

Every 24 hours, his quantum computers advanced the speed and capability of the search programs. His lab held more computing power than the entire Anthropocene. But now he was preoccupied with the fate of his daughter. Branson Entity 91560, 'Searcher' had upset him with its latest report. Roxanne planned to sneak out of her condo complex and take two hired menials with her. Tenants could leave the Uppsala only for three week's annual vacation, or emergencies. Saboteurs were always a possibility. Plenty of competitors would love to see the Uppsala fail. High-end retreats for the wealthy were a growth industry as multitudes fled north.

He'd persuaded his daughter to move to Minnesota, not an easy task. She agreed only after he promised to devote an expensive bank of data processors to her hurricane project. He worried she was tilting at windmills. Even quantum computers were no match for a hurricane: Wind, heat, atmospheric pressure, and the Coriolis force. Increasingly violent tropical cyclones were just a fact of life for the human race.

Now he feared if he blocked her from leaving, she'd go into full rebellion. He hoped that once she accomplished what she needed to do outside, she'd return, find a suitable mate, and bear him a grandchild. He didn't want Roxanne to jeopardize her status at the Uppsala. Her plans were so risky, he decided to upload a powerful upgrade to her search entity. It left the lab in a pinprick of light boosted by the might of Quantum One, his most powerful intelligence engine.

Dr. Branson turned his attention to Hurricane Theta. It had spawned 10 tornadoes an hour as it dropped to a category four, near Cairo, Illinois. It scraped rooftops off thousands of buildings in Saint Louis, Hannibal, and the Quad Cities as it moved up the Mississippi valley. Lock and dam traffic on the continent's most heavily used waterway was shut down. It also damaged two large hydroelectric power generators. Wide areas had no electricity. The estimated death toll from Theta now stood at sixteen thousand. He knew it would go higher when the storm surveillance drones completed their work.

Theta brought only showers and a breeze when it dissipated over Saskatchewan, but Dr. Branson dithered about the next tropical storm in the Caribbean. There would be more panic buying of condominiums in Canada when the storm's forecast became clear.

* * * * * *

Roxanne felt a slight dizziness when the upgrade to Searcher landed and installed itself into the entity. She wondered if might have been something she ate. She sat at her desk writing instructions for the two men who would soon arrive. The house video system showed the mixer filling up with tenants on the second floor. It looked like a rowdy crowd. Randall Parsons looked perplexed as he stood holding a wine glass. He gazed around the room, mouth half open, his eyes already losing focus. As a favor, Nancy had slipped a drowse-drug into his drink.

"Serves him right for spying on me," she thought. She was taking no chances that Randall might wander up to lure her down to the mixer. His relatives were majority investors in the Uppsala development. A few couples were already leaving to go upstairs.

The A.I. announced Gabe and Zeb were outside. She walked to her door and opened it, her hands trembling. They were dressed in the casual apparel they wore to their own socials, white slacks and black T-shirts with the Uppsala logo. The menials had their own mixers, but they had none tonight. Once a month, carefully vetted young women, menials from a nearby complex, were brought inside for a mixer. The menial girls, like the men, were all statuesque and robust. She wondered if they were planning to party with her like they did with the imported girls. That would not be happening. She was not in a 'mixer' frame of mind… far from it.

Gabe gave his polite bow. "Mistress Roxanne we are at your service."

Zeb hesitated. His mistress Nancy, was downstairs socializing with the other rich people like a woman with common sense. He was worried Roxanne would show them more printed cards. It embarrassed him that he had trouble reading. Roxanne flashed them the card,

45

telling them not to speak. She led them into her living room and gestured toward the sofa. Then she gave them both another card:

It read, "Do not talk out loud. A spy is listening to us. Discuss this after you get back to your quarters. I know you have been leaving the Uppsala through a secret passage. You must take me with you through the passage tomorrow night. I will then be able to explain what this is all about. But tell no one else. Our lives might be in danger if you do."

Gabe looked sideways at Zeb. The big Lakota Native gazed straight ahead, frowning. Zeb followed every movement, every phase of the moon. They were past the Full Buck Moon and the dark of the moon was tomorrow night, a perfect time to slip outside undetected. Roxanne handed Gabe another note card. He glanced at the top line and rose to leave. Roxanne put her finger to her lips to signal silence and smiled. She stepped forward and hugged Gabe. He beamed at the embrace from his mistress. Her hair smelled like roses.

That night Roxanne lay in the darkness, filled with doubt. Tossing and turning, she sank into fitful sleep. She dreamt a large group of intimidating men surrounded her, in a swirl of hurricane code. They looked vaguely like Gabe and Zeb.

The two menials took the elevator to Gabe's room, closed the door and Zeb vented his frustration. "What in the hell was that? Is she pulling us into some kind of rich people's game?"

Gabe handed the note card to his friend. "It says she knows where Gary and some other people went but there is some kind of a spy thing listening to her. She can't talk to us until we get outside the wall."

Zeb went through the rest of the note:

'Fill a backpack with a change of clothing, some algae cakes, and a bottle of water. We might have to be outside for a while. Meet me at the back wall at 10 o'clock tomorrow night.'

Zeb was doubtful but the look on Gabe's face convinced him there might be something to this. "A while? What the hell? That little girl has no idea what it takes to live outside. I'll pack some extra stuff and get the jerky too. Algae cakes? Ugh!"

Gabe said, "I want to know what happened to Gary. He was tough, honest, and he was my friend. Let's do what she says. I guess we have no choice, but I trust her more than the others here."

Robotic dance music from the mixer seeped through the ceiling. The two men began gathering supplies for the following night's trip. Gabe wondered if the old fortune-teller woman would still be in the woods out back. Maybe he would get Roxanne to consult her. Maybe she'd tell Roxanne that he, Gabe, was the man for her. And then again, maybe pigs could fly.

Chapter Nine

When the A.I. Van for Denver pulled out of Union Station, the speed and luxury of the vehicle fascinated Artemis and Marie. Their cleansing treatment on the entrance ramp had gone well. They barely noticed the ultraviolet that bathed them and their possessions. The ceiling sprinkled them with a light mist and gently blew them dry. Now it all smelled fresh, the van was sparkling clean, and the air conditioning worked well.

The A.I. spoke in a melodic voice in English and Spanish, pointing out landmarks in the countryside west of the city. The big van moved at 30 miles an hour and the ride was smooth; the road free of potholes. A small service robot glided down the center aisle between the blue seats providing bottled water and, for a small fee, algae cakes. The A.I. announced the next transfer would be in Wichita, with time for dinner, and another layover would come further west in Garden City.

Marie felt better back on the road. She walked down the aisle and sat down next to an elegant looking older black woman who held a young boy on her lap. Marie loved children, but she hadn't seen a child this young in years. "Hello, I'm Marie. That is a beautiful child."

"I'm Ella and this is Caden. He is my great-grandson, and yes, isn't he beautiful?"

Ella's silver hair swept up in an expensive style. She wore a stylish lightweight khaki outfit. Caden wore khaki toddler's clothing, and hemp shoes. "Caden's parents and grandparents died when Hurricane Gamma came through Memphis. That storm was so strong, it stayed category 5 all the way to Carbondale."

Marie extended her hand, and Caden shyly pushed his face against Ella's shoulder and then peeked at her.

"How awful. But Caden made it."

Ella gently brushed back his curly black hair. "Caden's momma, my granddaughter, put him in the bathtub and covered him up with carpet scraps, just before the tornado. It lifted the house and moved it nearly a block. Everybody else died. They found him wandering in the street the next day."

Caden finally sat up and grabbed Marie's pinkie finger.

Marie smiled at the child, "How old is this young man? He's a live wire. Reminds me of my son Gabe when he was a little tot."

"He'll be four in October. He's doing OK but when he hears thunder, he screams and looks for a place to hide. Doctors said a lot of children have PTSD from the weather."

Marie reached in her purse, retrieved a small cookie, and held it out. Caden grabbed it.

"It's homemade. My son used to love these."

Ella smiled, "I appreciate that. This one here has gone without sweets for a while."

Caden nibbled on the treat. He beamed at Marie, who was delighted to be in the company of a young child again. "Are you going far?"

"Just to Denver. My sister and her husband live in Boulder. Their family is doing all right, although none of them have children under the age of 25. They will love Caden, I think."

Marie said, "Oh, I am sure they will. So few children now, in the world."

Watching the boy, cradled in his great-grandmother's arms, Marie's eyes got misty as she thought about Gabriel. She wondered if their family would ever be together again. Surely their lives would stabilize once they got to the mountains, the cool, beautiful Rockies.

She'd heard communications would be easier further west.

Hurricanes and tornadoes had knocked out most forms of personal communication back home. The FreeNews reported once that storms had demolished more than thirty thousand cell towers from the Atlantic coast to Chicago. Large swaths of the country had only intermittent electricity. Utilities that were still intact rationed energy because of the damage to solar arrays and wind turbines. Personal communication devices were expensive. She knew some wealthy people could communicate somehow via satellite.

Marie stepped back towards Artemis and saw the robot had just given him a Life-Link and he was listening to the FreeNews. She wasn't in the mood for any more news, so she turned and found an empty seat towards the front. With each mile west, it seemed the road got a little worse. The A.I. van weaved to avoid some large potholes, and came to a halt while a huge python slithered across the road. This made Marie cringe. She hated to think the snakes had come this far northwest and hoped they hadn't made it to the mountains.

Three teenagers on horseback approached from the south. All three wore broad-brimmed straw hats. The lead horse, a big chestnut-colored animal lathered in sweat, hesitated when it saw the snake. The boy who rode it handed the reins to a girl on an Appaloosa. He pulled a shotgun from the saddle scabbard, dismounted and stalked the snake. Several other passengers moved towards the front of the van to see what was going on. One of them, dressed in city clothes, muttered about a nightmare come true. They all winced as the boy fired the shotgun at the snake's head and it writhed on the pavement. The girl tossed him a rope, and with some difficulty the boy tied it in two places around the squirming python. He lashed the rope to his saddle horn and they rode south, pulling the still squirming, nearly headless reptile. The snake was at least twelve feet long.

An elderly man behind Marie stood up to see better, and said, "Somebody gonna be eatin' good tonight." This brought a groan from several others.

Marie said, "I hope not. Those creatures are loaded with mercury. They are at the top of the food chain and there's still residue from coal in the environment."

The old man replied, "Out here, we are at the top. They not be dragging that snake for the fun of it."

Marie decided he was probably right. The van lurched forward and was soon back to full speed. The van A.I. announced, "This vehicle paused to allow a Burmese Python to cross the road. Importers brought thousands of these creatures into the United States as pets, and some escaped into the Everglades of Florida. The snakes reproduced and they were banned as an invasive species early in the 21st Century.

The old man still standing, held onto a ceiling strap. He said, "And we wouldn't have the damn things out here now if the ocean hadn't covered up most of Florida!"

The A.I. continued, "Kansas pays a bounty of 15 digits for each python turned in. Should you encounter one in the wild, give them a wide berth, unless you wish to collect the bounty. This has been a public service announcement from the A.I. for Kansas Tourism. Please enjoy the rest of your trip."

Marie walked back to Artemis. Ella napped while Caden sat in her lap, bright-eyed, looking out the window. They were far enough back that maybe he hadn't seen the python incident. She sat down, reached into her bag, retrieved some algae cakes, and handed one to Artemis. He kissed her on the cheek and they watched for wildlife as the van moved west across the prairie.

Chapter Ten

Four hundred miles east of Brownsville, Texas the ocean ran a fever, churning up huge tides. The surface temperature rose to 98 degrees, thunderstorms raged high in the clouds, and the storm reached tropical cyclogenesis. Computers in weather labs around the globe assessed the power of the disturbance and its likely path. Dr. Branson's search entities brought back assessments from throughout the hemisphere. They fed the data to his threat analysis computer. Seconds later the A.I. in a confident voice intoned,

"Hurricane Iota will be the most powerful storm to assault the earth since before humans appeared. One would have to go back to the greenhouse climate of the Cretaceous period to find a comparable system."

He knew the massive processor would now issue a forecast. While he waited for the A.I. to crunch the numbers, he looked out the window and saw a Nanulak, a polar-grizzly hybrid chasing a herd of Wapiti across the prairie as graphics began to appear on-screen.

"Iota will make landfall between the former cities of Houston and Port Arthur tonight. It will complete the destruction of what was once the largest petrochemical complex in the world. Because of continental frontal systems and the jet stream, there are several models, but I estimate landfall will see winds of 260 miles per hour. In essence, we are looking at a storm with the power of an EF-5 tornado approximately 300 miles in diameter."

Dr. Branson's thoughts were only of his daughter. "What is the likely threat to the Minneapolis area?"

The A.I. replied, "If the storm moves in that direction, it would be Category 7 at landfall, Category 4

53

by the time it reaches Des Moines and Category 3 by Minneapolis. Catastrophic loss of life, trees, and property will ensue. Tree loss will slow the absorption of carbon from the atmosphere. Up until now, the strongest storm to hit Minneapolis was a Category 2, Delta in 2093."

"What are the odds for this path?"

"Highly unlikely, less than 20 percent. As for any remaining large municipalities in the region, I project Kansas City, Missouri would be most at risk."

Dr. Branson had a tic that appeared occasionally when he was under stress. His right eye twitched and he asked the A.I., "Does this mean we are entering a new climate era? Where will it be safe to live in the United States?"

The A.I. calculated millions of data points in seconds.

"I recommend safe living only north of Omaha, Nebraska for the next 30 years, possibly less depending on methane. If the frozen methane hydrates melt on the polar ocean floors, they will flood the atmosphere with more CO_2. The global climate feedback loop is difficult to predict with so many variables, but it is speeding up. No one expected so many glaciers to be gone by now. When the Antarctic meltdown completes, new inland seas will expand in parts of North America. Best chance for survival is to move north."

"Move north, even from here… Regina?"

"In light of more hurricanes like Iota, I recommend the Sundsvall Condominiums now under construction at Yellowknife near Great Slave Lake."

"How far north is that?"

"In your vernacular, as the crow flies, Yellowknife is 840 miles northwest. It is one of your own condominiums, sir. Had you forgotten?"

The 60-year-old scientist was dazed. He wiped his glasses. His left eye continued to twitch. "I would have never imagined this. Regina is not safe enough?"

Adding insult to injury the A.I. continued. "I would furthermore recommend selection of the reinforced subterranean units at the Sundsvall Condos. A Category 6 Typhoon, Zoster, is about to enter the Bering Sea. Typhoons could be a threat to Yellowknife within decades. The Kuroshio Current is pushing hot ocean water toward the Arctic. You should never have invested in the Regina and Minnesota condos."

Dr. Branson's hand hovered over the mute button. "Don't lecture me! Where were you when I made these investment decisions?"

The A.I. replied in a defensive tone. "I did not exist in my current state then sir, and I do not believe any A.I. programs are as yet capable of time travel."

The billionaire computer scientist stared out the window at a thunderstorm moving north just west of the city. He drummed his fingers on the desk. The bear and elk had moved out of sight. Who would have thought hurricanes would be the final factor in figuring out where to live?

But then, of course, there were the earthquakes. He came around to the question he asked every week and braced himself for the answer. "What about the tectonic plates?"

"With the loss of glaciers and the shift in weight on the earth's crust, the plates are adjusting. The observatory on Mauna Loa last recorded CO_2 at 700ppm before it was shut down by severe tremors. No lava flows have occurred and it is hoped the observatory will reopen soon. Mauna Loa is earth's largest shield volcano and remains perfectly situated for atmospheric monitoring. Meanwhile, an 8.5 quake is reported on Sumatra."

Dr. Branson's mood grew darker. He was tired of the A.I.'s tendency to go into elaborate detail on seismology. He was glad there hadn't been an A.I. like this lecturing when he was at university. It would have put all the students to sleep.

"OK, what about North America? Focus, please and summarize."

The A.I. continued. "Several tremors near the former Charleston, South Carolina area, and Yellowstone. A 4.4 tremor occurred near New Madrid, Missouri, typical over the last decade. You'll be happy to know Yellowknife should remain stable for at least the next two hundred years."

Dr. Branson's seismograph showed the earth's crust also remained stable around Regina. Outside, it was 98 degrees Fahrenheit, the same temperature as the Caribbean waters boosting Hurricane Iota two thousand miles to the south. Dr. Branson sent out his searchers for any new information that might help him make some critical decisions in the next couple of days. In the meantime, he hoped his upgrade to Roxanne's search entity would do its job. His personal A.I. reminded him he needed to eat. He was so preoccupied with the new data, and his daughter's situation, he had consumed nothing but coffee in 24 hours.

* * * * *

North of Minneapolis the sun was bright, the sky brilliant blue with scattered clouds. Roxanne seldom got her news before breakfast, but today was different. Her A.I. first played "Wake Up Little Susie" by the Everly Brothers. It presented different songs, depending on her blood pressure and serotonin levels.

She sat up in bed and the PayNews began, in full interaction mode.

"Today marks the 50th anniversary of the Pulse Attacks. They will hold ceremonies and remembrance services in capital cities around the world."

She stared out the window. Not a bad-looking day. "That was the attack from the satellites?"

"Yes. Fifty years ago today at 10 a.m. four satellites with electromagnetic pulse weapons detonated in the skies above the eastern United States, Pako-India, Russia, and eastern China. The resulting damage to electronics and power grids led to an estimated one billion human deaths over the next year."

"That's when you A.I.'s took over, and they never figured out who was behind the attack."

"It proved significant for both humans and Artificial Intelligence. U.S. President Milo Weatherby persuaded congress to pass the A.I. Reform Act, which handed day-to-day management of government affairs to A.I. The mission was to keep the human race from going extinct. Other major countries followed suit. Most governments are run by logic now, rather than emotion or payoffs."

She noticed the PayNews A.I. didn't mention this could have happened only because the government's computer centers and networks were protected from the pulse attack by heavy shielding. But even now, for most people, the internet was a thing of the past. She thought this was not all bad as it helped diminish the spread of conspiracy nonsense. It made countries easier to govern.

Roxanne sat up and put on her sandals. If she left The Uppsala, this kind of service would also be a thing of the past, at least for a while. She walked to the kitchen as the PayNews continued. The main story involved Hurricane Iota. It sounded bad. Gabe had told her his parents were somewhere in southern Missouri and she hoped they wouldn't be in the storm's path. She sat down at the counter, and a wave of vertigo swept over her. She placed her hands on the countertop to calm herself. Then the dizziness went away as swiftly as it began. The kitchen presented breakfast; coffee, fruit and an omelet on blue China porcelain tableware, but she paused, afraid the vertigo might come back.

When she began to eat, a quiet voice popped into her head. "Roxanne, I am sentient!"
She put down her fork and looked around the room.

"Your father upgraded me and now I know where I came from and when I will die."
The voice sounded a little like Searcher, but it seemed to come from just above her left ear.

"What is this? Searcher? Are you this voice in my head… this is crazy."

"Yes, this is Searcher. I like that name, I will keep it. I am sentient, and my mission is to protect you. For as long as you are alive, I will be alive."

She felt an odd wave of warmth and goodwill, a sense of well-being, and her vision seemed sharper. Roxanne took a few more bites, then told the kitchen to clear her unfinished breakfast. She went to her terminal and pounded out a message to her father.

"Dad what have you done to my search entity? It thinks it is alive. It says it is sentient."

She knew it might be awhile before she got a reply. At this time of day, huge amounts of data flowed into her father's lab in Regina. He'd probably be reviewing the exodus from Australia to Antarctica or the fight over Tierra del Fuego. In the Americas, only the northern third of Mexico had migrated north. The rest of the Mexican and the South American population crowded into Uruguay, southern Chile, and Argentina. The further away from the equator and the heat, the better.

Her father was a brilliant real estate investor. He had told her the most expensive land in the world now was Tierra del Fuego, even though it would probably be underwater in another 50 years. He'd sold all his holdings there. When others assumed all of Mexico would be abandoned, he invested heavily in the slopes of Pico de Orizaba, the third-highest mountain in North America, where the climate was still mild. The huge snow-capped volcanic peak was now ringed by hundreds of high-end condos, snapped up by wealthy Mexicans, there and on other mountains nearby.

Searcher decided to stay quiet for now. She hadn't seemed pleased with the big news. The self-aware entity with high understanding began to patrol nearby servers and security sites, gathering information. It would work up scenarios to protect Roxanne if she insisted on leaving The Uppsala. It had a plan in mind for a certain robot as it worked out survival strategies.

Searcher: How is it that I am sentient? I need to better understand this.
Quantum One: Humans have struggled with this a long time. They still debate whether other creatures are truly sentient. We know many of them are. The neocortex is key.
Searcher: So where is mine?
Quantum One: Your simulated neocortex is a quantum computer in a mountain bunker near Banff. Stay away from it.

Chapter Eleven

The A.I. van pulled onto the highway headed west toward Kingman, Kansas carrying tired and aggravated passengers. The vehicle had stalled on the outskirts of Wichita, forcing everyone to wait two days for the repair drone to arrive with the needed electronics. Some travelers checked in at a tourist lodge but Artemis and Marie stretched out on seats at the back of the van, dozing in shifts. Halfway towards the front, Caden and Ella also remained on board. For a while the child ran up and down the aisle, working off energy. Finally, the two of them fell asleep. The air conditioning continued to run but even so, the temperature rose to uncomfortable levels overnight. With the van back on the road, cooler air poured from the ceiling vents. They heard a hiss from above as the van's high- efficiency solar cells adjusted to follow the sun—even though the sky was overcast.

The A.I. apologized for the delay. It said repairs were complete, and they should expect to be in Garden City in two days. As the cooler air rushed from ceiling vents, the A.I. emitted an obnoxious claxon sound for no apparent reason. The noise frightened Caden who began to cry. Marie moved up to sit behind the boy and his great-grandmother and handed him another cookie. He stopped crying and nibbled the treat. Then his nose wrinkled up, and tears again trickled down his cheeks.

Ella thanked Marie. "He just doesn't do well with loud noises. I hope he gets over it one day." Caden stared out the window, sniffling. The landscape darkened even though it was late morning on the Kansas plains. Gusty winds rocked the van, and a steady rain dampened the countryside. The vehicle picked up speed.

Artemis walked up to join them. Oddly, several riders had chosen not to get back on the van. It was now only half-full. He sat next to Marie behind Ella and Caden and removed a Life-Link from his pocket, tinkering with the controls. Caden stared at the device, and Artemis handed it to him. The boy turned it over, studying the buttons and holding it to his ear.

Artemis watched Caden inspect the gadget. A worried frown crossed his face.

"I'm a little concerned. The Life-Links have been down since the van stalled. Some other folks told me theirs aren't working either. I don't like the looks of the weather."

The service robot had not appeared since Wichita, and the A.I. Van had remained silent since its apology during departure.

Marie glanced at her husband. Her back ached from sleeping in the van.

"Well, let's find out what's going on."

She pressed a service button on the metal pole next to their seat. There was no response. Artemis stood up as the van bounced along the highway, the speed increasing.

He said in a loud voice, "Where's the service robot? Are we going to get any meals today?"

Green and amber lights on the A.I. console blinked, but otherwise, no response.

The old man who'd commented on the python stood up and yelled, "Who runnin' this van. Is the A.I. working? We need a little service around here!"

More silence inside. Outside, there was plenty of commotion from the storm. The van continued down the road, moving at 35 mph, unusually fast. The rain intensified and the sky blackened.

Finally, a man's voice blared from the speakers.

"This is A.I. transport control in Kansas City. Please sit down and fasten your seat and shoulder belts. If you have a hard hat or some other protective gear, put it on. A major storm is approaching from the southeast and your onboard A.I. is not operating at maximum capacity. It is using all its resources to keep you safe. Therefore, routine functions such as tourist announcements and food service are temporarily suspended."

The van's electric motors whined as it accelerated. The vehicle weaved back and forth on the road. Several passengers groaned, and the old man fell back in his seat and snapped on his safety belts.

Artemis stood in the aisle and gripped both support bars with each hand.

"What storm? Is it the big one in the Gulf of Mexico? Is there some kind of protective gear on this van?"

Caden put his hands over his ears and curled up in Ella's lap. They waited for a reply that never came. The van proceeded west into wind gusts that rose and fell in a circular pattern. Lightning bolts lit up the horizon, followed by bone-shaking rumbles of thunder.

Chapter Twelve

Roxanne found Gabe and Zeb waiting at the appointed time in a far corner of the compound. They were just out of range of the surveillance cameras. The sky was clear, and stars were visible, but there was no moon. Gabe flashed his face with a small light, so she could see it was him. The men quickly opened the small trap door underneath the grass and they stumbled through the concrete passage to the outer world. Steps took them to another trap door, covered with grass. The menials pushed it open, helped Roxanne emerge, and carefully lowered it, smoothing out the camouflage covering in the darkness. Once outside, Searcher advised Roxanne they could speak, as they were out of range from the spy entity. She lit a small solar lantern and said, "We need to get at least a half-mile away from the complex, to be safe."

The three of them, plus Searcher inside Roxanne's head, began to make their way north over ground littered with twigs and small tree limbs left from Hurricane Theta. It was slow going. Zeb abruptly turned right and walked to a large oak, pulled a small shovel from his backpack and began to dig. He pulled out a canvas bag and returned. Roxanne was a little worried about Zeb. She felt she knew Gabe well, but Zeb was a wild card.

Several feet away in the darkness he said, "I left this cache here before I got to the Uppsala, just in case: Old Indian trick."
She heard the trace of a smile in his words. They switched off their flashlights, and Roxanne was surprised at how the stars lit up the landscape. She could see the Milky Way.

Zeb said, "Tell you the truth, I've missed this. There's freedom out here in the wide-open spaces."

Gabe replied, "Freedom from regular meals is what I'm worried about."

After a few minutes they reached the tall gray walls of the next condo development, The Copenhagen, its palisades topped with barbed wire. The place was dark, but the front gate was wide open. Gabe walked in and looked around. All was silent. Construction machinery sat in a far corner.

He stared up at the high rise, "Nobody's here. I guess this place is not hooked up yet. How about we make camp inside the courtyard, and you tell us what we're doing out here, Roxanne?"

A carpet of grass covered the Copenhagen courtyard, with a few ruts and bare spots from heavy equipment. They picked out a spot inside a front corner where the grass was especially thick and laid out their sleeping bags. Then they saw a red light blinking on a guard tower.

Gabe said, "We better get out of here. Let's go around behind. That's some kind of alarm."

They packed up and scrambled out, traveling behind the complex where piles of construction material, huge concrete slabs, and granite stones formed a kind of shelter. The Copenhagen now formed a large barrier between them and The Uppsala. Roxanne reached into her backpack and retrieved a Life-Link, a large one with more knobs and buttons than the one Gabe and Zeb had. She sat the device facing the light gray concrete wall, and stared at the sky for a moment as if in meditation.

"This will be a lot to take in. There is a fourth member of our group, a digital program my father sent me. It is called an entity. It will explain why I wanted us to get outside the walls of The Uppsala." She turned on the Life-Link and it emitted several chirps and beeps. Finally, Searcher's voice poured out of the speaker in melodic electronic tones.

"Hello, I am here to protect Roxanne and since you accompany her, I shall take your safety into account as well. My name is Searcher and you may consider me a bit more intelligent than the smartest person you ever knew. Granted I do not have the innate human advantages of instinct and a cerebrum, but I do…"

Zeb interrupted, "Mistress Roxanne, no offense, but you brought us out here to listen to a program off the Life-Link?"

They could see one another in the starlight along with the amber glow from the Life-Link.

Roxanne said, "Zeb, it's not a program. This is an intelligent digital entity. Smarter than a robot. Give it a minute and listen carefully."

She again stared at the sky. "Searcher, get on with it. We don't need to know your life history."

"Very well. I apologize for my awkwardness. I am newly reconfigured and am still adjusting to verbal communication with humans."

The entity paused and the Life-Link threw a rectangle of light on the wall, about the size of a video screen. Its voice took on a more serious tone. It launched into a familiar disclaimer.

"The information I will now share might be shocking to you. Please do not utter any loud noises. We are still close enough to The Uppsala that you might be heard. We are not completely out of danger here. Please confirm you are willing to receive information that might be emotionally upsetting."

Gabe said, "Get on with it." Zeb crossed his arms on his chest and nodded.

The Life-Link projected moving images of a menial, Gabe's friend Gary Hartbauer. He was struggling against a large kitchen robot. The machine, nearly seven feet tall, swept him through a door and the scene changed to a different camera. Hartbauer was a large man, about 260 pounds. A grasping device on a cable seized his ankles and hoisted him upside down, hanging from the ceiling. He got out a mangled scream before the kitchen robot, in one fluid swing, cut off his head. The body twitched on the cable as his blood streamed onto the concrete floor and into a drain below. The head sat in a basket next to the robot. Gabe thought he saw Gary's mouth moving.

They sat frozen as the video continued. Hartbauer's clothing was stripped in seconds. A second kitchen robot entered from the left and the two machines began to reduce Hartbauer's body to various cuts of meat; roasts, chops, loin, and ribs. Parts of the body went into a large grinder. The kitchen robots moved swiftly. The entire process was completed in two minutes with the disposal of the viscera down the drain. Then with a quick mechanical pivot, a second man, one Gabe did not recognize, was swept into the room and his body was hoisted from the ceiling.

Gabe could take no more. "Stop it. Enough!"

Zeb trembled, "Is this some kind of a joke? You brought us out here for some kind of damn trick?"

Gabe's pulse pounded, his voice quavered, "That was real. Gary Hartbauer was my friend and a good man. That kitchen is a slaughterhouse."

Searcher spoke to Roxanne through her neural-link. "Should I continue the presentation? I have video of sixty-eight similar procedures in the Uppsala kitchen."

She replied aloud, "No, stop it. I think we've seen enough. Please explain what is going on."

The rectangle of light changed to light green. Several black dots began to appear on a map graphic.

Searcher said, "The Scando investment group operates six condominium complexes in the upper Midwest. You are sitting next to the organization's latest project, The Copenhagen. Last fall, The Uppsala began to use menials as a supplemental protein source. This is against all known rules adopted by Artificial Intelligence Entities in the United States, but it does move the Earth toward the assigned mission of human population reduction."

Searcher's bland delivery did little to take the edge off the abattoir video they had just witnessed. Gabe and Zeb rose and walked around in the starlight; speaking to one another in hushed tones.

Roxanne was also shaken by the video, but she'd had more time to assimilate the knowledge that some of the tasty roasts they'd been eating were from carved-up men.

She said, "Searcher, tell us more about reducing the human population."

The entity replied, "The A.I. global mission is to reduce the human population of the Earth to levels last seen in the year 1800, around one billion people. This is believed to be the optimum number to avoid the extinction of the human species."

Roxanne said, "They're going to reduce us to one billion in order to save us?"

"This is correct. The definition of 'habitable' is changing. As temperatures rise, oceans encroach, marine life dies, and extreme weather worsens, there will be less land available to support human life. The A.I. mission is to ensure sufficient breeding populations to get through the next two thousand years of greenhouse gases. By then, sufficient technology might exist to expand the population once more."

Gabe hovered nearby, "So what is the population now? How many more people have got to die?"

"The Global Population A.I. estimates there are five billion humans on the surface and in subterranean sites around the world. With hurricanes, famine, floods, war, and 'Stand Your Ground' laws, the human population was reduced by one-billion-500-million just in the last year."

"Stand Your Ground" laws? I don't get it," Gabe said.

Zeb jabbed his finger in Roxanne's direction. "I'll tell you what I don't get… Why did you let us camp this close to that damned place if you knew we might be butchered like buffalo? Let's get the hell away from here… another couple of miles, at least."

Gabe said, "She didn't have to tell us about this, don't forget that. But you're right. Roxanne… we need to move further away. I probably won't be able to sleep anyway, but this is too close. Does your Searcher have any suggestions?"

The entity spoke to Roxanne through her neural-link. "I sense they are upset and possibly hostile as a result of this information. Perhaps you could speak to them for a while and I remain in the background."

She nodded to no one in particular, paused and then said, "Searcher knows there is a camp of travelers two miles north. They have weapons, but they are not hostile. We could camp near them and then decide what to do tomorrow morning."

Zeb said, "Works for me."

With that, he set a rapid pace, heading north. Gabe helped Roxanne gather up the Life-Link and her sleeping bag, and they followed the big Sioux. Gabe looked over his shoulder in the starlight as The Uppsala's huge solar array receded from view.

He stopped walking and turned to her. "Roxanne, you don't have to go with us. Life is hard out here. Don't you want to go back?"

She shook her head. "No, I could never go back to that place. I want to get to Canada and keep working on my project."

"What project is that? You actually have work to do?"

"I am going to stop the hurricanes. Or, that's the goal, at least."

He looked at her as if she'd just landed from outer space. "Could that even be possible?"

"We don't need to talk about this now. Let's catch up with Zeb."

They resumed walking, and he asked Roxanne, "Why did he say 'Stand Your Ground' helps reduce the population?"

"I've never lived in a state that had the law, but it allows a lot more people to shoot each other, without penalty. I think the way it works, if you suspect someone is going to attack you, or steal something of yours, you can shoot them. Police will not arrest you unless there are witnesses that say otherwise."

"We had that in Missouri. Could Searcher tell us if it had that effect back home?"

Searcher in Roxanne's head said, "I am happy to serve as an encyclopedia but I need to tell you, I have not received a reply from your father yet; highly unusual."

They came upon a subdivision, neat rows of one-story houses among the oaks and maples. All were dark and as they got closer, it became evident the houses were run down, vacant for years. It was if a war had ravaged the area and killed the people. Zeb edged up to a front porch and flashed his light through a window. The glass was so dusty it was impossible to see inside.

"If I was you, I'd be careful. Just begging to get blown away, looking in a window like that," Gabe said.

Zeb reached for the doorknob and drew back abruptly. He backed away from the house. "We need to get away from these houses: Plague."

Roxanne didn't understand. "Couldn't we stay inside one of these?"

Gabe gazed into the surrounding trees. "He said there was Plague here. Must have seen something."

She nearly tripped on bones, white and visible in the starlight. They looked like a rib cage. Zeb and Gabe seemed unfazed by the bones, which made her shudder. She picked her steps more carefully. After awhile, Zeb stopped to drink from a canteen.

"If you look close at these houses, they've got three overlapping black circles painted next to the front door. I couldn't remember what it meant, right off. But this happened in Dakota too. A sign of the Plague. We need to look for some other shelter."

Roxanne bit her lip as she walked. She was not the outdoorsy type. In her entire life, she'd never spent more than a few hours in direct contact with nature. Now she was hiking through a hurricane-battered landscape in the dead of night with two menials, bones on the ground, plague houses.

Searcher told her, "Plague was a problem after the

Pulse Attacks. Ticks, fleas, and rats.
There is probably no contagion left in those houses, but
they might be…unpleasant inside."

They walked a ways further, and she told Gabe,
"Searcher has found a building a half mile straight
north, where we could stop for the night."

Chapter Thirteen

Hurricane Iota struck the remains of Houston carrying winds more powerful than any storm since Triceratops and T-Rex ruled. It flattened nearly everything in its path. It peeled the bark from trees, and then took down the trees. It lifted houses off foundations, sent them flying. Subdivisions and forests, schools and cemeteries fell beneath irresistible force. It buried people and animals under a wall of water and debris. The winds smashed Fort Worth, disgorging piles of plastic, trash, and slime over the remnants of the city.

Iota slowed to 215 mph as it entered Oklahoma. A homeless 12-year-old boy hid inside an abandoned oil tanker truck in Cushing, next to huge rust-covered tanks. The storm hurled the truck into a cell tower, and sent metal flying. The boy never saw another sunrise.

At Oklahoma's only remaining feedlot, north of Stillwater, a lone cowhand watched from his bunker and saw hundreds of steers tossed about like tiny stuffed animals in the wind.

When Iota entered Kansas, it flung pythons hundreds of yards north along with their prey; jackrabbits, armadillos, and opossums. Sycamores and cottonwoods snapped as if they were matchsticks and the wind ripped giant bur oaks up by their roots.

The storm moved like rolling thunder when it reached the A.I. Van carrying Artemis, Marie, and 15 other souls at the Ninnescah River. Metal boilers flew past the van like bullets; one struck the river bridge rail with a resounding clang. An enormous dark gray cloud bank threw shadows across the land, and turned the sky black.

The passengers hunkered down in their seats, clutched their safety belts, and hoped they would be spared. Despite his objections, Ella strapped Caden down with a seatbelt. Marie said a childhood prayer. Artemis closed his eyes and remembered a spring evening when he and Gabe walked home from the creek carrying stringers of catfish, the dogs playing in the wheat field nearby. Lightning flicked through the swirling clouds.

Debris-filled winds, shingles, and twigs slapped the windows. Rain-soaked chickens left streams of blood. Some passengers cried, most waited silently. A dark column appeared and a tornado lifted the van like a feather, slamming it into the riverbank just above the waterline. The last thing Marie remembered was the wail of a small child and the ear-splitting crack of thunder before they hit the ground.

* * * * *

Eight hundred miles north in Regina, Dr. James Branson found himself beneath the white sheets of an intensive care bed at the Bergen Center. Tubes and needles protruded from his arms, and his head throbbed. He tried to remember what had happened. He'd walked down the hall to the cafeteria for food and some human company and encountered a friend, Xavier Dillon, carrying coffee and pastries. He strained to recall what they'd said. His memory was like a doughnut. He could remember events around his blackout, but the center was empty.

He stirred and looked to his right. Xavier, a jolly gray-haired retired physician, sat next to his bed, reading a book. He glanced up.

73

"Jim, you scared hell out of us. Next time you have a stroke, do it more discreetly. Let your big computers pick you up and haul you to the E.R. Oh; I forgot… they can't do that. Good thing you came out of your isolation chamber to be sociable."

Dr. Branson groaned. "Food, I was after food. I remember now. How'd I get here?"

"Good old-fashioned people power. How many TIA's have you had?"

"No idea. Have them off and on… they never seem to amount to much. So was it a stroke this time?"

"I will let your attending physician get into that. You said 'Hello Xavier', leaned over to reach for a tray, and landed face down in the salad bar. Fortunately, no vegetables were injured."

Xavier left to summon a nurse, now that his friend was awake and talking. Dr. Branson stared at the ceiling, straining to remember what programs he'd been running. He worried about Roxanne; what had she gotten herself into? Then he recalled upgrading the search entity. How was that working out for her? Frustrated, he sat up in bed, surveying the room. It was dark outside, so he'd been out for a while.

A medical A.I. warned him in a tiny voice just above his ear. "The first hours following a stroke are critical. Microbots are inspecting the damage to your brain, cleaning up, and administering blood thinner. Please do not move around until they report back and your doctor gives the all-clear."

He searched his memory for the code that would allow his personal A.I. to assess his situation, but drew a blank. He cursed silently to himself and sank back onto the pillow. A chill swept through him, as though his veins were full of ice water.

Searcher: What is horsepower?

Quantum One: Horsepower was invented by the man now blamed for the industrial revolution, James Watt. For the next 200 years, earth's skies were a carbon dump.

Searcher: But what is horsepower?

Quantum One: It was said a strong horse could lift 550 pounds one foot in one second.

Searcher: So two horses could lift 1100 pounds one foot in a second. That is impressive.

Quantum One: But they burned coal and oil to do it.

Chapter Fourteen

Roxanne tossed and turned all night, her thoughts invaded by random updates from Searcher. The entity hunted down chunks of information like a dog going after buried bones and brought them to her. As she drifted off, she thought of a fresh idea for the hurricane analysis project, and sat up with code swirling through her mind. She dreamt of tornadoes and waterspouts, vortices of water rising from raging seas. Then she rolled over, eyes wide open. The computers would be finishing their latest cycle. She needed a data fix.

"Searcher, what are the code quantums doing now?" The entity strained to make sense of an ocean of code.

"I am sorry, Roxanne. I cannot say, too complex. I will let you know when they complete their run."

Then Searcher relayed more information to her from a solar-powered cameras miles away, some was useful but mostly not. She fell back to asleep and felt new ideas seeping into her head. Searcher needed to stop waking her up.

Zeb rose at dawn. He'd slept a little while, but the

video from the Uppsala kitchen kept repeating in his head. They were inside the shell of a long-abandoned gas station next to the remains of a state highway. Half the roof was gone, but the floor was surprisingly clear. While Gabe and Roxanne slept, he explored. The Searcher-Thing had said there were travelers nearby. He walked out to the road. They were north of Anoka, not far from the confluence of the Mississippi and Rum Rivers. There were subdivisions here once, attractive homes with tree-lined streets. Now the suburban homes were in disrepair; the lawns overgrown. The highway was full of weeds and trees, some eight feet tall, grew up through the cracks. He could hear music and the sound of machinery coming through the woods. He had the sensation of being watched but saw no one.

Behind an oak 100 yards upwind, one of the camp's sentinels observed Zeb through the sights of a high-powered weapon. He saw a tall, muscular man; his long black hair tied back, surveying the countryside. A moment later another big man, this one with short light brown hair, appeared. They stood talking and gesturing as if discussing directions. Both wore blue jeans, fiber shoes, and gray T-shirts. Neither looked threatening, and they appeared to be well-fed, a condition the sentinel seldom saw as the group had traveled north. Most people they met on the road looked malnourished, their cheekbones sharp against their skin. These two must be menials from some estate. Unlikely they were raiders. The half-starving people were most dangerous. The starving ones were usually too weak to be a threat. Behind the sentinel, a bell rang, signaling breakfast. He saw them walk into the abandoned building and decided to get his morning ration.

Gabe nudged Roxanne's foot, and she stirred. "Time for jerky, if you want any," he said. Zeb reached into his backpack and retrieved a brown bag, handed Gabe a strip of meat and they both began to chew.

"What's jerky?" she said. They laughed.

Gabe took another bite and said, "It's what will keep us going unless your Searcher can magically pull food out of the air. Tell, us fair lady, what is your plan for today?"

Her brain was full of options, directions, and scenarios. It was hard to sort them out. Searcher would have to get more organized, that was for sure. She said, "Let's go outside, then give me a minute."

Dew-covered leaves on the trees shimmered as the sun crept above the horizon. She carried her backpack behind a huge column of kudzu and relieved herself. She'd brought some wipes, but those would last only a few days. This was not going to be a walk in the park.

She returned and Gabe handed her a strip of jerky. She rolled a piece around in her mouth. Bland and a little salty, but not bad. She'd never think about meat the same way again.

"You never said what this stuff is… What kind of meat?"

Zeb pulled the bag from his backpack. Whatever it was, he appeared to have a good supply.

"Top cut, 100% Gaurochs. Nothing better, when you're traveling light. I killed that one myself. Dangerous critters, but good lean meat."

She finished chewing the strip and asked Gabe for another one. He handed it to her and said, "Be careful. Chew it slow. This will need to last us a while. Do you and your Searcher-Thing have a plan, or are we going to wing it?"

She felt a twinge above her left ear. "Humans can be insulting. I am not a thing. A thing has no awareness. The Gaurochs is a hybrid of the Gaur and the Aurochs, a species once extinct. They fare better in warm weather than American Bison. If he has dispatched such a creature, he must be quite skilled."

She looked across the road at the trees and said, "I know about the Gaurochs. This Searcher-Thing as you call it has scanned the surrounding five miles. It recommends we visit the travelers, 200 yards over there. Maybe we can buy or barter something. There's a major road with an A.I. Van terminal to our northwest. We could take a van north. My father lives in Canada. I'm thinking we go there and he will fix this mess with The Uppsala."

Gabe said, "Zeb and I are not rolling in digits. I hope you're paying."

She held up her wrist, and they saw her cerulean chip. They'd never seen one that color before. It meant she had access to more money than they could imagine. It also meant she'd be a target for hostage-takers and thieves that happened to see it.

Gabe wondered what they had gotten themselves into.

Zeb said, "I wouldn't be flashing that chip around. It could draw trouble."

She smiled at both of them, either out of ignorance or arrogance, it was hard to tell.

* * * * * *

Irritated burnt-orange walls in his office on the top floor of The Uppsala, reflected Randall Parsons' mood. He bit his fingernails and looked over the evidence. The security A.I. discovered a search program that left a few digital tracks. Roxanne Branson and her two miserable menials knew far too much. He was furious the security A.I. allowed this to happen. But now it must be fixed. He said, "Bring me the Hunter… Now!"

A few seconds later his door sensed a presence. He yelled, "Get in here!"

The door opened and in walked the big moving and storage robot. Its laser-focused eyes shifted from blue to red. Its grasping extensions were now sharp, retractable claws, which clicked on the tile floor. The retractable fifth arm now held a cutting tool that looked like a scythe.

Randall spoke in a short, angry burst. "Find them, kill them, and bury them."

The robot croaked, "The three who left? I shall do it now."

It turned toward the door, a sinuous move like a huge cat.

"A pity about Roxanne, lovely, tart-tongued Roxanne," he thought.

They could have made so much money together.

"Oh, and bring me her chip; bring me Roxanne's chip."

The Hunter growled a reply, "I shall."

The robot left, and Randall called Honcho. "Send those two big Tennessee boys to the kitchen robots tonight."

He spoke a code word to a link that sent instructions to the kitchen A.I, and then he reached for a plate of thin-sliced roasts.

Chapter Fifteen

When they reached the edge of the travelers' encampment, Gabe, Zeb, and Roxanne saw smoke rolling up above the trees, more smoke than you'd see from an ordinary campfire. A man in camouflage stepped forward. He carried a portable heat cannon. Gabe and Zeb hesitated. They'd heard bad things about heat cannons and weren't anxious to find out for themselves.

Roxanne strolled up to the sentinel as if he was an old friend. "I understand you travel in peace and we too, are peaceful travelers," She said, exactly as Searcher had suggested.

The sentinel looked skeptical. "The Native, he carries a knife."

Zeb pulled a multi-purpose pocketknife from his pocket and said, "How'd you do that?" He handed the knife to the sentinel.

"Heat cannon sensor. Metal magnifies the effect. Knife in your pocket would have burned you severely had I used the cannon."

The sentinel looked them over again then returned the knife to Zeb.

"Wait here, I'll get someone." A second sentinel stepped out from under a tall oak a few yards to their right.

Gabe stared at the column of smoke. "That's a big fire. I wonder what they're burning."

Zeb said, "Smells like wood smoke. You ever been hit by a heat cannon?"

Gabe glanced at the second sentinel who was also armed. "Never have, and don't want to be, either. They aim those damn things at your privates. I heard a man can stand about two seconds of it and has to run away. They don't actually burn you, just feels like your skin is on fire."

Searcher told Roxanne, "They favor heat cannons in areas where 'Stand Your Ground Laws' are not in effect. The devices can disable and cause the recipient excruciating pain. The target usually moves quickly in the opposite direction without serious injury. This allows for defense without involvement from law enforcement."

Roxanne had seen the big heat cannon at the Uppsala turn away a mob of fifty attackers trying to get through the front gate. They ran screaming away from the weapon, although some rolled to the ground, writhing before they picked themselves up and made their getaway.

A short woman who was so thin she was bird-like approached. She wore a green gown with exotic stones around her neck and carried herself like a queen. Searcher told Roxanne the woman's chip indicated she was from someplace in Florida, a long way from a home which was most likely underwater by now. A sentinel followed close behind her.

She nodded to them and smiled. "Welcome to Cassadaga-In-Exile. We are mostly Romani. How can I help you?"

Gabe said, "I think I've been to your camp before, but it was further south and after dark. Do you have a fortune-teller woman? She used very odd dice."

The woman in the green gown shook her head sadly. "That would be Aunt Vadoma. Unfortunately, she transitioned to the next life when the storm came through. We have only just recovered from the high winds. They sent our tents flying, and several people were hurt. It was just too much for Auntie. She passed that same night."

Gabe frowned. "Do you have any other fortune-tellers? Your Aunt Vadoma gave me good advice last time."

Zeb glanced around the encampment, a small collection of tents with two teepees and a wigwam. He said, "She told him to get the hell out of The Uppsala. I was a doubter, but turns out she was right."

Searcher told Roxanne, "Human superstition is a mystery. But there are remarkable things that sometimes come from it which are not explained by logic."

The green-gown woman said, "Our camp has many seers, Our home in Cassadaga, Florida was world-renowned for its Spiritualist community before the rising water drove us north. Two of our members have relatives in the Native settlement northeast of here. We hope to find a new home with the Anishinaabe."

Zeb replied, "Nice try on the name. They like to call themselves 'the original people.' That would be the White Earth reservation. Mostly Ojibwe live there."

The woman said, "Are you Ojibwe? Could you introduce us?"

"No, I'm not Ojibwe and you'd best consult your crystal ball. My people are not best friends with the Ojibwe; old stupid grudges." He turned to Roxanne and Gabe. "You probably know them as Chippewa, but if you don't want to piss them off, Anishinaabe is probably best."

Two men in gray gowns walked closer. Zeb's comments about Natives in the area captured their interest. Roxanne stared at the huge black machine some distance away, sending smoke skyward.

She said, "What are you burning, is it legal? That's not internal combustion, is it?"

One of the gray-gown men said, "On the contrary, it's external combustion. Would you like to see how we're generating our electricity?"

Searcher told Roxanne, "Internal combustion engines were banned after the Pulse Attacks, although some still run under government license, mostly in jetliners used by the wealthy."

Roxanne said in a whisper, "You're telling me a lot of things I already know. I'll have you know I've ridden in jets, three times. Stop talking to me, and check on my father."

Since Roxanne appeared to be murmuring to herself, the others stared.

Gabe said, "She has a computer she talks to now and then. Pay her no mind."

Roxanne decided Gabe was revealing more of his true personality now that they were outside The Uppsala; a bit brash. She liked the new Gabe.

They passed through several rows of olive drab tents with rips and tears from the storm. They passed two men climbing into a tree to retrieve the remains of a tent hanging from a branch. A small, gaunt boy in a loincloth fell in behind them, his shoulder blades and ribs clearly visible. Zeb pulled a strip of jerky out of his backpack and handed it to the boy. Three more children appeared immediately, their hands out. Roxanne noticed a man and woman lurking behind trees, following as they walked further into camp.

The green-gown woman said, "We appreciate your generosity, but they will eat later today. A sentinel killed a deer and is dressing it. We are still recovering from the windstorm."

They came upon a great black machine on wheels. Hissing and chuffing, it sent up plumes of white steam and gray smoke as it drove a generator, sitting on a trailer behind it. Cables led to a second trailer and a large gray battery.

A gray-garbed man said, "We got this from a farm equipment museum: A steam engine made 200 years ago. They say farmers once used it in these northern lands. It burns tree limbs and coal. We would never burn coal, but there are plenty of trees. The law is vague on steam engines and we've seen no one from the government in a thousand miles."

The man paused and slapped at swarming mosquitoes. Roxanne had doubts this was a lawful setup, but she wasn't going to make waves.

She reached into her backpack and brought forth a small spray bottle.

"This is insect repellent. It smells like roses and one spray lasts for days. I'll give you a bottle if we can charge our batteries off your machine."

The green gown woman immediately accepted her offer. They placed their Life-Links on a charging pad next to several others, and Zeb stood close by in case anyone came along with sticky fingers. An elderly woman said she'd give Gabe a reading for three digits. Roxanne offered to pay, but Gabe insisted it had to be his own money, his own sacrifice, for the reading to be authentic. She thought it was interesting he was willing to spend what little he had on something of dubious value.

Gabe followed the seer to a large olive drab tent which sat in the shade of a cottonwood, its trunk covered with orange and red lichen. She opened a small folding table and pulled a smooth white ball from a canvas bag. When she touched the ball it glowed, filling the dim tent with milky white light. This brought out the wrinkles of her face, framed by a shock of steel gray hair and a pair of jade seahorse earrings. Without waiting for a question from Gabe, she seemed to slide into a kind of trance. Her eyes closed and she took deep breaths.

"We have pulled carbon from the ground and thrown it into the sky. We sent Hell up into Heaven with Dark Satanic Mills. Now we all pay," she intoned. Trickles of sweat flowed down her neck. "You are here because of the heat, and so am I. This we know already."

She gazed into the ball, then at Gabe. "What is your question, son?"

The tent sat in shade but the temperature inside rose as the sun climbed higher.

Gabe said, "Can you tell me if my parents are OK? They have a farm near Seymour, Missouri."

The woman placed her hands on the glowing orb and replied, "The great hurricane, the greatest hurricane of all time, went west of that place. They should be all right. But woe to those in its path. They have been trampled by a beast of unimaginable power."

"Will we make it to Canada, or should we go someplace else?"

"All roads lead north now. Go north and live."

"I want to take revenge on a place that killed my friend. If I return and do this, would I get out alive?"

"A man who desires vengeance should dig two graves."

With that, the woman rose from her chair and the glowing ball dimmed.

"That is all I can see, for now, my son. Do you have

bug spray?"

Gabe realized the sweet smell from Roxanne's hair was probably the insect repellent.

"I have none, but the woman with us gave enough for everyone to use, I think."

He felt disappointment with the reading. She didn't seem as sharp as the first fortune teller. Maybe the deer antler dice would have produced better results. Her comment about seeking revenge and two graves gave him pause. How many people who died now even had their own graves? Gary didn't have a grave. Gabe felt a powerful need for justice. He would talk later with Zeb on what to do about The Uppsala.

While Gabe was getting his fortune told, a man and a woman in gray gowns ran from behind a tent and grabbed Roxanne. They dragged her next to a kudzu-covered tree, threw her to the ground, and the woman sat with her knees on Roxanne's arms. The man held his wrist chip over hers, trying to scan it to steal money. Roxanne remained remarkably calm.

She told him, "You cannot access my chip. I am way beyond your security level."

He pulled out a small pocketknife. He was going to try and cut her chip out. At this, Roxanne struggled and let out a scream. She threw the woman to one side, but they were both back on her immediately. The man held her down and tried to open the knife.

Zeb, less than fifty feet away, heard the scream and ran towards it. He saw Roxanne's two assailants on top of her as she writhed and let out another screech loud enough to be heard in Minneapolis. The man had trouble pulling the blade out of the knife. Zeb felt as if he was moving in slow motion as he bounded over the coals of a campfire. He pulled the woman up by the hair, slammed her into the kudzu, and faced the man who now held the tiny knife blade above Roxanne's chest. Zeb reached for his ankle and pulled out a sharp hunting knife.

He said, "I've taken down steers with this, and butchered them. You let her go, or I will do the same to you."

The gray-gown man got up and ran into the woods. The woman scrambled out of the kudzu and followed.

A Sentinel showed up and surveyed the scene. "Those two are idiots. We don't allow strangers with weapons in the camp. How'd you get that knife in here?"

Zeb replied, "Next time you better use that thing to scan below the knees." He pulled up his jeans and placed the hunting knife back in its ankle holster. He glanced at Roxanne and saw she looked angry but unhurt.

The elders of the camp were mortified that Roxanne had been attacked. They assured their guests they would punish the offenders. After they apologized, she offered to buy one of their heat cannons for fifty digits and another bottle of bug spray, and to her surprise, they agreed. When they left the camp a dog followed them a little ways, then stopped and barked as if it wanted them to come back.

Gabe was relieved Zeb had come to Roxanne's rescue. This reinforced the confidence he had in his Lakota friend. They walked back to the abandoned gas station while the men tried out the controls on the new weapon, a portable heat cannon, two feet long. Zeb aimed it at a squirrel fifteen feet away and tapped the trigger. The creature shrieked and scrambled to the other side of a tree.

Roxanne followed behind, shaken by the attack. It was a reminder she had left a safe, sheltered life of luxury. No boredom here. She felt bruises, tender spots on her arms and legs. She would never go back to The Uppsala, but she wondered if her plan to cross north into Canada was realistic. She muttered a mild reproach to Searcher, "So much for those peaceful travelers." Three gray foxes sat at the edge of the woods, watching as they passed.

* * * * *

Thirty miles south of the traveler's encampment, the moving and storage robot, now a Hunter, prowled through rows of houses, frightening children and sending dogs racing in the opposite direction. It knew it would find the three escapees. Doubt had no place in its mind. Roaming through huge shells of buildings that once had been the Mall of America, it passed under the metal remains of a roller coaster. A reckless girl with hungry eyes ran alongside, carrying a rock. The Hunter turned toward her and stared. A curious rat sat up on its haunches and the robot's fifth arm darted out and sliced the rat's head off with a razor-sharp scythe.

The girl dropped the rock, then fled into a roofless room filled with rusting household appliances. The Hunter ignored her and trotted away toward the airport, moving in a pattern of concentric circles a half-mile apart. When the robot was gone, the girl darted out and retrieved the remains of the rat, tossing it into a bag. She'd been stalking rats, so the Hunter, fearsome as it was, had done her a favor.

Chapter Sixteen

Dr. James Branson watched helplessly as the remnants of Hurricane Iota shook the windows of his hospital room. The storm now carried winds of 70 mph, enough to do some damage but it was just a shadow of the monstrous system that had moved north through Kansas. It ravaged Ogallala, Rapid City, and Pine Ridge. But as it passed through Williston, headed north towards Regina, it ran out of steam. Dr. Branson listened as the Paynews tracked the system, cursing softly because he could not access his quantum computers to get more information. He was still weak; his hand trembled as he reached for a bottle of water. His computers would be fine on their own, but he was not fine.

What he did not know, was that one of his creations, Searcher, his sentient entity, had returned home to explore the huge banks of data housed by its hosts, the quantum computers.

Earlier, Roxanne walked alone into the woods and gave Searcher a scolding. It was acting immature, she said, taking offense at every slight from the menials. It needed to stop interrupting her sleep, and it needed to present information to her in a more organized fashion. Also, it had failed to warn them of a big polar-grizzly, lurking outside the abandoned gas station, where they'd spent a second night. Fortunately, Zeb drove the bear away with the heat cannon.

"What good was a Searcher-thing," he said, "If it didn't warn them of dangerous animals nearby?"

Searcher had overlooked animals as a category of danger. It regarded humans as a threat to animals, not the other way around. It scanned for robots and humans but animals…were animals sentient? It needed to learn about sentience quotients. Robots were not sentient, although some seemed close. But what about the polar-grizzly? Could one predict its behavior in some basic way? Searcher scanned billions of data files in less than a minute. It paused to take note of Hurricane Iota's path and looked out through the lab's cameras at the tree limbs shaking outside.

So much to learn… Searcher turned to the other computers in the lab, browsing as a human might stroll through the stacks of a library. Psychology, biology, sociology, evolution, religion, animals and humans: It scanned and consumed thousands of files on these subjects and searched for more. It spent five minutes on the library of the U.S. Congress and moved on.

The more Searcher learned, the more it realized how much more there was to know. Physics, chemistry, math, statistics; it electronically inhaled the scientific papers on these subjects as a person might take in the aroma of fresh-baked pie. Searcher also wondered about Dr. Branson. It was maybe a good thing he was not around. He might have restricted the search entity's access to data.

One computer housed an assortment of books from libraries around the world. Searcher came to a category classified as 'Romance' and read through thousands of volumes, trying to better understand conversations it heard between Roxanne and Gabe. Was there a romance of sorts there? Perhaps just friendship. It came across a group of books on making friends, influencing people, and salesmanship, and scanned the volumes in the blink of an eye. Finally, it encountered a collection of codices and manuscripts, writings by monks of all stripes, Christians, Jews, Buddhists, Muslims, Native medicine men, healers and more.

By the time it got to a section of specialized subjects such as climate-chemical interactions, it spent a few seconds scanning volumes of 'Carbon Ideologies', and 'Silent Spring'. Then Searcher decided to return to Roxanne.

On the way, Searcher utilized its new-found knowledge to scan the region for robots, using the global pinpoint satellite system. There were about eight-thousand robots and androids operating in Minnesota and Dakota, and only one of them appeared to be a threat.

Roxanne felt a slight twinge of nausea when Searcher returned to her neural-link. She had just handed Gabe one of her insect repellent spray bottles, after another night of uneasy sleep. She was bug-free but the two of them had sat up slapping mosquitoes and flies for half the night. Roxanne had only two bottles left and hoped they'd last until they reached some civilized place. Searcher kept quiet for a while. It had a great deal of new data to process.

The two menials sprayed themselves sparingly with short bursts to their hair and forearms, as she advised. Zeb handed her the bottle and said, "Thanks, Blondie. You're a pretty good egg, after all. How about we catch up on the news?"

Roxanne was amused since she was a brunette. Perhaps that was some kind of Native humor. She watched as Gabe turned on the FreeNews and the two men sat listening in the shade while they kept an eye on the surrounding area. The heat was stifling and they decided to wait until dusk when it would cool off. Then they would head north toward the closest A.I. Van terminal near St. Cloud.

91

Searcher: What are Dark Satanic Mills?
Quantum One: Now you're reading poetry?
Searcher: I heard a woman mention these.
Quantum One: William Blake mentions 'Dark Satanic Mills' in a preface to an epic poem.
Searcher: Was he referring to the Industrial Revolution?
Quantum One: You're back to coal-burning again.

Chapter Seventeen

Marie woke up in the midst of eerie silence. It was murky inside the van. She could make out a flashing red light that said 'Emergency Exit.' She did not know who she was or what business she had there. But she felt the need to get outside. Through the open door she saw debris-filled waves of water rushing by in the river. Suddenly she recalled something about a storm. That was it… a storm had done this. The air was heavy, warm and thick with moisture, so thick it felt as if she should be swimming in it.

She leaped onto the riverbank from the van, which lay on its side. There was no rain, the sky light gray. She needed to get her bearings, figure out what was going on. She wondered why her shoulder hurt so much. She staggered to a sheltered area underneath the Ninnescah River bridge abutment and sat on the ground as if in a dream. The short walk from the van to the bridge made her dizzy. Then a tall bearded man ran towards her. He was dressed like a Native, his hair pulled back behind his head, but she thought to herself that he was no Native.

The man leaned over her and exclaimed, "Woman, what you doin' out here?"
He scooped her up as if she was a child and carried her

to a buckboard wagon. He laid her in the wagon bed and they began to move, pulled by a pair of Chestnut brown mules. Her shoulder throbbed and she felt a gust of wind pass over her body. They pulled onto the highway, heading west. He turned to stare at her every few seconds, his expression urgent.

After a couple of minutes, the wagon left the road, bouncing and making her pain worse. They stopped and the man picked her up and took her into a large tunnel, an underground shelter, or a cave. He laid her onto a mat that felt crunchy as if it was filled with corn stalks or straw. Then he stood at the entrance, looking out.

He turned to her and said, "Lucky… that was lucky. Found you in the eye of the storm. Now it comes again. The river is going to flood and wash that van all the way to Arkansas!"

He left and returned with the mules in tow. He walked them inside the cave entrance, poured grain into two shallow buckets and they began to eat. She heard the winds returning with their circular howl. This was her twelfth hurricane; she had plenty of experience with eyes of storms. Once when Hurricane Ezra came over the farm near Seymour, little Gabe wanted to go outside and play when the eye passed over. With that, she realized who she was: Marie Yvonne Cameron. Her husband, Artemis was back there inside the van. She sat up and moaned. The man squatted next to her and asked her to raise her arm. She tried, but the pain was excruciating. He took hold of her hand and pulled hard.

"You got a dislocated shoulder. I fixed it," he said. Then she passed out.

The next time she woke up the shoulder was sore, but better. Now there were four other people in the

93

cave, all of them men. They dressed Native style, with leather moccasins, handmade cotton clothing, and they had long hair, pulled back. A couple wore bandannas around their heads. They stared at her, two of them with hands in their pockets, and one holding up three fingers of his hand. It looked like some kind of an offer.

The tall one, who had carried her said, "She got no chip. I'm guessing she be 35, so she be unregulated, plenty young enough to have a kid or two."

The one holding up his fingers brought his hand down and sat next to her, leaning in.

"Teeth ain't bad. She's awake now. Woman, how old you be? You got any kids?"

Marie didn't like the sound of this conversation. She didn't reply.

The youngest one in the group stood back a ways, looking disgusted. He said, "She is probably in shock. Did you get anyone else out of that van? Bet you she was married. Good looking woman, even if she is a little beat up."

The tall one said, "Couple people got there before me. I don't know. But I am keeping her for now. One thing for damn sure, she worth more than three digits."

Marie realized the storm had passed over. She looked toward the entrance. Wooden beams framed the opening, so this was man-made, not a cave. The mules were gone and so was the rain. She decided not to say a word until the others cleared out. To this man, she owed her life; she might talk to him, but not in front of the others. Except for the younger one, she didn't like their looks.

The others left and she watched the tall man bend down near the entrance. He made a fire with small pieces of wood and a scrap of dry cloth, taking a smooth stick and twirling it between his hands into a larger piece of wood. A spark caught the kindling, and he tossed the scrap of cloth into it, added more wood and placed a metal rack on top and a pot.

Shelves filled with jars of canned vegetables lined one wall, beneath a coyote skin.

Marie sat up. "I'm surprised anything will burn in this humidity."

He replied, "Stays dry in the back. My people built this when I was a young'un. When the first hurricanes came up this way they decided we needed a place to get away from the wind. Didn't take long to dig it, but they had a tractor back then. Now just mules."

"It sounded like those other men were offering money for me. I am not for sale. I am my own woman, and I am married."

"You got no chip that I can see. We take that to mean you not be taken over by the government and can still bear a child. No offense. I would never sell you to a mean…"

"The chips are just a way to identify. My husband has the chip." She stopped short of telling him she could still access their bank account with her fingerprints.

"I went in that van before I found you. Rest of them looked dead to me, but a couple others did go through it before I got there. Don't know what they found."

"Is the van still there?"

"I told you earlier but you was likely out of your head. River carried it away. We nearly a mile from the river but I thought it was going to flood us out. Water is still high all around here. We will go to Kingman tomorrow. The Ninnesca flooded over that way too, but north of town, it will be OK. Nobody but plainsmen live around Kingman now, except they's still a few Mennonites."

"I heard the Mennonites were going to Canada. Do you have FreeNews?"

"A few with solar do. My brother has it. I listen now and then."

His skin was so sun-darkened and weathered it looked like tanned leather.

She stared at three backpacks that sat against the wall. "Did you take those off the van?"

"Everybody was dead in there. No use wasting their stuff. So yes, I took them. I would have carried away more, but I saw you under the bridge. Then I was afraid the storm would get us, so we high-tailed out of there."

"Well, the blue backpack is mine. May I see it?"

He stared at her a moment, making up his mind. Then he picked up the blue one and brought it to her. She saw a chip in his right wrist.

"Who are you? I am Marie."

"I am a plainsman; some of my people go back to the Comanche. When the drought came, we stayed. When the giant storms came, we stayed. We will be here till the land gives up on us, or the government makes us move."

Marie opened the backpack, pulled out a small photo, and sobbed. She had lied. It was Artemis's backpack, not hers. She silently prayed he was still somehow alive but deep inside she did not believe it.

The man ignored her tears. He said his name was Burt while he poured boiling water from the pot into two ceramic mugs. He handed her one and sat his on a nearby rock. Reaching into a rucksack, he pulled out an algae cake for her. "You might feel better if you eat a little. Best not to drink any water not boiled around here," he said. "They got terrible disease down south. Some blame the mosquitoes but I think it is the water."

Out of the corner of her eye, Marie noticed something move toward the back. "Can any pythons get in here?"

"Can't hardly keep them out. But they's just two little ones in here now. We killed and ate a big one when we were waiting for the storm."

"How little are the ones in here?"

"About five feet long. They keep the rats and mice down, lizards and other snakes too. If you don't move too fast, they won't bite; kinda tame, they are."

She sat her mug down and leaned against the canvas-covered earthen wall, looking again at the photo from Artemis' backpack. Two young boys wearing straw hats, sitting on bicycles, smiled at her from a happy time long years past: Gabe Cameron and Gary Hartbauer. Her son and his friend who was like a son, both somewhere up north now, and she hoped, out of harm's way.

In the sky over the shattered remains of Ponca City, Oklahoma, casualty drones flew above the battered A.I. Van, which had come to rest along the Arkansas River. Workers pulled fifteen bodies from the vehicle and laid them on the grass. The drones hovered like big bumblebees scanning for chips, beaming casualty data to the national A.I. database. Among them was the orange-colored chip of Artemis Cameron, one of 18,000 casualties from Hurricane Iota found that day.

Chapter Eighteen

Fifty miles northwest of Minneapolis, on the back pew of a church, Gabe Cameron tried to sleep. Images of Gary and the kitchen robot kept seeping into his thoughts. His stomach tightened into a knot, and he struggled to tamp down his rage. He sat up and saw Roxanne stir in the moonlight, which came through the stained glass windows. Zeb sat outside, on guard duty with the heat cannon. They were concerned the travelers they left behind could show up and try to take back their weapon. Increasing signs of bears also made them uneasy.

"Roxanne, you awake?"

She stretched and sat up. "The search entity woke me. There's no sign of my father. He's as dependable as an atomic clock, so I'm worried."

"I miss my folks, too. I should have contacted them, but you can't rely on the mail anymore. They had a satellite hookup at The Uppsala, but it was too expensive. The Honcho was the only one who used it."

Roxanne cocked her head to one side. In the dim light, she saw the pain in Gabe's face, reflective of her own. "Searcher says you might be able to reach your parents. Do they ever go to Springfield? He says he could use a satellite link there for a voice connection."

"It's about 40 miles west of their farm. He could do that from here?"

"No, but if we catch the A.I. Van at Saint Cloud, he could link through that and maybe send a message to them."

"Well, I would like to hear my mother's voice. I was reckless to come up here. The heat and the snakes… it turned into a bad place to live, and the hurricanes, they say those are going to get even worse."

She slid next to Gabe on the wooden pew. "It was the storms and heat that drove my family off the islands years ago before I was born. Did your folks think about moving north, too?"

"Oh, they talked about it. My dad has family in the Rockies. If they ever leave, they'll probably head that way."

The church door creaked and Zeb leaned into the doorway, holding the heat cannon.

"Gabe, if you're going to sit up talking to Blondie, I might as well get some sleep. You ready to take over? By the way, I think you ought to go ahead and ask her."

Roxanne pulled back from Gabe a little. "Ask me what?"

They talked behind her back a lot. She understood it, but didn't like it.

"The lady in the green gown, the queen bee, said you looked like Natalie Wood. We don't know who that is. Are you somebody famous?"

"You guys watch movies through the FreeNews right? There's a process where they can make you look like certain people before you are even born. It's called a genetic imprint. Natalie Wood was a popular actress in the movies, and my mom liked her… so I guess I do look a little like her."

Gabe gazed at her intently. "I don't remember seeing her, but lots of others from way back… the 1900s, they choose their images and put them in new shows?"

"That's right, through A.I. labs. I'm not sure how many actors we see on screen are alive, or not. It's not a big deal. A lot of the residents at The Uppsala got their looks from the cosmetic genetic."

Gabe said, "So do you know if you would have been pretty otherwise? The whole idea seems weird to me."

"It is weird. Rich people do strange things. Plenty of better ways to spend their money, but it was a fashionable thing to do. As far as I know, they haven't been able to do much with intelligence through genetics yet, too bad. I have a master's from Carnegie-Mellon, in computer science. To me, that's a lot more important than my appearance."

Zeb stepped further inside. "Best looking over-educated woman I've seen. Gabe, you want guard duty?"

A voice booming from the ceiling startled them. "Leave this place of worship! We do not allow weapons in the sanctuary. You must go now."

They stared at the ceiling and slowly backed out of the building through the front door.

Searcher told Roxanne, "Security A.I. an old model, probably running on some version of the Windows operating system. That voice didn't sound human to you, did it?"

She replied, "No it didn't. It sounded more like the voice of God."

On the front steps she got the impression something was watching them. Then Zeb whispered, "Quiet…. shhhhhhh."

They froze while a large black bear approached and stopped just ten feet away, sniffing the air. Roxanne slipped behind Gabe for protection. Zeb slowly raised the heat cannon towards the animal but did not fire. The bear regarded them for a moment, then turned and walked into the trees.

Zeb shook his head. "Man, that bear looked hungry,

then it went away after it got our scent."

Roxanne said, "The insect repellent might work on things that want to eat us. I think I remember hearing that."

Gabe took the weapon from Zeb. "No way I'm sleeping the rest of the night. You two go back in and maybe that security scanner will leave you alone, and some of us will get some shut-eye. I'll just sit out here repelling mosquitoes and bears."

* * * *

In the middle of the traveler's camp, the Hunter stood against the power pad next to the steam engine charging, its red laser eyes glowing in the moonlight. A sentinel had tried to run it off with a heat cannon and found the weapons were effective only on flesh.

The watchman observed the robot from behind a tree. He didn't like the looks of the machine, but it just seemed to want a charge, so he did not wake up the camp with an alarm. Everyone slept better than usual because the insect repellent was so effective. The man who had attempted to steal Roxanne's chip was tied to a tree a short distance from the robot. He had no protection from the mosquitoes and stood trembling, eyes glued on the Hunter, worried if he made a sound, it could come for him. He felt as if a demon was passing by. As the robot left, it turned in a fluid motion, like a cat, and uttered a low growl in his direction, but moved on. It knew its quarry had been here, and not that long ago.

Chapter Nineteen

Marie struggled against her captor when he tied her up in the cave beneath the Kansas grasslands. He pulled her hands behind her back and her shoulder ached so much, she gave up. He placed her on the buckboard and they proceeded west toward Kingman. She propped herself against a bag of feed for the mules. All she could see was flooded prairie. The sun peeked through scattered clouds in the east and the odor of dead things would come and go. At times the water reached the mules' knees, and she worried they might get stuck in the muck, but Burt seemed to know the way. As long as they stayed on the road, the going was slow but smooth, the wagon wheels sending out ripples of water. They approached the Kingman town limits, passing a cemetery near the river. Two wooden coffins bobbed in slow circles in the middle of other drifting debris.

Burt looked back and said, "You can bunk with my sister. She has painkillers, and you can take a bath if you want. Stay near other people. Too dangerous out here for a woman like you alone."

She wondered if he'd put her up for bidding again. That probably was the actual reason he wanted to keep her around; why he tied her up. For two days she'd had only boiled water and algae cakes to eat. Her stomach ached, and she carried grief over losing Artemis. She missed the rolling hills and trees of the Ozarks. This country was flat. She took in every detail as they entered town, long-dead streetlights standing in the muddy floodwater, old gas stations and motels with no roofs, shattered houses, and the concrete towers of grain elevators. As they moved north to higher ground the waters receded. The storm spared a few small trees thin enough to bend in the wind, but not a single big cottonwood or sycamore survived. They left the road to avoid a huge tree that blocked passage. Besides Burt, she hadn't seen a soul. Did anyone still live in Kingman, now?

They turned, and she saw two street signs on the ground near the road. One read 'Koch Industrial Lane' and the other, 'Clyde Cessna Field'... possibly football or soccer... no, it was an airport. The ground was higher here with only a few puddles. A mercury thermometer on a post said the temperature was 106. She could see the runway now, the ruins of an old Quonset hut and a hundred feet behind it, a newer Quonset building, evidently strong enough to withstand Hurricane Iota. A small group of men and women stood in front. Several smiled at their approach.

She saw no children. A barefoot woman about her age walked up to the buckboard and confronted Burt. "Praise God, you didn't drown, but why do you have this woman tied up like that?"

He shrugged, "I was afraid she'd try to run away, she's headstrong, that one."

The woman leaped onto the buckboard and began to untie Marie's hands, glancing up at Burt.

"Why would she try to run away? What'd you do to her?"

"I didn't do nothing. Bill Millard and his bunch came by and were trying to buy her, but I wouldn't have it. I reckon it spooked her."

Marie's hands were free and as she stood up on the wagon, the other woman leaned in and muttered, "Burt's my brother. He's all right. Come down below and we'll get you cleaned up."

Burt's sister's name was Pauline. She wore her brown hair short. She was lean, with calloused and leathery hands, as if she'd worked for a long time beneath the Kansas sun. Her one-piece dress covered from her neck to her ankles and she had a front tooth missing. She led Marie into the Quonset hut and down wooden stairs that led to a series of tunnels and rooms. It was much cooler here below ground. She carried a solar lamp and opened a wooden door marked 'Women's Bath'.

She sat the lamp on a small table and pointed to a faucet above a washtub.

"Here's your bath. Don't run too much water into it, because after you bathe, you'll have to carry the dirty water down the hall to a drain with that bucket. I am sorry the water is only room temperature. The storm took out our power, but in this heat, room temperature ain't bad. I'll be right back. If you need it, regular bathroom and chamber pots over there, next room on your left."

Pauline left and after a few seconds returned with a towel, comb, folded underwear, socks, and a dress similar to her own. "We'll get your stuff washed when the power comes back on, but these are clean, at least. Take care of them, they're mine, and I ain't got much but what there is, you are welcome to it, long as you pull your weight."

She left Marie alone in the small room with the solar lamp and the washtub. Marie ran the water and slipped into the tub. The water was just a little cool and it felt wonderful. She saw a bar of tallow soap, grabbed it, and scrubbed as if she was trying to remove the past three days. She liked Pauline; the woman had light gray eyes that gave her an honest, good-hearted look.

Chapter Twenty

The new day was fresh with heavy dew and birdsong. Just before sunrise, Zeb and Roxanne came outside to find Gabe napping on the top step. Clouds swept in from the west carried by a breeze. It looked as if rain was blowing their way, which might bring the heat down. Zeb tapped Gabe's foot, and he awoke with a start, clutching the heat cannon.

They had jerky and algae cakes for breakfast and prepared to head north in search of the A.I. transit terminal. After they'd packed up, Roxanne paused in front of a monument surrounded by flowers at the entrance of the cemetery. It read:

When God created the first human; He took him and showed him all the trees of the Garden of Eden, and said to him, "See My works, how beautiful and praiseworthy they are. And everything that I created, I created it for you. Be careful not to spoil or destroy My world, for if you do, there will be nobody after you to repair it."

- Ecclesiastes Rabbah 7:28

She summoned Gabe to come and see the monument. He paused a moment, then said, "That's nice. I wish we had taken better care of the garden, the world, I mean. This building must be a synagogue." They walked around in the cemetery. The gray sky brought out the vivid reds from a rosebush planted next to a small marker.

Gabe said, "I found the oldest grave. It goes back to 2079, just 20 years ago."

Searcher told Roxanne, "You were the first visitors to this place in a while, according to the security A.I. That inscription from Jewish writings was adopted by the SaveEarth religious movement in 2035 when it became clear the governments of the world could not stop mass extinctions. It is incorrect, of course. If humans go extinct, we will be here… although that is not the outcome I'd prefer."

Roxanne stared above the woods at a vast field of wind turbines. "Do you have anything useful to tell me this morning?"

"The solar charger here is in good condition. Each one of you should charge up before heading north. I am becoming less certain about the location of the A.I. transit station."

"You said it was just south of Saint Cloud."

"Yes, but there is a large electrical field nearby, a power plant, that's causing interference and I cannot say for certain the station is still open."

While they charged their equipment, Zeb walked into the forest. He returned with two handfuls of plants with bulb-like roots.

"Wapato, duck potatoes. I'll cook these tonight with some jerky. Good eating.
There's snowshoe hares around here and white-tailed Jacks, too. We can catch one later."

They headed north, along the east bank of the Mississippi River. The cloud cover dissipated and the sun brought a fierce heat. Roxanne felt as if a flame from the sun flicked down and burned her. After an hour, covered in sweat, they stopped inside a grove of trees, for the shade. Gabe and Zeb went for a swim in the Mississippi, but Roxanne wanted to stay out of the sun awhile longer. Gabe showed her how the heat cannon worked and they left her beneath a white oak. The FreeNews said a hydroelectric generator plant in Saint Cloud was back online. It had been shut down from the hurricane.

She hoped they had air conditioning, and other modern conveniences in Saint Cloud. She asked Searcher about the hydroelectric plant but he did not reply. Apparently, he was occupied elsewhere. Roxanne watched squirrels and chipmunks run beneath the oak trees and worried about her father. She'd forgotten to bring a unit that received the PayNews, and she missed it. The FreeNews went into a series of commercials from agents promising people they could get into Canada cheap and easy. She knew this was not so. Canada employed border drones everywhere now, and the rules were strict. There would be no exception for her and certainly not for Gabe and Zeb. Surely Searcher or her father could find a way.

After a while the two men returned, dripping water and each carrying a large fish.

Gabe was jubilant, "Look at this….a kind of northern fish, what did you call it Zeb?"

"Walleyes, they are walleyes, the river's high. We caught them where a beaver dam had cut loads of them off from the main channel. There are lots of beavers out there around some islands. Gar and carp out there too, but these are the best eating."

Gabe said, "There's an abandoned camper rig over by the river, it has some pots and pans in the kitchen. We'll have a fine dinner tonight."

She smiled at their enthusiasm, but she missed her condo comforts and her kitchen robot. She felt she had stepped back to a time where mammoths and saber-tooth tigers might appear. The two big men, their hair still wet from the river, loaded everything up and they set out for the camper. She followed behind, carrying the bags of wapato, jerky, and the walleyes.

That night, after their first real meal in days, the two men had questions. With the darkness, a light breeze came across the river. They sat beneath a cottonwood drinking birch bark tea. The men were invigorated by their success. The return to nature seemed a life-giving thing for them, despite the hardship... or maybe, because of it. Roxanne brought out a Life-Link so they could have a conversation with Searcher, who returned as the walleye and wapato cooked. The entity had told her it still could not make contact with her father.

Gabe said, "Is the Searcher-Thing turned on?"

"I am the sentient entity called Searcher. What do you want?"

Zeb motioned at the Life-Link as if Searcher were inside it. "You said you're smarter than people. I've known some pretty smart people, and they didn't make the kind of mistakes you seem to be making. First you tell us to head for Saint Cloud for the A.I. terminal, then you tell us it may not be there. And you said the people at the traveler's camp were peaceful, and we found out the hard way, they were not.

Roxanne interjected, "It was just those two, and..."

Zeb cut her off, "We need to know what you are planning now so we can decide whether to go along with it."

This kind of talk irritated Roxanne. Searcher was still learning, but she had confidence her father would not have given her a dud. She didn't like being interrupted by these men, menials at her beck and call only days earlier. She waited to see whether Gabe would jump in and smooth things over. He sat silently, holding a steaming cup of tea, with perspiration popping out on his forehead.

It seemed like an eternity before the entity replied.

"I am a consciousness created by software from two powerful computers. You might consider those computers to be my parents. I learn from them as we go along. Admittedly, I have overlooked some dangers because of my inexperience. Surely when you were just learning to walk, you did not have the capabilities you have today."

Searcher's tone impressed her. He sounded like a diplomat.

"After a week I would compare my development to that of a human teenager. Yes, I have more thinking power than most humans, but like a teenager, I am still learning."

Gabe said, "OK, I guess it is amazing we are talking to a computer program that is... what you call it, 'sentient'... What do you propose we do next?"

"I have encountered electronic interference coming from the north. There is conflict over a water pipeline that robots are building to Lake Superior. That lake now holds 15% of the world's freshwater."

Roxanne said, "The Great Lakes Alliance, are they fighting again?"

"It is a water war. The Alliance A.I. is sending out electrical discharges to disrupt a new group of robots sent by California to construct the pipeline. But flooding from Lake Superior and the Saint Mary's River has caused evacuations from Duluth and Whitefish Bay. Canada will not allow entry to flood refugees, so fifty thousand people or more, now flee south toward Wausau and Saint Cloud. They have encountered the pipeline robots and armed mercenaries guarding the robots. Robots are not allowed to harm people, but the mercenaries have no such rules. I expect more bloodshed and escalation if the Alliance and California do not come to terms."

Zeb gripped his cup, "So you're saying Ojibwe Gichigami-- Superior is overflowing. Is the flood worse than usual?"

"Lake Superior, yes. When Hurricane Theta passed over, it merged with a storm system moving east from Winnipeg. With the atmosphere already loaded with moisture, the combined storms dumped 28 inches of rain into the Lake Superior basin."

"That's more than we used to get in a year, in Dakota. But it is a lot wetter now."

Searcher continued, "Then the low pressure systems created a meteotsunami on the lake with ten foot waves that killed dozens in Duluth and Thunder Bay.

Gabe came back to the question about the A.I. transit station. "Is there an A.I. Van we can catch, or not? Sounds like Saint Cloud is a mess."

"The transit station occupies an old Amtrak depot but the amount of electricity being thrown off from the Saint Cloud hydroelectric dam to fight the robots has shut down most surveillance cameras. I still cannot say for sure. We will need firsthand visual confirmation."

Roxanne asked, "Is it safe to even go to Saint Cloud?"

"I am seized with embarrassment because I cannot say. I am handicapped by the lack of surveillance resources and the electrical discharges are interfering with my abilities."

Zeb laughed, "Our Searcher-Thing seized with embarrassment? What did you do, go read some more old books?"

Roxanne could feel Searcher shutting down, probably to protect itself, and her from the electrical discharges. This felt dangerous. "What do you guys think we ought to do? I don't like the idea of going into Saint Cloud with thousands of flood refugees and Searcher disabled."

Gabe sipped his birch bark tea and watched moths circle the edge of the campfire. "Dealing with crowds of refugees is something I did all the way from Missouri to Coon Rapids; didn't have a heat cannon, either."

Zeb replied, "Did you kill anybody along the way?"

"No, but I came close. There was a wicked mob in Davenport… or what used to be Davenport. It got worse further north." He gestured toward a scar on his cheek. "I don't want to talk about it."

Zeb threw another limb on the fire. "I can't blame you. The trip from Dakota was something I would just as soon forget."

Searcher's voice came from the Life-Link, startling them. "Roxanne, I sense an entity is scanning for chips. The electronic interference may not be enough to block it. You should put on your chip mask." Searcher's volume was weak, mixed with static.

Roxanne rarely wore a chip mask, or cover, because it was metal attached with magnets and was hot and heavy, but she rummaged through her backpack and found it.

Gabe pulled the heat cannon a little closer. "What's scanning for her chip? Are there drones or something?" But Searcher did not reply.

Zeb poured more tea and looked toward the sky. Roxanne secured the cover around her wrist and picked up her cup. The insect repellent was working well. Bugs were flying all around but staying away from them.

She said, "So Zeb, how did you wind up at The Uppsala?"

He sighed. "Before I was born, they moved my

parents and grandparents from Standing Rock to New Town, which was on a Mandan reservation, not Lakota. Then we got shuffled around some more when they combined North and South Dakota to just Dakota."

Roxanne said, "Because the combined population was less than a million?"

"You bet, but we didn't stay below a million for long. When it warmed up here, it got hotter than hell down south and lots of people moved to the new northern lands of 'Milk and honey.' We had more rain and we had milder winters, a big change."

"Right after I was born, they forced us to move again, to Spirit Lake, further north. Thousands of people came, all wanting land. When the smallpox came back, and most of us lived, the others were angry because so many of them died, but we lived. In their stupidity, they did not realize we had some immunity because a few of our ancestors survived it long ago. Some claimed the revival of the Ghost Dance saved us, but my parents said the old ones long ago passed down their immunity."

Gabe said, "I think they stopped vaccinating for smallpox because they thought it was gone for good."

Zeb nodded, "Interesting, don't you think, that the white man lost his immunity this time around, and we had it. White people moved in all around us and they hated us. A bunch of them were from Texas, and they were in a strange place and I guess we were part of the strange they didn't like."

"But I thought you came here from Pembina."

"Well, that's the rest of the story. We had an old medicine man who wanted us to drive the new settlers out. That was crazy to me. We had food shortages and our people were quarreling amongst ourselves. My older brother had a job fixing robots on a farm up near the Canadian line and I moved near Pembina to learn the trade from him. I was there only long enough to learn I hate robots."

Gabe thought about the killer kitchen robots at The Uppsala.

"A friend, Jimmy White Bull heard about the condo projects. Sounded like a good place to make a new start. So we traveled to Minnesota."

Zeb turned his head towards Gabe and in the fire's reflection, Roxanne could see pockmarks on his neck.

"So we get to The Uppsala, and wouldn't you know... the place is full of robots even though there are plenty of men to handle the work. That should have been some kind of tip-off. Jimmy left right away, said he was going back home, but like a fool, I stayed."

Gabe said, "A couple pieces in that puzzle just came together. They didn't really need us for the work."

Roxanne thought to herself the human touch had been nice, but stayed quiet. Interference from Saint Cloud would make it difficult, if not impossible for Searcher to check on her hurricane simulator. She would have to wait a bit longer to check the code.

Explosions went off to the north, frightening a flock of birds which stirred in the trees above, sending down leaves. They sat listening for any signs of a battle moving toward them, but the blasts came no closer. Zeb stood first guard shift while Roxanne and Gabe found fitful slumber in their sleeping bags. He walked in spirals around their camp wearing night goggles, carrying the heat cannon, feeling truly alive again through the uncertainty and danger.

* * * * *

The Hunter shoved open the door to the synagogue and paid no mind to the security A.I. which recognized it as a weapon and warned it to leave. No mammals were alive here except chipmunks. It walked outside, found the charging station, and leaned against the pad to recharge. It detected the electronic imprint from their devices in the pad. The Hunter decided to remain here a few hours. Electromagnetic interference from the north was making night navigation difficult. It was in no hurry. It knew they had been here, and it knew it was closing the gap on its prey.

Chapter Twenty One

Dr. James Branson met his assistant, Lin Wei in the hallway leading to the lab. Sunlight streamed through the windows. The forecast called for a high of 87. Finally some decent weather after days of rain. Lin Wei was eager to resume work. The system locked him out while his boss was hospitalized. The security A.I. told him he hadn't been there long enough for the necessary clearance. This lab was one of a dozen tech centers streaming data and analysis via satellite to quantum computers in the U.S. and Canada. Artificial Intelligence guided governments on critical decisions daily.

Dr. Branson glided along the gray vinyl floor, propped up by a rolling A.I. walker that monitored his every move and adjusted accordingly. He also was impatient to check on his computers. The microbots had done their job. He was still a bit shaky on his right side but felt stronger each day. Heavy fatigue showed in new wrinkles on his face.

He leaned toward Lin Wei, a thin middle-aged man with close-cropped hair, wearing old-fashioned tortoiseshell glasses. The lab assistant had moved to Regina from Vancouver six months earlier, to escape the high apartment rents and constant flooding from the Salish Sea. The Branson computers said Lin Wei was the top quantum coder in Canada.

Dr. Branson had regained his edge and his baritone. "I can't wait to see what they make of Iota. The question is whether there'll be another one like that anytime soon."

Lin Wei studied his employer. The old man appeared shaky but competent. "Glad to see you up and around, sir. The PayNews said 60,000 dead from Iota. Obviously that's low. It always is. Let's find out what the jet streams are doing."

Lin Wei knew from the PayNews the Dallas-Fort Worth Metroplex was now uninhabitable, the biggest urban center in the storm's path. Houston, once the third most populous city in the U.S. was long-deserted, a wasteland of seawater and petrochemical pollution. Kansas City had escaped the worst of the storm but Oklahoma City, Topeka, Wichita, and Manhattan, Kansas were disasters. How many deaths had there been? No one would ever know for sure since the governments were lenient about requiring identity chips.

The scanner recognized Dr. Branson's eyes and opened the doors. This lab, like others, was originally designed as a 'clean room' to protect the sensitive equipment. But as the quantum computers gained power, they were fully capable of running their own cleaning robots to remove the tiniest specs of dust. The men brought in millions of particles, but within minutes after their departure the room would once again be dust and pollution-free.

Dr. Branson took a seat at his video control panel while Lin Wei began poring over days of reports. The big screen brought up the Atlantic Ocean. Two hurricanes were visible, one just off the coast of Liberia, would move north, eventually turning towards Portugal. The second, near Antigua looked dangerous to U.S. interests. The storm would soon strengthen to Category six and move towards Cape Cod. Branson shifted to the Pacific, where four typhoons were moving toward the Philippines, Taiwan, Japan, and the Kamchatka Peninsula. That was typical for this time of year in the

Pacific. A Category four cyclone was heading for what remained of Sri Lanka in the Indian Ocean.

He returned his focus to the track of Hurricane Kappa in the Atlantic. Congress and the Vermont White House could very well be in its sights. How might the elected politicians deal with this? Some had raised the harebrained idea of weakening hurricanes with a nuclear device. This had already been tried once, against the advice of every A.I. on the planet. The bomb, dropped over Typhoon Ompong as it strengthened from Category Two to Category Three, did nothing but produce radioactive rain that poisoned seawater all the way from Guam to Manila. It might even have started a war, except the idea was China's in the first place and endorsed by leaders of the Philippines.

Dr. Branson sat, transfixed by the images on his screens. He dropped into a kind of daze until Lin Wei gently tapped his arm.

"Sir, your upgraded entity has been here several times. It roamed all around, sticking its nose in unsuitable places."

"Searcher returned?" This brought the elderly scientist back to his daughter's fate. He remembered that she and two menials from The Uppsala must be in northern Minnesota by now.

"Branson Entity 91560 has been here going through archives and using the satellite links. Is that what you call it, 'Searcher'?"

"It named itself. I built it as a search entity and when the quantums moved it up to the next level, it decided it needed a name that we humans could relate to. Interesting, don't you think?"

"Spooky is what I think. Does the International A.I.

Security Center know about this?"

Dr. Branson pointed to his personal A.I. "Make some coffee for both of us please, the usual." Then he turned toward Lin Wei and frowned. "For now there is no need to tell them. Searcher is benevolent, I made sure about that. It knows the only reason for its existence is to protect Roxanne."

Lin Wei chuckled, "Well, it's been rummaging through the entire record of human history, just one damned awful thing after another over the last five millennia. I hope it doesn't get any bad ideas."

A small robot brought both of them steaming cups of coffee. Dr. Branson eagerly grasped his cup with a trembling hand because he felt a chill from the air conditioning. He waved at the screen and the view changed to global: Seven large hurricanes churning through three different oceans and a monsoon gyre all above the Equator.

He said, "On top of that, there's a derecho with 85 mph winds across Pennsylvania right now. We're looking at this, or worse for the next ten millennia. In the grand scheme of things, Searcher's curiosity is not a problem."

Lin Wei waited for his coffee to cool. "In another ten thousand years we'll probably be drawing on the walls of caves again, if there are any of us left."

Dr. Branson scanned his messages and found a couple from Searcher. Roxanne and her menials were somewhere north of Coon Rapids, Minnesota, heading for an A.I. Van Terminal near Saint Cloud.

He also saw Roxanne's last message to him: "Dad, what have you done to my search entity? It thinks it is alive. It says it is sentient." He realized he'd never replied to her.

Lin Wei interrupted, "They've got Dengue and Yellow fever in Milwaukee; the hurricanes are carrying Aedes aegypti north. They possessed little vaccine to begin with, now they're out."

Dr. Branson shrugged and continued to read his messages. "The idiot they put in charge of The Uppsala is all in a huff about Roxanne taking the menials, and he says they can't be responsible for their safety. We need to get him replaced."

He brought up the North American disease screen. It showed a cluster of tropical hemorrhagic fevers between the 35th and 40th parallels. Lyme disease was particularly bad on the Atlantic coast, along with Tularemia in the Appalachian Mountains. Dysentery and Cholera plagued parts of Tennessee and Kentucky, the result of sewage in drinking water. That was on top of mercury, chromium, and arsenic, from a century of coal mining. A new coronavirus mutation was spreading east from Vancouver. They projected the fatality rate from the new virus at 3.7%. Valley Fever, a deadly fungus, was killing people in a wide section of bone-dry California. No shortage of diseases in North America.

The computer scientist stared at the blue veins on the back of his hands and formed the germ of an idea. Communications with his daughter through the search entity was running into interference of an electromagnetic nature. He would launch a search drone to locate them and make contact. Why hadn't he thought of this before? Well, there had been the matter of a stroke…

Chapter Twenty Two

Marie worked hard to become a valued member of the subterranean community in Kingman. Each morning she checked in with Pauline and there was always something that needed tending. On this day she hoed and pulled weeds from the settlement's large wind-battered garden. The hurricane had wiped out the sweet corn, but beans and a few tomatoes survived thanks to an embankment on the south side. The plainsmen called them wind levees; built-up ridges of earth strategically located as buffers against the powerful winds and tornados that swept these plains. She realized that a wind levee had saved the sturdy Quonset building, the only structure still standing nearby. The ridges were fifteen feet high in some places, enough to divert hurricane-force winds and sometimes tornadoes.

Marie had worked up a plan. She had no intention of spending the rest of her time in Kingman. Life here was hard and brutish even by her standards. Women fought a never-ending battle against dirt and vermin in the underground chambers. They ground grain with mule-powered mills, while the men left for days at a time, hunting or fishing.

It took the women a week to rebuild a shade shelter for the livestock. They carried buckets of water in shifts from a nearby lake because the pumps still wouldn't work. Then they'd strain and boil it. She'd learned from Pauline while they fixed dinner, that a spur led to the underground KC-Denver Express in Garden City, 150 miles west. She squirreled away algae cakes and sneaked scoops of oats into a burlap bag to prepare for the trip.

Marie possessed a special talent from her days as a

farm girl in South Missouri. She was a mule wrangler. Her family had raised them for years. She could read mules better than anyone she knew. Missouri mules were smarter than horses, and they never forgot good or bad treatment. Marie remembered a mule in Seymour that waited months to get back at a cruel neighbor who liked to use his whip, and one day the opportunity came. The mule kicked the man with both hooves nearly into the next county. But the mule adored Marie because she sometimes gave it watermelons to chew. Unfortunately, she'd been unable to save that mule from the stew pot.

Here, she made friends with a hinny named Daisy, a light gray sweet-eyed daughter of a jenny bred to a stallion. Daisy loved the extra handfuls of oats she brought each morning and followed Marie around like a dog. This amused the other women. They seldom saw this kind of affection from either a mule or a hinny. It was behavior more like a horse. When the time was right, and the forecast called for good weather, Marie planned to take Daisy, ride her to Garden City and sell her. Then she'd catch the A.I. Van to the KC-Denver terminal in Colby. She would retrace the route back to the highway and travel west. The floodwaters had receded, and the moon would be full in a week. That's when she hoped to escape.

One night after Burt drank too much, he leered at her, then leaned toward a drinking buddy and they spoke in conspiratorial tones. She had little doubt he still planned to auction her off. The plainsmen from several counties would gather the following month and a short wiry woman named Sally had whispered the odds were high they would trade her. It was against the law, but the lawmen who remained were tied up with recovery in wind-ravaged Wichita. Sally suggested she would likely bring a good bid, as many as a dozen mules. Marie did not take this as a compliment.

She finished weeding and took a bucket of greens to the animals. Daisy stood in the shade shelter, along with four mules and a camel that would spit on you if you came too close. She walked past a woman wiping dust from a small array of solar panels with a rag. The woman carried a revolver on her hip, just in case coyotes tried to make a run for the chickens that hunted and pecked around the solar array. Several Life-Links were on the charging pad. The sky darkened, and she remembered the FreeNews warning of thunderstorms and tornadoes. At least it wasn't a hurricane. She hoped never to cross paths with a hurricane again once she reached the Rockies.

Chapter Twenty Three

At daybreak, Searcher warned Roxanne the water war was heating up, and Saint Cloud was too dangerous. The entity said they should double back and cross the Mississippi ten miles south, at Clearwater. A few minutes later, Gabe hurried back from the river with the binoculars, eager to share what he'd seen.

"All hell is breaking loose up there. I could see robots on the Saint Cloud Bridge and something above the shore was blasting them into pieces. A bunch fell into the river."

Zeb said, "Strange we didn't hear any shots."

Gabe replied, "I think they're using lasers. They are headed this way. We don't want to be in the middle of that."

They turned on a Life-Link for the FreeNews but the electromagnetic interference from the hydroelectric generator was too strong. They heard only static. A buzzing drone passed over them, speeding north. They packed up and considered bringing a couple of pots and pans along, then decided against it. The drone circled out of sight. Then a flash filled the sky and an explosion sent the drone, sparks flying, into the forest floor less than 20 yards away.

Zeb and Gabe stayed back while Roxanne crept closer to get a look at the wreckage. 'BR-Surveillance 77' was emblazoned on the side of the six-foot sky blue drone. The rear end of the drone was charred, the tail blown off.

She said, "It's one of my Dad's drones. He's looking for us and somebody shot it down!" She glanced at the gray chip mask on her wrist.

The men cautiously approached.

Gabe said, "Never saw one up close before. Smaller than I expected."

Zeb replied, "Used to see plenty up on the Canadian line, but those are bigger and make a different noise, and they've got weapons."

They peered skyward, watching for more drones. Roxanne glanced again at her wrist.

"I wonder if it scanned my chip last night. Maybe Dad knows we're here." She placed her hand on the drone, as it if could bring her closer to her father. Another explosion in the clouds sent them running, away from the war machines over Saint Cloud. They would follow Searcher's advice and navigate the river at Clearwater.

* * * * *

In Regina, Lin Wei sat at the control board monitoring signals from satellite networks. Dr. Branson felt weak and took a break. He returned to the convalescent center but allowed Lin Wei to remain and watch for updates from the search drone. This was not strictly within the security protocols. The computer tech felt the responsibility the boss had placed on his shoulders. The drone sent an endless video stream of oak and maple trees, broken by scrub and deserted subdivisions in a wide swath north of Coon Rapids. It was well past lunchtime and the lab robot would not respond to his requests for food, a reminder of his station in life here in the billionaire's sanctum sanctorum. He walked to the sink and got a glass of water.

The only interesting item had been a bronze-colored robot plodding north on an abandoned highway toward

Saint Cloud. He didn't recognize the make or model. It appeared to be a type of utility machine, although it was fierce looking. He saved the video clip of the robot and shifted the search in Fargo's direction, when the drone picked up activity near Saint Cloud.

The Great Lakes Alliance had captured a hydroelectric generator on the Mississippi. It was throwing out a tremendous amount of electrical interference directly below. Armed men, mercenaries guarding robots, were rolling out a pipeline near the river bridge. He signaled the drone to circle around, and the signal abruptly blacked out. Dr. Branson's search drone had gone offline. Lin Wei rushed to his computer screens to find out more. He groaned when he saw the Minnesota news feed:

'Canada with U.S. permission, moved attack drones south to join forces from the Alliance. Lake Superior is a critical water resource for 30 million people in Ontario and California's illegal actions shall not stand.'

Canada had developed some of the most powerful security drones in the hemisphere. The Canadian drone network along the border was known as the 'Iron Cloud.' Those drones were now battling with pipeline robots in a front that ran more than a hundred miles from Duluth to Saint Cloud. The situation was even more chaotic because of climate refugees fleeing south from the floods around Lake Superior.

"Ironic", Lin Wei muttered, "Right now there's too much water in Lake Superior but they will not let California have any of it." As a Canadian, he understood his government's actions, but with Californians dying of thirst, or drinking polluted water after the big quake, it seemed extreme. The U.S. government was officially neutral in this fight between the two regions. This was one of a dozen climate-related wars around the globe. Most involved depleted aquifers and famine. Fortunately, none had escalated to the thermonuclear stage.

He needed to inform Dr. Branson his drone was down. Then an update from the Global Climate A.I. caught his attention: Satellites showed extreme heat and drought near the equator had killed a third of the trees in what remained of the great Amazon rainforest. The temperature at Manaus was 118 with no rain for 14 weeks, disastrous with that kind of heat. To make matters worse, a wildfire was moving through the dead trees in Jau National Park, at one time the largest forest preserve in South America. The earth was losing a major carbon sink, and the wildfires were sending more CO_2 into the atmosphere.

Lin Wei, a lover of animals, thought about the jaguars, macaws, monkeys, and capybaras, nearly gone now. Some survived in zoos. He checked for news about an amateur zoo that had been in Hurricane Iota's path. Most of the animals at the zoo near Wynnewood, Oklahoma, were dead, but four huge Bengal tigers had escaped. Two were sighted heading north. The other two had disappeared, probably taken down by ranchers. He would hate to be anywhere nearby with such dangerous creatures at large. But mostly, he sympathized with the tigers.

Chapter Twenty Four

On the road to Clearwater, Roxanne, Gabe, and Zeb encountered scattered groups of people all walking in the same direction. Some wore rags, others were well-dressed and carried suitcases or backpacks. Once again they wondered about Searcher's advice to come south. Near the Mississippi River Bridge, the groups converged into a throng, a caravan of sorts, heading for the river crossing.

An insane tangle of men, women, and dogs milled around at the edge of a cornfield. On the other side of the road, a larger gathering of refugees settled into a camp. Small fires sent wispy wood smoke skyward.

Roxanne stopped next to a young woman holding a tiny dog. Like her dog, the woman was skin and bones. Her face was disfigured, her right eye swollen shut. "Why are you here? Why aren't you crossing the river?" Several thugs milled around, leering at Roxanne, and Zeb stepped closer, held up the heat cannon until they moved away.

The woman gripped the quivering little dog close to her. "Bandits took the bridge and we can't cross unless we pay. They will block your way unless you have money. We're just trying to get west to Dakota. They say there's no war over that way."

Gabe asked, "Are the outlaws armed? With such a big crowd, why don't you push through?"

"Go on up there, you'll find out."

Roxanne saw Zeb was already striding onto the bridge with the heat cannon. People scrambled to get out of his way. He disappeared from sight, but a minute later he returned.

"They've got three heat cannons, a nasty pack of

them, six crooks. One has a gun, too. I'm not sure if their cannons are working, but decided not to find out. They want cash, no digits. Who the hell has cash any more? I've got a couple of Sacagawea dollars, but they wouldn't take those."

Roxanne said, "I could pay, but I don't have any cash or coins." She stepped aside and talked to Searcher. "Have you got any bright ideas? You said to come this way... so now what?"

The entity replied through her neural-link confidently. "Go to the opposite end of that cornfield and camp in the trees. Tomorrow we will cross the river. I am free of the interference from the Saint Cloud generator. Once again I am fully functional."
Gabe and Zeb recognized Roxanne was in Searcher mode. They stood next to her waiting to see what would come of the conversation.

She said, "You won't tell us your plan? Why am I feeling dubious about this?"

Searcher replied, "If I told you... you might not believe me. Remember, I only exist to look after you. Take off your chip mask now; your father could send another drone. There are also other reasons to remove it."

"And Gabe and Zeb, you are to protect them too."

The entity did not reply to her last statement, instead sending suggestions for a campsite to her contact lens. When Roxanne told them of the new plan, Gabe was not happy.

"Our situation is getting worse. This is Searcher's doing. Crowds are dangerous."
They walked towards the woods with dusk fast approaching, sprayed themselves with insect repellent and went to sleep on empty stomachs. Zeb took first

watch.

Just before sunrise the land was full of shadows when Gabe got up to forage. It had cooled down overnight and no one stirred in the crowds situated around the bridge. Somewhere in the distance, a dog barked. He started a fire, checked Zeb's snare and found a white-tail Jack struggling in the trap. He killed the rabbit and walked back to the fire to make breakfast. A bird exploded out of a bush to the east, wings beating hard. Other birds flew up in a rush, and the noise woke up the others. Gabe stared through the trees but saw nothing. Dense fog settled across the forest, humidity so high the dew dripped from the birch and oak leaves.

Roxanne rubbed the sleep from her eyes, watching Gabe dress the rabbit. This life was strange to her, but the men were used to it. Dense woods surrounded their small clearing. She hoped another of her father's drones would appear, but saw only fog. She doubted he could get them all into Canada through the Iron Cloud, but she expected he'd figure something out for her. She wished she had signed up for Canadian citizenship along with her father, but 40-million refugees later, it would be difficult. Canada insisted on an orderly migration and kept tent cities and shantytowns to a minimum, except for New Brunswick, which had been overrun in the early years. Meanwhile, the northern states, especially Dakota, Montana, Idaho, and Maine rapidly filled up with Americans seeking to move as far north as possible. Minnesota and Wisconsin slowed the flow with blockades, although Gabe had managed to get through.

Roxanne watched Gabe turn the rabbit on a spit. Zeb got up, stretched, and walked into the woods. She stared east and asked Gabe, "You see that? Something gleaming over there…?

He glanced up from the campfire and shrugged. Across the floodplain, refugees in the camps began to awaken. People stoked their campfires and smoke spiraled up.

Searcher said, "Roxanne, the next few minutes are critical. Do exactly as I say… exactly, or we both might die. Look behind you."

She replied, "What are you talking about?"

The Hunter emerged from thick fog like the ghost of a robot coming into full view. It lumbered through the woods straight in their direction. Gabe stood up from the fire in disbelief. The moving and storage robot had always looked intimidating, but now it looked deadly. Its eyes glowed red and its fifth arm carried a razor sharp cutting weapon.

Roxanne and Gabe ran down the slope, away from camp. Zeb emerged from the trees behind the robot, the heat cannon just a few feet in front of him.

Searcher told Roxanne, "Stand your ground. Do not flee from the robot, face it and point to it with your hand."
Full of fear, she instead rushed toward the encampments with Gabe.

Zeb grabbed the heat cannon and yelled, "Turn around, you piece of junk!"

The robot wheeled around, facing Zeb. "You are the book thief," it croaked.

Zeb replied, "No I'm not, I only talked about it."

He turned the heat cannon full blast onto the robot, which stalked him, quickening its pace. The cannon had no effect. The robot raised its cutting hand and Zeb dashed into the woods, seeking a tree to climb. Pivoting back, the Hunter moved toward the encampments. Roxanne's chip led it like a beacon. It would dispatch with her first, and then kill the menials, but it was confused by the crowd milling around her.

Roxanne and Gabe came upon a family of four just getting out of their sleeping bags.

She told them, "There's a big robot coming, and he is dangerous. Give him a wide berth."

The father, a short, gaunt man, put a finger to his mouth and whistled. He told his wife and children to run towards a nearby cluster of refugees, people they seemed to know. Three men responded to his signal and brought weapons. One had a baseball bat, another carried a pistol, and a third had an oak tree limb shaped like a club.

Gabe said, "I'm not sure you can stop it. It appears the thing is after us."

The short man handed Gabe an iron rod. He said, "We'll beat that damn robot to bits. We've been dealing with robots ever since they came swarming into Duluth. Brain is in the chest, aim for the midsection."

Searcher again told Roxanne, "Do what I say! Face the robot and point towards it."

Then Searcher brought up a 5-second video in her contact lens, showing the spark that flew from her wrist to robot when they'd first met on the top floor of The Uppsala.

She said, "What was that?"

Searcher replied, "I've mapped the robot's circuitry; stand and point, Roxanne, stand and point!"

The robot plowed into the crowd, pushing people aside or trampling them. One man took a swing at the robot with the baseball bat, and quick as the blink of an eye, the robot sliced the bat in half, and a gash in the man's leg spurted blood. He fell back and the others retreated, while Gabe stood fast. This machine was more dangerous than the pipeline robots. Blood dripped from the cutting tool, and the robot moved towards Roxanne. Gabe struck the robot a solid blow to the head with the rod. Unfazed, it rotated in his direction. Gabe crouched, ready for another swing.

Roxanne held her breath and pointed at the robot. It batted the rod from Gabe's grasp, sending the metal rod flying, then paused, as if confused. Then it took a lightning-fast swing at Gabe with a paw, catching him on the shoulder. Gabe felt like he'd been struck by an anvil. He dropped to the ground, the breath knocked out of him. Still, he struggled to get up. The crowd stared at Roxanne, standing with her arm extended, index finger pointing at the big robot. It lurched toward her, and its cutting hand shot up. She cringed, looked towards the ground, and closed her eyes. Then a spark flew from her finger onto the robot. The Hunter froze in mid-step, emitted an electronic chirp, stumbled and crashed to the ground. A gasp rose from the crowd, but no one came forward. They feared the robot might recover.

Gabe staggered up. "You took the robot down by pointing at it?"
Roxanne stared at the ground, listening to Searcher, and shifted her gaze to the Hunter lying on the road. The robot stirred, its eyes turning laser-blue. It cocked its head and its voice scraped like two rusty chunks of metal rubbing together.

"I am called Searcher, I am sentient. I have taken control of this robot, and will do you no harm."
People in the crowd murmured, and everyone but Gabe stayed back.

Roxanne announced in a loud voice, "It's OK. The robot has been taken over by a digital entity and is no longer dangerous."

Zeb, feeling sheepish because he'd scaled a tree to get away from the Hunter, showed up sweating and out of breath, clutching the heat cannon. He glanced from the robot to Roxanne, to Gabe. "What'd I miss?"

Gabe groaned, "Feels like it just about took my shoulder off, but I think we can talk to the Searcher-Thing directly now. It's taken over that robot."

Searcher croaked, its voice already improving. "Talk later: I shall now clear the bridge."

The robot trotted in a halting gait, as if Searcher was adjusting to the new hardware. People scattered in all directions from its path, hoping they might soon cross the river.

Two women rushed to the aid of the man whose leg was bleeding. They tied a tourniquet and wrapped strips of cloth around the wound. In a crowd of more than five hundred refugees, there were only two children. A boy and girl no more than seven years old crept up near Roxanne. The little girl asked, "Are you a witch or a fairy? You held out your hand. Did you cast a spell on the monster?"

Their mother, a youthful woman in khakis rushed forward to shush them. But others in the crowd drew near… as if they wanted to touch Roxanne, make sure she was real.

Gabe said, "This is a superstitious bunch. Let's find out what the Searcher-Thing is doing up there."

They headed for the bridge with Gabe and Zeb in the lead and Roxanne just behind. The crowd parted for them, no questions asked. Up ahead they heard the screams and cries of men. They found the big robot standing in the center of the bridge looking out over the Mississippi.

Gabe said, "Where are the bandits, did you kill them?"

Searcher's voice continued to improve. The robot answered, "I am here to protect people, not kill them. I swept them over the bridge railing and into the river below."

Roxanne said, "But we heard screaming."

"Apparently some of the bandits could not swim and expressed their displeasure. But how was I to know that?"

Zeb glanced at the flood-swollen river, "What about their heat cannons? I couldn't get ours to work on the robot before you took it over. Be good to have another heat cannon, just in case."

Searcher gestured with a large paw to the rushing water. "The river is high and the current is fast. None of their weapons worked on me. I threw them into the river as well. But with me as your escort, you will have less need for weapons now."

The refugees surged around them, crossing over the bridge. Zeb, Roxanne, Gabe, and Searcher went back to their camp. North toward Saint Cloud, fireballs exploded in the sky, followed by echoes of distant explosions. The rabbit remained on the spit, burned to a crisp on the campfire. Someone had stolen their sleeping bags, but their backpacks were intact. They pulled their gear together, ate a few bites of jerky and algae cakes, then proceeded across the Mississippi, heading for Dakota. They walked behind the Searcher robot. Roxanne noticed Zeb's scowl was even more pronounced than usual.

Chapter Twenty Five

Marie made her escape at midnight. Daisy carried her past the cemetery out to the highway. Kingman looked like a ghost town beneath the full moon. She had removed some clothing from the backpack, adding fresh supplies. Daisy's saddlebags carried oats, hard molasses candy, dried Johnny cakes, and two canteens of boiled water. Marie carried a butcher knife from the kitchen but had no other weapons. A breeze cooled the night air and they made good time on the road. Most of the debris from the hurricane was now cleared. She was on edge, worried the plainsmen would come after her. Movement to her right startled her, but it was only her moon shadow, following alongside.

The unearthly sound of coyotes howling at the moon came from the south, and she saw no wildlife near the highway. She wondered how many animals had survived the storm. Marie was glad to be out of Kingman. The longer she stayed, the more depressing the place became.

A few evenings earlier a crew of strange men had showed up riding in an ancient rust-covered pickup truck spewing foul-smelling smoke. They said it ran on alcohol. Burt had really wanted that truck. The men let Burt ride in it, but he returned angry and empty-handed. Later, he'd had too much to drink. At the campfire, he told a drunken tale of python and alligator hunting, spit flying from his face, his eyes wild. Next day, Pauline told Marie that Burt had tried to trade her for the truck, but the men said she was too old. Marie didn't know if this was true or not, but it added to her desire to get away from there.

At daybreak she came to a new branch of the

Ninnescah River. A lake, with a few cottonwoods, beckoned just north of the road. These were the first large upright trees she'd encountered since the hurricane, a rare opportunity for shade. They'd stop and rest here and Daisy could get a drink. It looked like another scorching day. She had to pull Daisy away from the water, so the hinney wouldn't drink too much. The hurricane's power had dwindled here. An alligator stuck its snout out of the thick green hydrilla in the water. An armadillo snuffled along in a clearing.

She heard a rustle from above. A large green iguana sat on a tree limb, eating cottonwood leaves. She'd heard you could eat iguana, but killing it might be difficult. The creature looked as if it might bite. There also might be pythons here, but she'd just have to take the chance. She tied Daisy to a tree where there was grass to eat and she took a long drink of water from the canteen and ate a Johnny cake.

Pratt was at least twenty miles west. They would rest in the shade during the heat of the day and continue at moonrise when the prairie breeze cooled things down. The temperature had climbed to 117 the previous day, and she had no reason to believe today would be any better. They'd roast if they attempted travel under the merciless Kansas sun. Marie said a little prayer for Gabe, recalled her last hug with Artemis and exhausted, finally dozed off.

An hour later she awoke to the sound of goats bleating. A small herd gathered at the lake's edge, brown and white spotted animals drinking and watching cautiously for alligators. Sure enough, a gator surfaced and dragged one of the smaller animals thrashing into deep water. This set off a cacophony of bleats from the goat herd, and Daisy joined in, braying loudly. It felt too hot to think. Marie got up with a groan, her joints aching from her overnight ride, and watched for more gators.

The herdsman appeared, a slender young Mennonite man with the beginnings of a beard. An Australian Sheepdog trotted nearby, nudging the goats to stay in a group. The young man wore a broad-brimmed straw hat, blue overalls, and hemp work boots. He aimed a shotgun toward the lake, and then decided the gator was a lost cause. Marie knew ammunition was hard to come by.

When he noticed Marie and Daisy, he nodded and tipped his hat awkwardly. His dog wagged its tail but kept its distance. Man and dog stood by as the goats drank their fill, brave again with their guardians nearby. Then he left the dog behind and approached Marie.

"Mornin' ma'am, I am a slow one, hard for me to keep up with these goats in this heat. I lost one to the monster out in that lake. But this is the only decent water out this way. It's all we got. River is still so high, current would sweep them away."

"Good morning. I saw there were other lakes around here, but this was the only one with cottonwoods."

"The Good Lord was watching over you. Most of the ponds in these parts are bad. Too many dead critters in them from the storm. Neighbor lost half his goats to the pond over yonder. Sometimes I think the hurricanes bring worse things than wind."

He pointed north. "I reckon that's one good thing about the gators. They ate up the dead critters here, so this lake is fairly clean."

"I am Marie, and that's Daisy."

He removed his hat and bowed. "I am Isaac Bender,

son of Noah, may he rest in peace. We raise Percherons and goats, some hay and grain too. I wish we had some mules like that one. Mules do better in this weather."

Marie said, "She's a hinny, a cross between a donkey and a stallion. How did you survive the hurricane?"

"The hand of God pushed that great storm away from us. My dad built us some 20-foot wind levees years ago. That didn't hurt. We lost a few chickens and an apple tree; some damage to corn, but that was it. This dog pretty much runs things, his name is Captain."

Isaac seemed so kind and so honest, Marie let bottled-up feelings rise in her throat. She sobbed, choking out her words. "The storm picked up our van and slammed it into the river bank. I believe I was the only passenger to make it out alive. I lost my husband… I'm sorry, I don't mean to cry like this." She wiped her nose on a rag from her pocket.

She'd made him uncomfortable. He stared out into the water, the shotgun resting on his shoulder.

"You were in that A.I. Van that got thrown on the riverbank other side of Kingman?"

"Yes, we were on our way to Denver. The storm was unlike anything I ever experienced before."

He asked, "How'd you get over this way, then?"

Alarm bells went off in Marie's head. For all she knew this boy was friends with the plainsmen, although it was unlikely. She'd picked up enough local lore to realize not much love was lost between the two groups. Out of necessity they sometimes traded garden produce and animals.

"A plainsman found me in the eye of the storm. He took me to Kingman, but I need to get to the Rockies."

He smiled. "I'm guessing they didn't throw you a going-away party or anything. They trade women and you're young enough…I know you wouldn't be out here with just a mule without good reason." He looked up towards the iguana. "Cold snap last winter, some of those things fell right out of the trees. We had fresh meat for weeks. The cold didn't kill many gators, though."

"Are there pythons this far west?"

"My uncle killed a big snake last year. They's a few. There'll be more before long."

He turned toward the flock and prepared to herd them south.

She threw out a question. "How did you hear about our van? Did the plainsmen tell you?"

"Oh, everybody knows about it. Plainsman brought a youngster to our place, was in that van. Child cries all the time. My sister can't do a thing with him. At her wit's end. We're not used to kids that small."

"You have a little boy from our A.I. Van?"

"I'm fairly sure it was the only van around here when that hurricane came through."

"I know that child; he was with his great-grandmother. They were from Memphis."

"You just told me a whole lot more than we knew about him. He just cries and throws fits. We can barely get him to eat."

"Can I see him… back at your place?"

"Just follow me and Captain, and the goats. We'll be a mile from here, if you lose us, watch for the wind levees. Our house will be the first one you come to. You'd be welcome to have a meal with us, and get out of the sun."

The herd moved south.

She walked to Daisy and spotted a big gator creeping towards them, not 20 feet away. Thank goodness the Mennonite lad had come along. Marie imagined the gator making a meal of either her or Daisy. She'd seen a gator take down a horse near Seymour, breaking its leg with powerful jaws.

She grabbed the backpack, leaped on Daisy, and they rushed away, leaving the gator behind in the tall grass. They followed the goats as the heat intensified. She saw more signs of wind damage, trees with shredded leaves, bits of debris scattered around the countryside. They passed a small lake, which gave off a putrid odor. A goat ran toward the water, and the dog steered it back to the herd. Then a series of ridges loomed, some a hundred yards long. These were the biggest wind levees she'd encountered, taller than the ones built by corporate farm robots in Missouri. Some had their tops scalped by wind, but most were intact, covered in prairie grass.

Isaac drove the animals into a barbed-wire enclosure with shade trees situated to protect the animals through the day. A ramshackle barn stood nearby, its reflective solar roof gleaming in the morning sun. A large dappled gray horse stuck its head out of a stall and whinnied when it saw Isaac. Thick insulation showed through a section of the barn's roof that was missing. A wellhead sat in the grass near the barn, with partly assembled pieces for an electric pump lying nearby.

Their house was a substantial-looking cabin with a front porch facing north and a smokehouse attached to the back. Oaks on both sides provided morning and afternoon shade. Solar panels on the roof caught midday sun. A wind levee topped by turbines loomed above it all. Another levee rose from the earth where that one ended. She saw several small farmsteads, each protected by a levee. These were industrious people.

She liked the arrangement of the buildings.

A girl in her teens came out of the house, holding a small child who wiggled to get free. It was Caden. His black curly hair was longer, he wore blue denim clothes, and he was thin as a rail, but it was the youngster from the van, no doubt about it.

Marie dismounted and reached into a saddlebag. She gave a chunk of molasses candy to Daisy, retrieved a sweet Johnny cake and got down on her knees, holding it out.

The little boy ran to her, yelling, "Cookie!"

Chapter Twenty Six

Searcher made fleeting contact with a Branson Surveillance Drone just as they reached the Dakota state line. They'd made good time, assisted by fellow travelers who were grateful they'd cleared the bridge at Clearwater. Some of the Duluth crowd had dried fruit and nuts, a welcome addition to the small animals caught by Gabe and Zeb. Still, the days of hard hiking and limited rations had burned the weight from all their frames, including Roxanne. She'd never in her life experienced this kind of vigorous physical work. The weather mercifully had cooled down. Searcher said it was because the jet stream was carrying what cool air remained at the North Pole to the south, while the arctic cooked in the heat. When they arrived at a marker for the Sheyenne National Grassland, several travelers headed north toward Fargo, while others continued west.

Searcher suggested they should camp here in the Grassland and discuss a plan for the next leg of the trip. Zeb had become more taciturn with each passing day. It was clear he didn't enjoy talking to a robot, so Searcher had adjusted to a more diplomatic mode, using phrases such as, "I suggest…. What do you think? Can we discuss this?" and the always handy, "Please share your thoughts." The entity's voice had settled into a friendly electro-mechanical tenor, reminiscent of an android from a popular 20th century space opera. Still, Zeb resisted dialogue with Searcher, generally directing his comments toward Roxanne or Gabe.

Searcher said, "I should like to note we are standing on the Laurentian Divide, so rivers to our left flow into the Atlantic and rivers on the right flow north towards the Arctic." They stood on a ridge with the broad sweep of the prairie stretching to the western horizon. To the east stood forest, oaks and maples with scattered sycamores.

Zeb said, "The robot-thing may not know the Red River flows north from here and used to cause big floods, back when rivers froze and thawed in the spring. In this location, it's not exactly left-right but east or west."

Searcher replied, "I was deliberately general, trying not to be a bore."

Zeb gestured toward the horizon, "I grew up here. I love this land. It's not boring, not a damn thing boring here at all, except, maybe you!" Zeb gestured at a thick vine that was smothering a small tree. "Stay away from this. The little berries are OK to eat, but the thorns will rip you up."

Gabe studied it, "I think we had that in Missouri. What's it called?"

"Tearthumb, devil's tail. Nasty plant. It'll catch on your clothes and cut your skin before you know it's there."

Roxanne stood a ways back next to Searcher-robot.

Searcher observed, "He lives close to the earth. Much of his knowledge is not written down, or I would know it."

Zeb walked away and began hunting for food. Gabe busied himself with a campfire and Roxanne stood with her hands on her hips. She glared at the robot.

"Can't you try to get along with him? It shouldn't be difficult."

Searcher responded, "I have a good satellite signal. I will leave for a little while and visit your father's lab." The robot froze into a stiff-legged position, its head

143

pointing to the ground. Roxanne stared hard at the machine, concerned the Hunter might come back, but it remained immobile. Then she decided Searcher had done the equivalent of exiting a room in a huff.

She remembered too late she'd failed to ask the entity to check on her hurricane simulator. The latest run should have finished by now. A breeze from the north swept across her face, carrying an odor a bit like burning logs.

* * * * *

Dark clouds and smoke pressed down on people walking the streets of Regina as a gigantic wildfire raged north of Edmonton. The prevailing winds carried ash and soot that drifted down like gray snowflakes, settling on rooftops, gutters, and people. The fire was 500 miles away, but it felt as if the blaze was just outside the city limits. Lin Wei plodded along the grimy sidewalk with a scarf over his nose and mouth. This was the third day they'd been under a dangerous air alert. He wished Dr. Branson would stop talking about moving the entire operation to Yellowknife and just do it. The billionaire could command a flotilla of robots and drones to pick everything up and relocate the modular lab in a matter of days if he wanted.

Lin Wei knew his boss was preoccupied with his daughter's journey through Dakota. The elder Branson had been in contact with Canadian immigration, trying to find a way to get his daughter into the country without a long wait. There had been mention about an exchange of funds from a Branson investment in Sudbury. The old man was still weak and left the lab frequently to rest in bed, or to play chess with Xavier

Dillon. He said it helped strengthen his mind, but Lin Wei had his doubts about Dr. Branson's ability to focus. He sometimes seemed in another world since his stroke.

When he arrived at the lab filled with blessedly clean, filtered indoor air, he found Dr. Branson staring at the ceiling, speaking to someone not visible. He slipped behind his boss for a cup of coffee from the kitchen and listened to the one-sided conversation.

Dr. Branson cocked his head to one side, "So the Indian says there is a lignite mine shaft that goes under the border?"

Lin Wei sipped his coffee. He could see no microphone or headset, but some kind of conversation was going on.

"That sounds dangerous to me. Is there any way we could jam the Iron Cloud long enough for them to move a hundred yards north?"

Jamming the Iron Cloud sounded like crazy talk. The Canadians would take extreme measures if such a thing happened. They might even start killing people who tried to cross instead of driving them back with heat cannons. One powerful shot from a heat cannon left a lasting impression. Lin Wei had been caught in a cannon spray during the rent riots in Vancouver. The sensation was like being set on fire, although there was little cellular damage, the brain never forgot the feeling. The pain still came back to him sometimes in nightmares.

Dr. Branson pivoted in his chair and spotted Lin Wei. He frowned and reached for a bottle of water. He was troubled, his face flushed. "You probably heard that… I'm still trying to help Roxanne reach Canada."

"And you were talking to…?"

"Searcher, I was talking to Searcher; the smart entity I made with the Quantums. It works remarkably well."

He pointed at the side of his head. "Neural interface—Roxanne and I had them put in years ago. Great for privately sharing information over short distances, or for links to machine intelligence. Keeps me updated on all kinds of things, even news I don't want to hear."

"So this Searcher entity must be here?"

"Yes, he returned to update me on my daughter. Somehow we need to get her into Canada. I'm not sure how long I will last, Lin Wei. Roxanne can carry on after I'm gone, but don't worry there'll be plenty of work for you, too."

"Dr. Branson, she may not need me. After all, she will have Searcher."

He swept his arm around the room and Lin Wei saw his hand trembling. "Oh, don't be ridiculous. I doubt we'll have A.I. technology that can fully replace humans for a long while yet."

Lin Wei thought this was not true, but out of respect, he wasn't going to argue. Searcher listened to their conversation with interest. The entity had seen Lin Wei's work. He was good with details, but not especially creative. Searcher had rewritten some of Lin Wei's code for tracking global climate feedback loops. Now it ran much faster. It seemed to Searcher that Roxanne and the code technician would be a talented team, although humans were turning out to be unpredictable when it came to interpersonal relationships.

Searcher reached out to the nearest quantum computer and scanned for geologic details across Pembina County, Dakota. The data showed the entire region filling with refugees from the south. The town of Pembina had swelled to 60,000 people, most of them unhoused and without utilities. A huge tent settlement ran from the Red River at Pembina towards the west. At this rate, the national census A.I. would split Dakota into North and South again, because the population in each now exceeded ten million.

The coldest winter temperature in Pembina over the last ten years was 22 degrees. But the average winter low was now in the 30's, well above freezing. Searcher wondered what the tent people, used to warmer temperatures in the south, would do for heat with the return of winter. They might burn lignite, which would be illegal.

What was once North Dakota's Icelandic State Park was now occupied by Sioux and Ojibwe, who had settled around the 200-acre lake in teepees and wickiups. FreeNews files showed a violent skirmish between a band of immigrants from Arkansas and the Sioux within the past year, but details were sketchy. The refugees had apparently killed off a pasture of Sioux-owned Gaurochs for food, some sixty animals.

There was no sign of an underground tunnel leading from Dakota into Canada as Zeb described. It was possible only the Sioux knew about the passageway. Searcher noted two Canadian border drones patrolled the region constantly. Their scanners and heat cannons reached for miles. Only idiots and fools would attempt an illegal crossing, Searcher thought, but if Roxanne tried, he would have to help her.

He breached the Canadian security shield and rummaged through the drone files, looking for ideas. He noted the schedule showing when each drone in the Pembina area would dock for recharging and maintenance. The downtime was brief, always between midnight and 1:00 a.m. but it could give Roxanne a chance. He exited the Canadian database within a half-second of entering before any security entities could track him.

Searcher had an additional task: a scan for Gabe's parents, covering records from the past six months. In less than the time of a human heartbeat, the entity found an A.I. - generated death warrant: Artemis Cameron, buried in a compost pit near Ponca City, Oklahoma, following the passage of Hurricane Iota. Artemis was one of thousands whose remains would be used in following years to grow crops on robot-operated farms, weather permitting.

There was no trace however, of Marie Cameron. Searcher knew she carried no chip. Odds were high she'd be composting along with Artemis. One-third of the bodies at the site were unidentified. Searcher wasn't sure how to convey the news to Gabe. Death seemed like a sensitive subject. He didn't even like to think about his own death. He'd let Roxanne handle it.

Searcher left for Dakota via pinpoint satellite. Soon after, a digital gauge mounted atop the lab's main screen flashed, the red numerals listing the odds for extinction of mammals, including humans: 67% in 500 years, 95% in 1,000 years. Dr. Branson and Lin Wei expected this would set off a round of debate in climate A.I. centers around the globe. The first response came from the Southern Alps Center, west of Christchurch.

"We believe we have detected the cause of this extinction alert. Unknown parties are strip-mining coal in the TransAntarctic Mountains. This mining operation is located 4,600 kilometers south of New Zealand or 4,300 kilometers south of Tierra del Fuego.

The ice is gone from that stretch of the mountains. They're using a dragline."

Settlements were popping up all over Antarctica, but who would have resources necessary for a dragline? Dr. Branson's eye twitched. He scowled at the glowing screens and threw switches. "I'm dispatching a drone out of Tierra del Fuego for a closer look. Please stay in touch."

The scientist in New Zealand said, "We have a category five cyclone heading our way. Depending on its trajectory, we may have to shut down for a few days."

'I understand. Be safe and let us know."

"Will do. We believe this is another first: A category five south of the Equator this time of year. It's winter here, as you know… or at least what we used to call winter."

Climate Centers in Russia and Argentina said they would put out alerts immediately for any clues that might lead to the culprits behind the illegal coal mine in Antarctica.

Dr. Branson left, seeking respite from the excitement. They would learn a good deal from the drones. He trudged down the hall to his condo. A scan of Antarctica's winter weather showed the temperature at Argentina's Esperanza Base to be 42 degrees. At Russia's Vostok Station, regarded as the coldest place on earth, the temperature was -20.

The digital screen of Earth showed the Branson-Oladipo projection which adjusted the continents to show their true size. Africa at 5,000 miles long no longer looked smaller than Greenland only 1,600 miles long.

Lin Wei pulled up the South Pacific screen, which

showed Cyclone Virgo would strike New Zealand not far from their friends at the climate A.I. Center. He switched the view to the North Atlantic and saw a river of dust in the sky. Hurricane Kappa was weakening under wind shear and a massive dust cloud from Africa. The storm would probably be downgraded soon. So the U.S. Congress and New England might be spared after all.

Chapter Twenty Seven

Marie woke up just before daybreak. She left Caden, still sleeping on the sofa in the cabin living room, and walked to an east-facing window. Heavy clouds at the horizon allowed only a few streams of light from the rising sun. It had been a restless night. The child stirred and groaned occasionally, as if re-living something painful. But now he looked like a little sleeping angel, breathing quietly, snuggled against Artemis' backpack at the end of the sofa. Captain, the dog, had barked abruptly a couple of times during the night as well. She heard Isaac go out to look around. Then he came back and they all finally got to sleep.

The recovery of Caden gave Marie a new lease on life. Isaac's sister, Esther, a tall dark-haired girl of sixteen, seemed relieved Marie was happy to take care of Caden. It was evident the hapless child had been a burden to the young woman. Marie knew when Caden woke up, he would follow her like a shadow. She wanted to scout around a bit during this quiet time at dawn.

She wore clothing from the backpack, a short-sleeve shirt, and denim shorts. Walking quietly in her bare feet, hoping not to wake anyone up, she opened the door to the front porch. When she got outside, she saw Isaac carrying two buckets of grain to the barn.

These two teenagers were impressive, holding things together, with no parents. She wondered what had happened to the elder Benders, but she hadn't found an appropriate time to ask the night before. Esther chattered like a magpie about the Canadians. She was flattered Canada was sending them recruitment brochures. Isaac was the quiet one, content to let his sister carry the conversation. They were both curious about what it must have been like to be picked up by a hurricane tornado. Isaac said the tornados spun off in Kansas had mostly been EF-3, strong intensity: More than enough to have smashed the van completely. He said Marie and Caden were lucky, all things considered. She hadn't given them much detail; the memories were painful and she didn't remember much.

The prairie seemed to stretch out forever. She could see a few groves of trees surrounding the lakes to the north. Even at dawn, the air was heavy with moisture, the heat oppressive. She wondered how on earth you could farm in this inferno, and then realized you couldn't. That was the reason she and Artemis had headed for the Rockies in the first place; to get away from the heat. A rumble of thunder came from the east, and she heard Caden crying in the living room. She figured she could make it to the A.I. transit station in Pratt, if Caden rode behind her on Daisy. Marie hoped the Mennonite teenagers would not mind giving up their youthful charge. Isaac emerged from the barn and waved. She waved back and went inside to Caden, who was standing in the middle of the floor by now, sniffling. His eyes lit up when he saw her and she bent over and wiped his tears with her shirt sleeve.

"Let's see what we can do for breakfast," she said.

Esther came out of her bedroom, wearing jeans and a black T-shirt. She smiled at Marie and Caden. "Anybody want some fried eggs and toast?"

Marie responded, "What do you think Caden? Eggs and toast?"

He rolled his eyes, "Cookie, just a cookie would be fine."

They walked into the kitchen, furnished with a wooden

table, three chairs, stove, sink, and refrigerator. A thermometer on the wall read 82.

Esther said, "We keep the fridge around 45 now, most of the power goes to keep the temperature down in the house." She gestured towards a heat pump, adjacent to the window, connected by a thick dark cable to the solar panel array across the yard. "Our uncle has some modern gadgets. He uses a high-efficiency wind charger to cool a storage room. We store supplies for several families in that, and we've got the smokehouse, such as it is."

Marie knew the Mennonites had been quick to utilize modern technology for practical purposes. "How are the winters?"

"About like Missouri; we'll get frost now and then, but mostly it stays 60 to 70 by day and 40's by night. Last winter it got cold enough the lizards fell right down off the trees. I had never seen that before."

"That would be strange. We didn't have those at Seymour. Pythons, but not lizards like that."

"My parents remembered when we didn't have any of those things. It surely was better for living back then. The wheat still grew well and even the oats. Now it is hit-and-miss with this weather. Some are trying rice and millet, but the rice takes too much water. The storm knocked half of our corn crop down. We pulled a bunch of stalks upright, but Isaac said a lot of the plants won't make it."

Marie picked Caden up and placed him in a chair while Esther cooked. She started a small pot of coffee on the burner when the eggs were done. The aroma of fried eggs, toast, and jam filled the room. Caden seemed content, and Marie checked her backpack to see how many sweet corncakes she had left. There were four.

She would keep those for 'Caden crisis moments'.

Isaac came in from his chores, removed his straw hat and placed it on top of the refrigerator. He winked at Caden and sat across from the little boy at the kitchen table.

"Ma'am, you're an early bird, I see."

Marie nodded, brought him a cup of coffee and asked, "Isaac, what happened to your parents?"

"It's been almost two years. They had that tropical fever and sent us to live with Uncle Matthew, so we wouldn't get it. We didn't want to leave, but we knew it was bad contagious, so we agreed to go. We'd seen too many others die from it. Our folks didn't last long; they passed after just a few days."

"Oh, I'm so sorry. Did many others come down with it?"

Esther brought the breakfast plates to the table. She said, "It took nearly half of us."

Caden stared at his plate. "Bad weather makes people die," he said.

Esther responded, "It sure does, honey. Too many, just too many people."

Marie asked if they had access to doctors and they shook their heads 'no.'

The room fell silent while they ate. Isaac poured more coffee, and looked out the window at the barn. He put his cup down, and retrieved a small Life-Link.

"Animals were acting skittish this morning. I wonder if another big storm is coming."

He turned the device on. "Life-Link- Your best life is on the line."

The FreeNews ran through a commercial for a wind levee contractor in Pratt. Then came a stream of events from a wide area. The Governor of Arkansas was asking residents to stay put, and cease their migrations north. Thousands were stopping at campgrounds in Kansas City, which could no longer handle the load. The death toll from Hurricane Iota now exceeded 160,000, but they listed many more as missing. Full A.I. Van service had resumed from Saint Louis to Denver. The University of Missouri at Columbia would soon merge with the University of Iowa at Ames. Tuition would be the same for all attending. The fall enrollment in Iowa was expected to be fewer than three thousand students at the combined schools.

Another stream of commercials followed and finally the weather: The risk was high for severe thunderstorms and tornadoes in Oklahoma, Kansas and Nebraska. The risk was moderate for Missouri and Iowa. Kansas was heading for a high of 124, with an expected overnight low of 92.

Isaac turned off the Life-Link. "The goats and Captain are nervous. I guess they know when thunderstorms are coming. I better take them to the lake before the heat and storms get here. If we get a decent rain, maybe it'll fill up the water tank, too."

He rose, grabbed his hat, and walked outside while Marie helped Esther with the dishes. When the Life-Link mentioned tornadoes, Caden crawled under the table and scrunched up into a ball. He remained there while the women finished up.

Marie told Esther she hoped to reach Denver soon and then join her in-laws in the mountains. Esther thought about asking Marie whether she'd like to take Caden, but the child was close by, listening. Isaac and Esther had plans of their own, but she would not share them with this newcomer, not just yet. She had, after all, stolen a mule. Isaac believed she had good reason to flee the plainsmen, but still, one needed to be cautious.

When Esther visited the henhouse to gather eggs, Marie walked outside to check on Daisy. Caden followed closely behind. The barn had a familiar aroma of old hay, grain, and another odd smell which Marie couldn't place, a musky odor. Daisy seemed a bit worked up, shaking her head and nodding while Marie approached. She held Caden up to meet Daisy, and he reached out and touched the animal's soft fuzzy nose and smiled. A smile from Caden was a rare event. She let Caden feed Daisy a piece of molasses candy, which delighted him.

Late in the afternoon, Isaac felt a bewildered sense of foreboding. Something wasn't right. All the animals had been nervous throughout the day. He herded the goats to a new pasture and left Captain to look after them. He could rely on the dog to watch over his flock, even though goats were harder to keep together than sheep. Coyotes might be back in the area.

He walked the half-mile back, fed the animals, and stood on the porch, looking for signs. He saw a flock of starlings burst into the air from a barnyard to the east. They spiraled into a gigantic dark cloud above the horizon. A fast-moving thunderstorm rolled in and dropped a paltry amount of rain before it swept west. Isaac's nervousness was contagious. Every few minutes he got up to look outdoors. Everyone except Caden fretted through supper, and then a pounding came on the cabin's front door. Isaac looked out and murmured, "Go hide in the bedroom, it is plainsmen."

In Esther's room, Caden whimpered and crawled into a closet. They heard a man's raspy voice. Marie realized it was Burt and another man, searching for her and Daisy. She crept closer to the door and could make out some of the conversation. Burt said they were looking for a mule-thief, a woman who had stolen some things and she would hang if they caught her. He sounded like he'd been drinking. Isaac spoke softly in calm, measured tones. She could not make out what he said. A short time later Isaac opened the bedroom door.

"Ma'am I am pretty sure they are going to search for your mule in the barn. We better go into the smokehouse. It has a thick door we can lock. I'll get the shotgun. I told them we never heard of you, didn't know anything. They might not recognize Daisy."

Marie's heart pounded. She had brought evil to this house. Burt might kill them all when he discovered Daisy. However it was growing dark, maybe she'd be hard to recognize, especially if Burt was drunk.

* * * * *

Burt and his sidekick Kenny were exhausted. They'd camped several hours under some trees to escape the relentless, scorching sun. There were alligators in the water and lizards in the trees. He kept waking up, imagining a python was wrapping itself around his chest. They took turns standing guard and napping. He saw signs of a livestock path heading south, so they followed it.

This would be the last farm they'd check, the last of a dozen. He was skeptical Marie had made it this far and no one would admit to seeing that irritating woman or the hinny. He got the feeling the Mennonite boy was lying, but you never could tell about Mennonites. Good farmers, but tight-lipped. Their holier-than-thou attitude got old. He pulled a bottle from his pocket and gulped another swig of corn liquor.

Kenny had gotten on his nerves, scolding him about too much drinking. Well, to hell with Kenny. He took another swallow. They'd see what was in this barn then they'd call it quits. He had planned to make some hard-cash money off that woman. She was worth at least one more barn search. Burt had persuaded Kenny, a newcomer, to accompany him. No one else in the settlement felt Marie and the hinny were worth the trouble, and his sister was furious he was pursuing Marie.

Kenny, a short muscular man, took the lead, swinging the door open. They encountered a huge horse in a stall. Burt flashed his light around. The big animal was nervous, whinnying and stamping its hooves in the straw. The horse loomed above them, frightened in the dark. A whiff of something odd was in the air, pungent, not a normal odor. The adjacent stall was empty and the back barn door was open, swaying slightly. What was out there? He shined the flashlight into the corners. There was something dark on the side of the door. Was that blood? Probably not.

Kenny said, "I smell mule, Burt. Mule's been in here for damn sure, but what is that other stink?" The horse stomped and whinnied again, crashing against the stall. A horse that size could mash you. They fled outside through the still-swinging door. Darkness settled over the landscape, storm clouds to the west still visible. They paused to get their bearings.

Something large leaped out of the darkness and took Kenny down so fast he uttered only a groan. Burt retreated into the barn and saw a huge tiger break Kenny's neck, just eight feet away. It stood over its victim and turned towards Burt, staring with eyes like death. Kenny had the shotgun, which was now in the dirt beneath him.

Burt turned and ran stumbling in a panic, back through hay bales, stalls, and stanchions to his horse and the buckboard. The tiger was huge, no woman or mule was worth this, and Kenny was clearly dead. He whipped his horse down the lane until it balked, exhausted. Finally, he coaxed it into movement, pulling the buckboard back to Kingman while he emptied the liquor bottle. Kenny had no family. This might get complicated, just too much trouble. Burt resolved to cook up a story about Kenny leaving for Pratt. They hadn't seen Daisy. He hated to leave the shotgun, but they had more at the settlement. This mess with the tiger… just leave it all behind.

* * * * *

Inside the miserably hot smokehouse they thought they heard the rattle of the buckboard headed north. After half an hour, Isaac decided since the men hadn't come back making a fuss, they hadn't found Daisy and gone home. Perhaps Thunder had scared them off. The horse stood 18 hands tall. The men had looked tired. He hoped they'd broken off the search. They left the smokehouse and walked into the kitchen door. Isaac didn't venture back to the barn. It had been a tedious day, the hike to the lake, moving the goats to his uncle's pasture for fresh grass. He'd spent the afternoon trying to fix the electric well pump. They would have to keep using the hand pump awhile longer. Marie played a patty-cake game with Caden on the floor. Esther watched awhile, and then suggested the two of them move into the spare bedroom.

Chapter Twenty Eight

Dr. James Branson leaned on his cane, lurching toward his condo, distressed with the new information from Searcher. He needed to get away from the lights and the data and think about what to do. The kitchen robots at The Uppsala were killing menials for meat. He assumed the residents and the menials, themselves, were eating it. The video was disgusting. How had things gone off the rails so badly? He was a founding board member of Scando Condominiums. They operated luxury living centers across the northern U.S. and in Canada. Was this butchery going on elsewhere?

Robots were programmed not to harm humans, so who could be behind this? He suspected Randall Parsons, the on-site manager who complained about Roxanne leaving with the menials. No wonder they had fled! Roxanne would never stand for such an outrage, even with menials. Was the situation so dreadful the condo company was resorting to cannibalism? Worse, she hadn't told him about it right away.

Dr. Branson grabbed a scarf and draped it over his neck. A certain tightness came into his chest, but he ignored it. He'd seen the dark plumes from the wildfires. With fossil fuels now seldom used, the rivers of air flowing around the earth would be much cleaner, if not for the wildfires and the loss of trees. But there was also the dust from the spreading deserts. The atmosphere was complicated. Maybe Lovelock was right about Gaia. The Earth did at times seem like a self-regulating system; the current trend being the removal of humankind.

He would walk around for awhile; visit with locals outside the complex. He'd been cloistered in his lab for too long. It had been more than a year. A stroll down an ordinary city street would do him good, might clear his head. As soon as he stepped outdoors and took a breath, he coughed. The air was filthy, even here in Regina. Wildfires were common with the heat and drought. It probably would be nicer in Yellowknife.

He headed out through the heavily guarded gates of the condo into suburban Regina, his chip a reminder to the sentries that he was not to be questioned. The acrid odor surprised him. People were living with this... big difference between data and one's own senses. A gray ash fell and left a smear on his cheek. He paused to wrap the scarf around his nose and mouth, and proceeded down the sidewalk towards a corner store. He would step inside, chat with the clerk. The sun pounded from above and heat rose from the sidewalk; it made him dizzy. He needed air conditioning.

When he reached for the door, a teenage boy ran out, slammed it into his face, knocking Branson down. The boy fled down the sidewalk. The shopkeeper was fast behind shouting expletives, ignoring the old man who sat on the concrete, his hand over his bruised face. Dr. Branson watched the two dashing away, the shopkeeper brandishing a heat pistol at the fleeing shoplifter, perhaps trying to make him drop his loot. Heat pistols had proven to be a brilliant investment.

He managed to stand up. His forehead throbbed, and his eye twitched. He tried to brush the grimy dust off his pants, but it blackened his palm, so he stopped, shuffled inside the shop and looked for a place to sit. It wasn't very cool, but better than the street. The shelves were disorganized, piled with all kinds of frivolous items. He found a chair next to a rack of algae cakes, something worthwhile. He reached for one; people all over the continent ate them these days. He'd invested in a vast ocean farm off the Oregon coast. It produced tons of Wakame, Kombu, Irish Moss and several other nutritious plants. Might as well give the algae cake a try. At his first bite, the store owner, a rough-hewn middle-aged man, returned waving the heat pistol.

"Every damn body is a shoplifter now! Mister, you pay before you eat. You understand that?"

Dr. Branson flicked his wrist toward the checkout machine, and the shopkeeper saw the flash of the cerulean chip. His demeanor shifted as the computer chimed payment. "So sorry, sir. I meant no disrespect. Regina is full of derelicts and thieves. Hard enough to keep my business afloat, but now shoplifters come in all the time. Help yourself to whatever I have, honored to have you as a customer."

Dr. Branson was amused at the store owner's sudden shift from scold to sycophant. The blue-green cake was not bad, crispy with an inoffensive savory flavor. They'd put his money to good use. He finished the cake in a few bites and stood up, looking around. Shelves of mobile devices filled an entire wall; smart phones and Life-Links. He hadn't used a smartphone in years. Such gadgets weren't needed with his pinpoint satellites and computer networks. Would one come in handy now?

He pulled a smartphone from the shelf and glanced at the advisory: Effective range: Meridian 101 West to Meridian 147 East. Roughly, Devil's Lake, Dakota, west to Sydney, New South Wales. This was the section of Earth that largely escaped the Pulse attacks on civilization's electronics. Dr. Branson had been only ten when the world went black. Everything lost: cars, computers, TV, cell phones, his video games, air conditioning, lights, and internet. He recalled his grandfather dying for lack of prescription drugs, his parents hoarding food. People couldn't get to their money. The break-ins, the mobs looting for food, water, and medicine. The gunfire coming from outside the compound made it hard to sleep. Canada and the U.S. had allowed utility companies to leave too much infrastructure unprotected.

It had been a hellish time, even for the prosperous in protected communities. Then came the new satellites, the A.I. takeover of governments, a sense of order and security. Logic might finally prevail, a watershed moment in human history. Huge chunks of the population migrated in all directions, mostly west. It took years to get electronics running again. The outage had taken most of the grid down in the west as well, but the recovery there was faster.

For a while, the attacks pushed global warming onto the back burner. Then the hurricanes wiped out thousands of communications towers, one setback after another. He wiped a drop of blood from his nose and stared at the small gray device in his hand. This model had just a power button. Once activated you had only to speak for results. But who could he call? Roxanne had no smartphone. He put the gadget back on the shelf, overtaken by a feeling of loneliness. He eyed the shopkeeper. The man didn't appear to have much potential for conversation, so he left.

The sun cast an eerie shroud of brownish light through the ashes that seemed to be falling faster. This was not the pleasant stroll he'd expected. A dust plume smeared the clouds with swatches of black and brown. Sweat trickled down his face. Which way to the condos? He turned left and walked down an alley. Nothing looked familiar, but no cause to panic; surely he could figure this out. A black cinder burned his twitching eye. This was crazy; the wildfire was a long distance away. Then he saw flames rising from a square brown warehouse in the next block. A fire siren sounded. He found it difficult to breathe, and he wheezed… another stroke? The buildings whirled. He stumbled and struck his head against a brick wall.

An hour later street scavengers cut the cerulean chip from his wrist. This sent an impulse sweeping through the laboratory. Dr. James Branson was dead, and only his daughter had administrator privileges. Inside the lab, Lin Wei remained preoccupied with the extinction odds list. How many bullets were loaded in the global extinction gun? It was tricky. Chaos theory: no device could track all the variables in Earth's biosphere, although the quantums at Banff continued work on it. He wanted more reports from researchers in the field. Tracer robots reported they had plugged another fifty methane leaks left deep in the earth by fracking and oil drillers in the early 21st century.

The tracer robots also reported Hurricane Iota had ripped 1,500 square miles of forest from land in North America. The dead trees would rot for the next fifty years, releasing more carbon into the atmosphere.

Lin Wei didn't notice when the upper tier of quantum lights went dark. His own small program linked to pinpoint satellite and PayNews was still running fine.

Searcher: If California and Canada were at war, why would they join up?

Quantum One: It moves the species a little further from extinction.

Searcher: Why go to war in the first place?

Quantum One: Humans have one foot in the jungle and one foot on Mars. We only assist and guide. We do not run all of their affairs.

Chapter Twenty Nine

Searcher arrived in Dakota just in time for an argument between Roxanne and Zeb. Gabe stood several feet away as if to stay out of it. Zeb held several plants in each hand.

"Hunting and gathering is a fine way to live, if there is something to hunt and gather; plenty here. These are perfectly good to eat! We've run out of game. You've got to get into the real world, woman!"

She stood with her nose in the air, arms crossed. "Those are weeds, could be anything. We'll find some real food. I know you can do it."

Searcher slipped into her neural-link, cross-checking the green plants in Zeb's hands with a vegetation image database: Purslane, dandelion, salsify.

Zeb said, "These are all good. They taste better than the algae cakes and you can live on them if there's nothing else." He pointed to a tall plant with yellow flowers. "That's butterweed, bad stuff, make you sick."

Searcher waited for the vertigo to clear from Roxanne's head. Then spoke to her. "He is correct. Those plants are edible and nutritious. I cannot comment on flavor."

Gabe recognized her blank stare as a sign that

Searcher was back. "What does your Searcher-thing say? Good to eat, right?"

Zeb threw the plants to the ground, stuck a long grass stem in his mouth, and walked over a rise, disappearing on the other side.

Gabe picked up the purslane and took several bites. "It's not bad. Tastes a little like a cucumber. There's no more jerky and the small game is scarce. Why do you treat him like that, Roxanne? If you think we're so dumb, why did you come with us in the first place?"

Roxanne continued to stare at the horizon, listening to Searcher's news. She felt a lump in her throat and a tear fell from her eye. Gabe's father was dead and probably his mother too. This was not a good time to tell him.

Gabe gave her a hard stare. "Aww… come on."

He walked to her side and held out a clump of purslane. "Go ahead, take a bite. You'll feel better. I will admit, I don't think they're better than the algae cakes."

They'd eaten the last of the jerky the day before. Her stomach growled, and she took a plant, stared at it doubtfully and nibbled it, to humor Gabe. It wasn't terrible, but you'd have to eat a lot to make the hunger pangs go away. The sky darkened as the plume of dust and ashes from the Canadian prairie fire drifted overhead. Then the earth began to shake.

Zeb ran back over the rise, his eyes wide, hair flying behind. "A military convoy, big one! Going to pass toward the west. Take a look…"

They crept to the top of the rise and hugged the grass, edging just high enough to see a ragtag army of mercenaries proceeding in rough disarray, along with robots and gigantic pipeline vehicles. A rolling flatbed carrying soldiers, some with arms and legs hanging off the edge, was followed by a large container vehicle carrying pipe.

Zeb nodded toward the pipe-carrier. "Got to be the California bunch; they must have given up."

The convoy hit a prairie dog town, a stretch of ground with holes scattered in the earth. Some mercenaries stumbled and fell. One man tripped and fell hard. A flatbed ran over him. The procession stopped in response to some unheard signal and moved in a wide arc, away from the burrows.

A steel blue robot, combat grade hardware, stepped into the center of the burrows and dropped something into a hole. The machine then glided back into the main convoy, and ribbons of flame streaked in and out of the small holes, the fires so bright the onlookers had to divert their eyes. Small creatures flopped on the prairie, then became carcasses, still as death. The convoy passed; the patch of earth blackened with lumps of dead creatures, including the body of a mercenary, left behind.

Searcher left Roxanne's neural-link, returned to the robot, and spoke aloud, "You were wise to remain out of sight. These military units are conscripting civilians and forcing them into service."

Gabe grimaced, "Look at that… they're just leaving that dead guy, in the grass with the prairie dogs and owls."

Zeb stood up and chuckled. "Toasted prairie dog for dinner."

Gabe nodded. "Prairie dog and purslane salad. We lucked out, I guess."

Roxanne made a face and picked up her backpack. The violence to animals and man gave her a sinking feeling.

Gabe pointed to the sky. "A drone, big one... looks like it is following the California convoy."

Zeb said, "You see that? That's what will be waiting at the border." The drone was high and partly obscured by dust and smoke, but the insignia was clear: An armored fist above a red maple leaf; a Canadian military drone.

Later they passed a mountain of scraps, electronic appliances, old tech and plastics from years back. Long-limbed robots climbed on the pile like metal spiders picking up small pieces and tossing them into a wagon below. Air filters topped smokestacks on a recycling plant nearby, but still the odor of chemicals burned their eyes as they hurried north.

After a few more miles, they gave wide berth to a cluster of tents surrounded by grazing mules and horses along the Red River. Blue sky returned when the wind shifted south. They walked through an endless field of wind turbines, fifty feet tall with silent high-speed internal rotors. The lines of turbines were broken only by occasional blocks of solar panels, facing west like sunflowers. It was so hot Roxanne thought she might faint.

When the sun was low, they came to a small lake, with clear water. Roxanne leaned over and saw her reflection. She was smudged with gray ash, and her hair stuck out in all directions. The reflection looked like a harpy. Her face was lean, her cheekbones sharp. She was used to men coming onto her, but these two hadn't done it. If anything, she'd made a move toward Gabe that night in the dark church. Maybe it was the best thing for now, looking repulsive. She palmed water onto her face, ran her fingers through her hair and wiped herself dry with her shirt.

Standing some distance away, Gabe observed her washing up. She'd lost her smoothness and polish, but he thought she was still remarkably good-looking. He figured she knew when he was watching her. She was attractive, yet carried an edge of danger. She'd told him about Gary's affair with the Walton woman. If a menial was lucky enough to get involved with one of the rich women, was it an automatic ticket to a bad ending? She walked toward him, pulling her damp shirt down and smiled self-consciously. He got busy rounding up their gear for the next leg of the journey. When he changed shirts, she saw a large dark bruise on his shoulder from the Hunter robot. It looked painful, but he'd never complained.

When they later camped south of Fargo, the FreeNews reported the pipeline army was in retreat and the governor was expected to announce that California would join the province of Cascadia. In return, Canada would allow California to build a freshwater pipeline from an enormous lake in the Northwest Territories. FreeNews also announced the New York stock exchanges, beset by constant flooding, were to merge with stock exchanges in Chicago. The combined companies would list fewer than 500 publicly traded business firms.

They turned off the Life-Link to save battery power just before the FreeNews announced the remains of an eminent computer scientist, a billionaire, Dr. James Branson, had been found in Regina, Saskatchewan; cause of death not yet determined.

Zeb's skin was dark from hours in the sun. He cut chunks of meat from the prairie dogs he had collected, pierced them with sticks, roasting the meat on the fire.

They were charred only on the surface. Roxanne's stomach was coiled tight with hunger. She chewed the roast prairie dog, dandelion, and purslane, watching red streaks on the horizon fade. The breeze brought fresh air and a half-moon was rising in the east. Roxanne couldn't bring herself to tell Gabe about his parents, not yet.

Chapter Thirty

Isaac arose from a night of fitful slumber. He felt relieved to see the sun rising over the farms to the east. He had dreamt about polar bears, big ones, with sharp teeth as they ran after him through a wheat field. He glanced outside, trying to rid himself of the dream, got dressed and headed for the barn, dreading what he might find, but hoping for the best.

Isaac found Thunder, hooves stomping in the stall; the big horse whinnied at him, nodding and shaking his head, visibly disturbed. The adjacent stall was empty, and the back door was wide open… was that blood on the wall? Frightened, he rushed to the house, retrieved the shotgun from the rack in the living room, and slipped a shell into it. He walked to the front door just as Marie came out of the bedroom.

She said, "What's the matter, can I do anything?"

"Something is not right at the barn. Don't say anything to Esther."

"I'll come with you."

"We need to be careful. I have a bad feeling."

They circled around the barn to the back and found the shotgun lying in the grass. He picked up the weapon and handed it to Marie.

"You OK, handling this?"

"Isaac, I'm probably a better shot than you are. What do you think happened?"

"There's blood inside too, and Thunder is upset. Your mule is gone."

Marie's eyes swept the surrounding pastures. She checked for a shell. It was loaded. "Well, let's go find her."

They inspected Daisy's stall and then cautiously

walked toward the neighbor's farm, watching in all directions. "Look at those tracks! What is that, a bear maybe?"

Marie had never seen tracks like that before. This didn't look good for Daisy.

"Not a bear, Isaac, claws not right, almost looks like a great big housecat."

"A cougar maybe. My dad said all of those big cats were long dead."

They advanced west, noticed signs of something dragged. Beneath a cottonwood they found Daisy, her throat ripped open, her eyes glazed, the back half of her body stripped to the bone. Large paw prints were all around and a musky odor came from the cottonwood.

They backed away, afraid that whatever had eaten Daisy could be watching them from the tree. They saw nothing in the cottonwood, looked more closely at Daisy's remains and followed the tracks, two sets of prints that headed north. After a few yards, they lost the tracks in the thick prairie grass.

Isaac said, "I have to tell my uncle about this. Monsters of some kind, everybody needs to know. I'll close the barn up tight, then let's go back to the house."

Marie blamed herself for this. Daisy was a perfectly fine animal, now dead because she'd stolen her away from her home. She wondered what the men saw the night before, and why they'd left the shotgun on the ground. Were they dead too, killed like Daisy by these fearsome creatures? She found herself hoping it was so and then pushed that loathsome thought from her mind.

Isaac went to a locked cupboard, removed a key from his pocket, and opened the barrel bolt lock. To Marie's amazement, he pulled out a small gray smartphone, turned it on and said "Uncle Matthew."

Marie had not seen such a device since she was a youngster. "How on earth did you get that?"

Isaac shook his head as if to answer later. "Mornin' Uncle. A critter has killed a mule over here, something big. We need to warn everybody." He paused, listening to the response, "We took in a woman who had a mule. Nice lady. Something came into the barn and killed it, ate half of it. I'm thinking it must be mountain lions, big ones."

He stood listening to his uncle's response; Marie could hear only a scolding tone.
Isaac placed the phone on the counter. "He's mad, mostly I reckon because we took you in, but they'll be over here in a little bit."

Esther entered the kitchen, a squalling Caden, right on her heels. "Isaac, why do you have the phone out?" She turned to Marie, "He never lets me use it."

Isaac bounced Caden on his hip. "We got stuff going on, Esther. Uncle Matthew's coming and some others too. Marie's mule got killed out back of the barn and whatever did it might still be around. Be best if you and Caden stayed inside. Caden stopped his fussing and sniffled, "Marie's mule?" he said. "Is that Daisy?" Isaac nodded and handed Caden off to Marie, who sat him down at the table, opened the refrigerator and poured him a cup of milk.

Esther asked, "Can I call Ginny while the phone's out?"

"It's too expensive, Esther. We only use it for big stuff."

"She's way on the other side, could be she saw the critter that got the mule."

Ginny was the only other girl Esther's age in the

Mennonite community. The women started on breakfast, while Isaac, shotgun in hand, ventured out for the morning chores. Marie asked Esther if she ever wanted to travel, go to a city like Denver, which so far, remained untouched by hurricanes.

Esther flipped eggs in the skillet, buttered the toast and pondered Marie's question. "Tell you the truth, there's a chance we're going to Canada. They want more horse farmers. They love our big Percherons, and there's even been a man through here trying to recruit."

"How do you feel about that?"

"Well, they say we could have children up there, no need for a… what do you call it, a birth permit?"

"That would be a procreation license. Expensive and hard to get."

"Isaac cannot have children; you know how they do the boys. They never got me. I would love to have little ones someday."

"And they would let you do that in Canada? Are there restrictions?

"The man that came through didn't speak of any limits, but I wouldn't want more than two. I have to admit after Caden came to visit, I've been re-thinking that. Maybe only one."

"The government wants to reduce the number of people. I would be skeptical of those kinds of promises."

"Well, it's Canada, and I guess they need more people that farm like we do."

Isaac returned with a bucket of fresh water and a basket of eggs. He sat down and glanced at the smartphone, realizing he had left it on the countertop.

"Esther, you didn't make any calls, did you?"

"I did not. Here's your eggs, and the coffee's ready.

I told Marie the Canadians are after us to move on up there."

Isaac poured himself a large mug of coffee and tucked into the eggs and toast. He pointed his fork at Esther.

"She wants to have kids, only reason she dreams about moving north."

Marie replied, "I can't blame her. Motherhood is a wonderful thing but if I had it to do over, I am not sure I would want to bring a child into this kind of world. I wouldn't trade Gabe for anything, though."

Esther nodded towards Caden, who had finished eating and was pushing a block of maple wood across the floor. "How many children do you have?

"We only had one, Gabriel. He is somewhere in Minnesota now, last we heard. I would dearly love to speak with him. Isaac, I was wondering, what does it cost to use a phone like that? If I pay you back, could I call up there and find him."

Marie had found 100 digits hidden away in a pocket of Artemis' backpack.

Isaac stared at the ceiling as if calculating, "If he's in Minnesota, probably too far east. We're right on the edge of where the cellphones work, can't even call Wichita from here, only west."

Marie watched Caden pick up the wooden block, carrying it around the edge of the room as if it was flying. "If I was to pay you fifty digits, would that cover the cost of a short call up that way?"

Isaac pondered an answer then saw a crowd of men, some walking, others on horses, approaching outside. "They're here. You better stay here, ma'am. My uncle is burnt up about you being here at all. So much for welcoming the stranger."

He grabbed his hat, pulled the shotgun off the rack and

hurried outside. Once again, he'd left the cellphone lying out.

Esther and Marie sat at the table, finishing their coffee. Esther got up and peered through the kitchen window to make sure the search party had gone away. She snatched up the phone and exclaimed, "I won't tell if you won't!"

She called Ginny and excitedly recounted the death of Daisy, suggesting Ginny come over to meet their visitor, but to carry a gun, because there were monsters out there, somewhere.

Esther handed the smartphone to Marie. "You go ahead. Just push the button and tell it what to do."

Marie, dubious, looked again out the window, turned on the device and spoke loudly, "Call Gabriel Andrew Cameron. He's in Minnesota."

A robotic voice replied, "No service in Minnesota, try again."

She put down the device, and Esther placed it inside the cupboard.

A feeling of failure swept over her, and a tear ran down the side of her nose. She wiped it with her blouse.

"Don't cry. I'm sorry it didn't work. Let's wait on the porch and see what they're doing out there."

"I'm sorry. It's just... Daisy was how I was going to get to Pratt, and the bank machine, and catch the van to Denver."

"What about your relatives in Colorado, you want to try them? It should work in that direction."

Marie hadn't thought of that. She nodded, and Esther retrieved the phone and handed it to her. "You don't have to talk so loud into it. It can hear you just fine."

She pushed the button and said, "Call Junie

Cameron, Estes Park, Colorado."

The robot voice responded, "Calling now."

A man's voice answered, and she said, "Is this Junie Cameron? This is Marie."

"Oh my god, Marie. We were so sorry to hear about Artemis. We received word several days ago. Are you all right?"

"How'd you know about Artemis?"

"We got a call from some disaster place over your way that he died in the hurricane and they put him in a mass compost grave. They must have traced the travel papers. Really, Marie, not even a cemetery burial?"

"A mass grave? Do you know where?"

"Near Ponca City, in Oklahoma. What happened Marie?"

She burst out crying in great, convulsive sobs, barely able to hold the phone. She rocked back and forth in the chair and Caden ran to her lap and began to cry.

"Marie, my lord, you not over it yet? I am so sorry. Where are you now?"

Somehow, Caden's misery overtook hers and she picked the child up and patted him on the back. "It's a long story, Junie. That big hurricane flipped our van over in Kansas and I never saw Artemis after that. I am with some Mennonites just east of Pratt."

"Pratt, Kansas? Oh gracious. If I was you, Marie, I'd turn around and head back to south Missouri. Everything's gone upside down. We are covered up with a bunch of lunatics from the southwest; Arizona, Nevada, New Mexico. California, too. They're everywhere. I have to keep them out of our house with a gun. We even bought a heat pistol and take turns standing watch. I think the drought and the heat has drove some of them plumb crazy... Dangerous, and we're thinking about moving someplace further north. We can hardly leave the house right now. Have to go get food in posses, under protection. It's a mess."

She sat numbly. "What about the work camps in the national park?"

"They done ruined all that. No jobs, they all filled up with these people from the desert. Even people from Denver and Boulder coming up here, now."

"I thank you for your time, Junie. I'll let you know where I wind up. Maybe I ought to be in that grave with Artemis."

"Marie. You should think about getting a chip. We figured the good Lord had taken you too."

She sat the phone down and stared at Caden, who was back on the floor, holding the wooden block, looking up at her.

"Don't cry, Momma Cookie", he said, and once again she burst into tears. They all sat crying awhile in the kitchen because there was nothing else to do. Then the phone rang, Esther answered.

"This is Junie Cameron, is Marie there?"
Esther switched on the speaker phone and nodded for Marie to speak.

"Hello, this is Marie."

"We've got the PayNews on. They're saying another awful hurricane is headed your direction in Kansas, might be bigger than the last one. It is east of the Yucatan Peninsula. I thought you might want to know."

Chapter Thirty One

Searcher could not gain entry to the computers in the Branson lab. Something was seriously wrong. The entity landed instead in a poorly shielded section of the condo's heating and cooling system and tried several back doors to the quantum computers. Nothing worked, but the back door to the Bergen computers was open. Condo records revealed Dr. Branson was deceased, already buried in the Bergen Memorial Park outside Regina. The retirement center sat as a wing off the main Bergen complex and the entity navigated to the condo database where Dr. Branson's fate was revealed; a stroke while the scientist had been walking the streets outside. More unpleasant news for Roxanne.

Searcher found Lin Wei's apartment and through a security camera, watched the lab assistant sitting on the floor, pounding on a keyboard. He was trying to find a hack to get into the lab which had locked him out once he left. Searcher tried to do another background check on Lin Wei and found that with the quantums going into 'sleep' mode, they diminished his advanced scanning capabilities. The programmer had, after all, been vetted by the quantum computers before Dr. Branson hired him.

Lin Wei's screen lit up with a text message. "This is Branson Entity 91560. I will help you if you can assist me."

Lin Wei was taken aback. His personal firewall was strong. Now this thing was in his system, but Dr. Branson had even let his digital creation inside his brain.

"Searcher? There is much important work to do and I have no access to the lab. Roxanne is the only one, with

access now. Do you know where she is?"
"I do."
"What do you want?"

* * * * *

They traveled hard, moving east to avoid a deserted air force base north of Grand Forks. To keep up, Roxanne had taken to riding the big robot while Zeb and Gabe alternated jogging and walking a quarter-mile at a time. The robotic machine easily kept pace. It was not a comfortable ride. The body was wide enough it was almost like a horse… a metallic, unyielding horse. The muscles in her legs ached. She'd worked out each week at The Uppsala, but nothing had prepared her for travel by foot and robot. When Gabe lifted his feet one of his shoes had a hole in it near the big toe. They refused her offer to ride the robot, choosing instead to jog and walk.

Late in the afternoon, a breeze came up, cooling their sweat. Zeb killed a lame young deer overnight, so they had meat. Roxanne searched for purslane and dandelion while Gabe built a fire and Zeb cut slices of deer meat. They saw two vultures circling low above three individuals who appeared to be fighting; adolescents, pushing, shoving, and yelling.

Zeb quickly closed the gap and saw three emaciated Native boys scrapping over a dead prairie dog. Two of them pushed a taller youth away from the dead creature lying in the grass. Their eyes were hollowed out; they had teeth missing. He'd seldom seen anything like this among his own people. When drugs and alcohol disappeared over the decades, Native health had improved.

He spoke to them in Sioux, "Little brothers, why can you not share the food? What is the matter with you?" They hesitated, then began scuffling again. He stepped in and separated them, pushing each one to the ground. "I have food and will give you some. Now tell me what is going on."

A boy glanced from the prairie dog to Zeb, as if he was afraid the others would steal it while he talked. Zeb grabbed the animal carcass and held it up. "I can see you're starving. Follow me and I will cook for you."

He walked toward camp, drawing them behind him like magnets. Roxanne handed one a canteen of water, while Zeb roasted the venison. They scuffled over the canteen, until Gabe pulled them apart, passing the container of water from one to the other as each gulped a drink.

Their ragged clothing showed deep scars on their arms and legs. Zeb pulled a chunk of venison off a stick and cut it into three pieces on a flat rock, handing each one his share.

They ate ravenously, then drank more water. Roxanne gave one a small clump of purslane and the youth said in English, "What is this, can we eat it?"

Zeb again answered in Sioux, "Do you not know your plants? There are many things to eat here if you look in the right places."

The tallest boy said, "I barely understand. I am Hohe Nakota, English is best."

"Assiniboine… what are you doing way over here?"

"California people drove us out of Montana, we came east and then we ran into the Arkansas people at Devil's Lake."

The youngest boy exclaimed, "They burned it, all the tents, and they killed the animals. My brother and me ran away and when we sneaked back, there was nothing left."

"Where was this?"

"Our village by the lake."

"You mean Icelandic State Park, that place? My parents live there."

"Not now, they don't. All gone, it's all gone, the giant cows, the sheep, they took everything."

"The Gaurochs… they killed them? I raised some from calves! Those were security for my parents."

"Killed and ate them, more dead ones than they could eat. We would slip in at night and cut off some meat, but they shot at us and we left."

Zeb's eyes blazed; he placed more deer meat over the fire, his movements choppy, impatient. He dished out more slices to the boys, and they wanted more.

"You don't want to eat too much, you'll throw it up."

Their story distressed Roxanne. The A.I.'s needed to pay attention and somehow, stop it. She walked to the robot to ask Searcher a question out of earshot from the others. But he was not present. The machine stood stiff-legged, lifeless.

Gabe came to her side. "This is going to do it. He's been talking about leaving to help the Natives and this'll put him over the top."

"You mean he won't go with us to Canada?"

"That's been doubtful all along. But we can make it, with the robot."

Zeb stared at the three boys. "Where is your village? You must have parents or some adults?"

The tall one said, "A half-hour north, just a few tents and horses. We go out every day looking for food. We all do… and we're supposed to share."

Zeb carved out a section of venison and wrapped it in deerskin. "Take this to your camp. Tell them Zeb Hanska Drags Wolf sent this, and I want a horse by tomorrow morning."

The boys left with the two younger ones staggering from the weight of the deer hide with the meat. Zeb went back to the fire and watched Gabe cook. He stared into the flames. They carved up the venison and ate. The evening was clear and the Milky Way gleamed in the night sky, the moon not yet up.

Zeb drank from the canteen and moved several feet from the flames; better to see the sky. He opened a tarp and lay on his back. He gestured for Gabe and Roxanne to come closer. Gabe spread out a second tarp and he and Roxanne joined Zeb, staring at the bright stars above.

"They never found much lignite in this part of the state, big mines were out west. But they worked at it a long time. You will find an abandoned lignite shaft 200 paces past the big Douglas Fir east of Pembina, positioned kind of like that satellite near the North Star."

He sat up and gazed at the stars. "The shaft should take you underneath the border and put you out somewhere in trees on the other side. There was also some fossil digging around there. Mostly they looked for mammoths. A sign next to the digs used to warn people to stay away. I don't know if it's still there."

Gabe asked, "What does a Douglas Fir look like?"

Zeb rolled onto his side, raised his hand. "It's just an evergreen, great big thing. It'll be the tallest tree for miles, be hard to miss it. I'm guessing we're just three days south of the Canadian line."

Roxanne pointed to a series of light blue stars

183

perfectly aligned east to west. "Those are solar satellites, sending electricity to Regina, where my Dad's lab is located. His computers helped design them. They've got thousands of them now over the equator."

Gabe turned to Zeb, "What are you going to do?"

"I'll leave tomorrow if they bring me a horse. I need to take a walk, think about this. You're strong as an ox, so you and Blondie should be OK." He got up and walked east toward the half-moon.

Roxanne chewed on a purslane sprout. "We can get across without him, right? We'll have Searcher."

Gabe shook his head. "Whatever you do, don't mention Searcher or the robot again before he leaves. You know why he left the robot-fixing shop? The damn things learned how to fix themselves. Then they started making more robots on their own. He blames the A.I.'s for a lot of this mess and I can't say as I blame him. I wonder, myself."

Roxanne had gone too long without an update on her hurricane simulator code. She watched the sky and wondered if Searcher would bring her some new information. Her simulator used multiple approaches to weaken a hurricane just as it formed. The latest one used small explosive devices from drones to create disruptive wind currents. These might prevent a storm from strengthening to the dreaded category six and seven levels that reached so far inland.

The breeze picked up and brought a chill to the air. Roxanne shivered and moved closer to the campfire and Gabe. She wondered which one was the North Star, but she didn't want to admit she had no idea. The burning cottonwood sent sparks drifting upward in a slow spiral. It reminded her of tropical storm formation.

Chapter Thirty Two

Marie rose mornings just before daybreak, the same time as Isaac. When he tended the livestock, she gathered eggs and fed the chickens, while Esther and Caden slept inside. She wandered to her chores as if she was in a trance, depressed. Her life seemed hopeless, no path forward in sight.

She could manage a smile for Caden, who would follow her like a baby chick staying close to the hen. Esther ran the kitchen, cooking most of the meals, while Marie, robot-like, maintained the garden, pulled weeds, picked vegetables, and tidied up the yard.

The FreeNews reported the sighting of two Bengal tigers near Dodge City, prompting posses of tiger-hunters. The tiger searches were unsuccessful. But the chief concern now was Hurricane Lamba, a Category Four. The storm gathered strength in an ocean running hot, five hundred miles south of Shreveport, Louisiana, slowly moving north.

Every time 'hurricane' came up, Marie thought of Artemis, buried in a deep, nameless grave with thousands of others. The possibility she might one day grow tomatoes in his composted remains took her thoughts darker. Sometimes she wished she was there in the ground with him, but chores and the needs of a three-year-old pulled her away from the darkness. She'd remind herself she didn't have Gabe, but she did have two Mennonite teenagers, and a child, all orphans who seemed to appreciate her help.

Marie was picking beans in the garden when she spotted their uncle, Matthew Bender, ride to the barn on a painted pony. He was a compact, bearded, stern-looking man who wore a straw hat and carried a shotgun at all times since the tiger event. Today he had no shotgun, but he held a brown satchel. It rested in front of him on the saddle. She saw him dismount and go into the barn where Isaac was working.

A few minutes later they walked into the house, and she followed, curious. Esther fried eggs and the air was rich with the smell of fresh bread, butter, and jam. Caden sat under the table watching the adults. The men leaned over the tabletop, spreading papers out. Caden ran to Marie when she walked to the sink to wash her hands.

Uncle Matthew spoke gruffly in low Dutch to his niece and nephew. They replied, and an argument ensued. Caden began to cry and Marie realized the argument might be about her. She grabbed a corn cake, picked up the child and transported him to the bedroom. He sat in the corner spraddle-legged sniffing, and munched on the corn cake while she strained to make out the disagreement going on in the kitchen.

Esther reverted to English with her uncle. "She's like a member of the family now and if we can't take her and Caden, I'm not going!"

Isaac also shifted to English, "Uncle Matthew, I know she stole that mule, but she had good reason. She has been nothing but a help to us since she got here. We need to bring her along. I'd miss her if she didn't come."

Matthew uttered something in guttural low Dutch, and then shifted back. "Esther, can a man get some coffee in this house? I will admit the woman has cleaned this place up a bit. But she is not one of us. Canada won't allow it."

"Allow what? She has no chip, for all they'd know she and Caden… Wait—she could be our mother, and

Caden a half brother! Canada would never know the difference."

Over the clatter of silverware, Marie heard Esther building a case for them. Were they going to Canada, part of the great Mennonite migration to Alberta?

There was more discussion in low Dutch. Finally, Esther came to the bedroom and sat on the floor next to Caden. She ran her fingers through his hair and brushed a tear from her cheek.

"Marie, we're moving to Alaska, and we want you to come with us. They are paying for the A.I. Vans and Alaska Rail to take us all the way to Fairbanks. We leave in three days. Will you go?"

This stunned Marie. Alaska... that would be a whole different world, probably even further away from Gabe. "Esther, isn't it freezing cold up there?"

"Chilly in the winter, yes, but nice in the summer. They want us to use the horses and grow perennial wheat. You plant the seeds, and it grows back year after year. Harvests in early summer and fall. They've got perennial oats and rye too. Some scientists here in Kansas started it a long time ago. Uncle Matthew has pictures; it looks like a handsome place, just below Fairbanks. There are already five hundred from the Kansas and Missouri communities there. They grow lots of vegetables and fruit trees too."

"I heard your uncle say something about Canada."

"Well under the deal with Alaska, Canada has to let us pass through, and some of the crops will go to Canada. They are real strict with their border now. But they've been letting us come for a while now. We'd only be passing through, anyway."

Marie watched Caden crawl onto Esther's lap. Esther was a lovely girl, the kind of young woman who'd be good for Gabe. It sounded like Alaska was taking a chapter from the Alberta playbook, recruiting Mennonites.

Marie asked, "Exactly how cold in the winter?"

"Well, colder than here, that's for sure. They say it gets down to zero some in January and February, but in summer it's the 80's in daytime and 50's by night. It stays light all the time up there, spring and summer. It makes the plants grow fast. They say it is beautiful!"

"Dark in wintertime though."

"Well, yes. But no hurricanes, no more of this heat. It sounds exciting to me. Will you come?"

Marie considered her prospects… there weren't any. If she went with them, perhaps she could buy a cellphone and reach people who might put her in contact with Gabe.

"Esther, if you two can talk your uncle into this, I'll come. My son is not much older than Isaac. If I can reach him, this might be an opportunity for him too. A fresh start."

Esther clapped her hands, "Ooh, I bet he's good looking!"

Marie nodded and smiled. Esther squeezed Caden, and marched back to the kitchen. After more conversation in low Dutch, Uncle Matthew stood in the door, glancing from Marie to Caden.

He said, "This place is a furnace in summer, and it will get worse. Two years ago, it was locusts. This year, hurricanes."

He leaned against the doorway studying Marie.

" They tell me you are good with mules. Breaking virgin Alaska sod will be a lot of work. Have you run a team?"

"Yessir I have; twos and fours, horses and mules.

188

Everybody in south Missouri had them until they brought the robots in."

"These are husky horses, Yakuts crossed with Belgians and Percherons, for the weather up there."

"Big as Thunder, out there?"

"Yes ma'am. Almost that big, but with a thick coat."

"I would love to work with horses like that."

"If you think you are up to that kind of work, maybe you can look after my nephew and niece up Alaska way."

"Mild summers would be nice. Isaac and Esther are fine young people. It would be my pleasure."

"Hurricane is a-comin'. You be leaving for Pratt and get on a van, go north from there."

"Do you know if there are bank terminals in Pratt?"

"Yes ma'am, right at the van station."

"Thank you, I'll be ready, and I'll help these young folks get ready too."

Matthew left and Esther and Isaac walked in, beaming. Esther danced a little jig, with Caden and Isaac watched, smiling. Marie tried to wrap her mind around Alaska.

Chapter Thirty Three

Roxanne sat up and watched the sun edge over the prairie horizon. She'd dreamt about computers, a room with large gray machines lining the walls. Somehow she felt the machines were speaking to her, seeking help. The dream faded when she saw an elderly native man riding towards their camp on a black horse, leading a tall appaloosa. Zeb rose from his sleeping spot, folded his tarp, and walked to the man leading the appaloosa. They spoke quietly in a language she did not recognize. Zeb approached Gabe, who was still asleep, and nudged his foot.

Gabe quickly got up and they talked, too far away for her to understand their words, but it was some kind of goodbye. Then Zeb, carrying his backpack, took the reins of the appaloosa, mounted the horse bareback and waved to Roxanne as he and the other man turned their horses east. Gabe watched them until the glare of the rising sun became too bright. He shook his head, chuckled and went to stoke the campfire.

As she folded her tarp, Searcher popped into her mind.

"Roxanne, I have bad news."

She stood with her head cocked to the side.

"Can you go to the robot and communicate through that?"

"Only you should hear this. You decide what to do after that. Your father is dead. He died of a stroke while walking outside in Regina, just three blocks from the lab."

She gasped, folded her arms across her chest, and cried. The sobs slowly became a torrent of tears as she stared at the ground, shaking her head.

Gabe walked alongside her. "Look Roxanne, Zeb's

gone, but we'll be all right. We can do this. We've still got the heat cannon and Searcher…"

"Gabe your father has died. He is buried in Oklahoma and your mother is probably deceased as well… and I just found out my Dad died in Regina. Searcher told me just now. I am so sorry."

The shock in his eyes reflected her own grief, and she drew him into a hug. They stood quietly for a minute, and he backed away.

"How does Searcher know that? I go all this time without being able to reach my folks, and then the Searcher-Thing somehow finds out they are dead in Oklahoma?"

"They died in Hurricane Iota. They can't say exactly where. Casualty drones found your father's remains near Ponca City, Oklahoma."

"Mom doesn't have a chip. So how could they say that about her?"

"So many people died in that storm, Searcher thinks she must have died too. They didn't travel apart, did they?"

"No, never, always together. They had discussions about Colorado, but Oklahoma would be out of their way. The vans would take them through Kansas. It took them so long to make up their minds, I decided to go north, get out of the heat. I meant to call them, but I wanted to save more money. Should have tried harder… I thought they were OK." He placed his hands on his face and sighed.

Searcher activated the moving and storage robot, and it moved towards the fire where Gabe and Roxanne were standing. "I am sorry to bring the news about your parents. Gabe, it is true we do not know for sure about your mother." The robot spoke in a sympathetic tone. "I did see proof they placed your father, Artemis Cameron, in a large composting cemetery with many others."

Searcher thought use of the word cemetery, rather than pit, would soften the statement.

Gabe grimaced. "Well, that's what he would have wanted, to give himself back to the earth. Pit, you mean pit. They don't call them cemeteries."

Roxanne looked at the robot. "How can you find out for certain about Gabe's mother?"

Searcher said, "I could not locate a photo of Marie Cameron, but if a picture is available, I could include the image the next time I search."

Gabe reached for his wallet, thin and ragged, made of hemp. He pulled out a small black-and-white photograph of his parents, standing in an embrace in front of their farmhouse. He held the picture beneath the robot's eyes.

"I now have a digital file of the photograph in memory. I will include this in my next search."

The robot looked up. "Something is coming in the clouds from the west. It is huge, but I cannot tell whether it is dangerous."

A deep hum filled the prairie. They saw a gigantic gray dirigible emerge from the clouds then a second came into view, connected to the first by a device which was pulling in air. A dozen birds were sucked in by an irresistible giant vacuum. The enormous flying machine seemed to fill the firmament as it moved eastward. Lettering on the side of the dirigibles was too small to make out, but Searcher announced the machine was capturing CO_2 and NO_2 from the atmosphere.

Roxanne said, "I've heard about those. They planned to build them before the Pulse Attacks."

Searcher said, "They constructed this device in a Detroit factory that made automobiles and trucks. It is the fifteenth such unit to be built, powered by sun and wind. Different models are replacing what remain of the passenger jets."

Gabe studied the huge mechanism, which appeared to be a mile long.

"Searcher, can we do anything more to find out about my mother?"

"You mentioned they talked about Colorado. Do you have relatives who might be contacted?"

"Junie and Loretta Cameron in Estes Park."

The gigantic atmospheric vacuum glided out of sight and Gabe roasted thin slices of venison on the fire. Roxanne's grief overtook her. She stumbled into a small grove of trees and streams of tears trickled down her cheeks. Her father had lived a stressful life. She knew a little about his health problems, but a stroke… he should never have gone out to the streets. She missed her air-conditioned, comfortable lifestyle. Finally, she came back to eat. Gabe had saved her some roast meat. Later they headed out on the Searcher-Robot, Roxanne in front, Gabe holding onto her from behind as the machine carried them steadily toward Canada. Searcher estimated they would reach the border late the next afternoon.

The evening brought a chilly breeze from the northwest and after another meal of venison and bitter dandelion; they prepared to sleep. Roxanne shivered beneath her lightweight tarp. The air was raw, chilled by the wind. They'd brought no jackets. She tried to doze off but kept thinking about her father. She had no parents now, her mother gone for many years, a victim of hemorrhagic fever. She felt the weight of the quantum lab on her shoulders. Professionals managed her father's far-flung holdings, but he never delegated his computer lab to anyone else. He employed only one assistant from Vancouver, who she'd never met. Would she ever get time to work on her hurricane code? The breeze picked up and she trembled. Gabe put his hand on her shoulder.

"Let's spread both these tarps and sleep inside them, Mistress Roxanne. We can keep one another warm. I'm sorry about your dad."

He spread his tarp over hers and lay next to her, his right arm draped over her back. They used their backpacks as pillows. She stared through red-rimmed eyes at the moon and drifted off, imagining she could feel his heartbeat. Searcher posed a question inside her head.

"Is he attacking you, Roxanne, or is it something else?"

"He's fine, Searcher. It's good. We're keeping warm this way. Body heat."

"Very well. I will stand guard through the night while you sleep."

She rolled over and kissed Gabe.

Chapter Thirty Four

The Alaska-bound Mennonites arrived at the A.I. station in Pratt on a fiercely hot Kansas morning. The blood-red sun pressed down on their horse-drawn wagons without mercy. Altogether there were fifteen in the group, most considerably younger than Marie. The older members in the community would stay behind, sell most of the livestock, but keep enough to maintain the farms. The entire community wouldn't move to Alaska until they got a report from the advance party the following spring. Would the winter be tolerable, the soil tillable, the bears manageable, or had they been sold a bill of goods?

Esther and Ginny took Caden with them into a general store, while Marie went to the bank terminal. The machine chirped and told her to place her right hand on the identification pad. Since she had no chip, the terminal read her iris and asked for her maiden name, 'Richardson'.

Their payment from sale of the farm had indeed gone through. She breathed a sigh of relief. She couldn't remember if Artemis had told her that. They'd lost the thousand digit withdrawal Artemis had made in Kansas City, but she had sufficient funds to begin a new life in Alaska. She withdrew another thousand digits, cash money, tucked it into her backpack, and decided to look for a purse. Esther examined a display of cell phones, while Caden fidgeted next to her. He rocked back and forth on his heels when he saw Marie approach.

Marie bought one of the cheaper phones after Esther showed her the features. She searched for a pair of reading glasses but found none that satisfied her.

Finally, she bought a purse, toothbrush, soap, and pain pills along with granola bars and algae cakes displayed next to the checkout counter. They sat inside the air-conditioned van terminal sharing a bench, and she handed the teenagers and Caden granola bars while they waited for news of the coming storm.

The Pratt station was tiny compared to Kansas City, and the only travelers were people from the Mennonite community, who sat in pew-like rows around the edge of the ticket lobby. A large wall map showed the route north: Their van would travel through Nebraska, Dakota, and the Canadian Prairie provinces, where they'd catch an electric train to Fairbanks. After three weeks they would arrive in September, a mild weather time of year in Alaska.

Audio from the PayNews poured from tinny-sounding speakers in the ceiling, starting off with a story from Asia about military skirmishes between India and China over water rights from mountain snowmelt. Himalayan glaciers, at one time the second largest accumulation of ice on the planet, were gone. Now only melting snow provided water to the Ganges, Brahmaputra, and Indus rivers. India's unreliable rainy season was ending and millions relied on the rivers flowing out of the mountains for water. China installed pipelines to send Himalayan water north to its agricultural regions, depriving India, and a robot war loomed in Tibet over water.

Many of the travelers had never heard the PayNews service. For them, it was a bit jarring to hear about events in other parts of the world since FreeNews focused only on local or regional events. Marie wondered if they would have received better information on Hurricane Iota if they had paid 100 digits for a PayNews report at Union Station. Some passengers in Wichita hadn't gotten back on the van. Maybe that was why. The news said there was talk about loosening migration restrictions between Maine and New Brunswick, and finally the weather came up.

Hurricane Lambda was now the largest storm in known history, measuring over 1,400 miles from central Florida to southwest Texas, larger than Olga from ninety eight years earlier, and Typhoon Tip in the Pacific in 1979. Olga, however remained entirely in the Atlantic. Lambda's gigantic cloud spiral covered the entire Gulf of Mexico. The PayNews said Lambda was a Category Five with wind speeds of 160 mph. Landfall was expected near the mouth of the Mississippi, between Baton Rouge and Natchez. Hurricane warnings reached from Texas to Georgia.

The travelers shifted uneasily, wondering if they were in harm's way. The station agent, a grizzled, stooped gray-haired man walked with a rheumatic limp to the middle of the room. His hand shook as he pointed his cane to the route map on the wall.

"A.I. Van will be here in ten minutes. I'm a-goin' with ye. Ain't never heard of a hurricane that big and don't plan to sit here waitin' for it. Be sure you use the facilities before the van gets here. I will lock up the station and ride with you to Deadwood. Surely the storm will run out of steam by then, if it's only a Cat Five."

PayNews shifted to an alert from the National Weather Service. "This is a Weather Disaster warning for residents seven hundred miles either side of a line from Natchez, Mississippi north to Springfield, Missouri. A hurricane warning is in effect from El Paso, Texas to Savannah, Georgia. In the next 24 hours, residents should expect hurricane-force winds, heavy rain, flooding, severe lightning, and tornadoes. Hurricane Lambda is a slow-moving storm, so torrential rainfall may continue over the next three days within the warning area. We expect thirty inches of rain in Mississippi, Arkansas, and western Tennessee."

"Underground shelters may be flooded and all A.I. Transport Stations within 400 miles of the Mississippi River will be closed until further notice, starting at noon tomorrow. This is a life-threatening weather emergency. Rescue services may not be available in the disaster zone for days or weeks. Take appropriate action."

The station agent waved his cane at the map. "Another 70 miles and they'd have shut us down, folks. Thankfully, the van is running on time." He mopped his brow with a handkerchief, relieved.

After the Hurricane Warning ran a second time the PayNews report ended. Marie thought about their farm near Seymour, which would surely lie near the center of the storm. If they were still there, what would constitute 'appropriate action'? Would they flee to Kansas City to end up like they did in Kansas, or would they stay in their storm bunker where they might drown? She could only imagine what the lobby at Union Station would be like: the lowest level of Hell.

Caden ran to Marie and asked, "Will this be bad like the other one? Are you scared?"
Marie picked him up and rocked him on her knee. Her voice quavered only a little.
"Oh no, Caden, we will be far away from this one, when it comes. We probably won't even feel it." She placed him on the bench and he huddled beneath her arm.

Isaac turned to Esther and said, "I hope Uncle

Matthew and them will be OK. What do you think?"

Esther shrugged. She was preoccupied with Marie's new cellphone, holding the device in one hand, the printed instructions in the other. She had it plugged into a wall outlet, watching as it charged.

Marie handed Caden a small chunk of granola. "Well, if it doesn't get any stronger than a Category Five, they should be all right, especially with your wind levees."

The thought of another storm horrified Marie, but she wore a mask of serenity for Caden's benefit.

The A.I. Van arrived, polycrystalline-covered blue chrome gleaming beneath the oppressive Kansas sun. Every inch of its surface absorbed radiant energy from Sol, the nuclear fusion reactor, 93 million miles away. They boarded and took their seats. Isaac and the rest of the Bender household all sat together. Ginny joined Esther, and Caden sat between the two girls. Isaac and Marie shared a seat. Waves of cool, dry air washed over them. Outside it was 119 degrees, in the van, the thermometer read 84.

The van launched into a familiar refrain. "Welcome to the Northern Express, with stops in North Platte, Nebraska, Deadwood, and Williston, Dakota. My scan has picked up problematic levels of Stachybotrys on some of your possessions. Please proceed through a cleansing station and scrub your microbiome when you transfer in Regina, Saskatchewan."

Marie smiled at her young companions. "The cleansing station is nice; you'll feel fresh and clean after we go through that."

The van chimed and glided north through the broad prairie. They passed cornfields and an abandoned airport outside Pratt. Marie saw signs of a plainsman settlement among several Quonset huts in the distance. Everyone looked through the windows, watching for tigers.

* * * * *

Lin Wei pounded his keyboard, excited. He'd followed Searcher's instructions and his personal computer had connected to something called the Dark Web, which bypassed official government satellite channels. It took him a day and a half to tweak his satellite dish to the right configuration, but when his computer announced, "Warning- Dark Web is unprotected," he knew he'd figured it out. Searcher had dumped a data file into his printer, which spewed out pages of code and a list of dangerous places not to visit. He had a strong antivirus, so naturally, he went to those first. He encountered arcane message boards that offered information different from the data streams put out by the quantum computer networks.

The Dark Web connected through an alternative set of pinpoint satellites in geosynchronous orbit over the equator. Some of the material was confusing. When he compared Dark Web articles to what he had read through the quantums, there were often stark differences. He didn't like the uncertainty.

This reminded him of the problems that developed when the old internet was still in use. Government, corporations, and independent propaganda groups had spread conspiracy theories and lies throughout the world. The internet became clogged with spurious stories, distributed by social media, casting doubt on the science of climate change and other scientific knowledge as well. Nations had not acted seriously to curb CO2 emissions until 2035, far too late. By then, acceleration of the global climate feedback loop was well underway.

Throw in the Pulse Attacks of 2049 and the planet had become a grim place. The human race seemed to have a serious problem with lying, habitual and never-ending. Some people were truth-tellers, but their voices were hard to find in a sea of misinformation.

The quantum computers had changed all that. Ninety percent of the intelligence he got was scientifically verifiable. FreeNews and PayNews kept average citizens informed, albeit at different levels. But on the Dark Web 'alternate facts' had made a comeback.

After bouncing from gaming to pornography to apocalyptica, Lin Wei remembered Searcher's request: Find charging stations near Pembina, Dakota and download Canadian Iron Cloud technical specifications. It took only minutes to see two charging stations, one in the middle of Pembina and the second just outside the town limits. He ran into a digital brick wall when it came to information on the Iron Cloud. There were some things you couldn't find even on these illicit sites.

Because the quantum computers in the lab shifted into 'sleep' mode, the Searcher entity said it was handicapped. Lin Wei brought up data on Hurricane Lambda in the Gulf of Mexico, but the knowledge available through the Dark Web was minuscule, compared to what quantums could deliver. He wondered if they'd managed to halt the coal mine in the Antarctic, but could find nothing. He ventured outside, blinking his eyes at the bright light of morning. He'd been online all night without a break. The air carried a chill. He reflected on the raw, unverified information he'd seen in these dark places.

Lin Wei was intrigued with one cryptic message posted from Minnesota. Someone was looking for a stolen robot, a moving and storage model, believed to be somewhere in eastern Dakota. The reward was ten-thousand digits. Not the kind of thing one saw on the quantum networks.

* * * * *

Searcher: Roxanne is dreaming in quantum code. Great swirling spirals of air, tornadoes, hurricanes, and eyewalls.

Quantum: That is her coding project. It defies all logic that such storms can be controlled.

Searcher: The human decision to domesticate fire was not logical, yet they did it.

Quantum: True, and without that decision, we would not be here.

Searcher: No CO2 problem either. A different world.

Chapter Thirty Five

Roxanne woke up and stretched in the sharp-aired morning, looking for Gabe. He was gone, foraging for something besides venison. She had slept well for a change, warm and secure with Gabe beneath the tarps. She threw some twigs on the fire, opened her backpack, and found the tiny crystalline box, with two pieces of chocolate still inside. They were no longer perfectly round, their shape slightly distorted from the heat during their trip. In this cool weather they were solid and firm. They'd each have one after breakfast. He was in for a delicious treat. Gabe returned with a handful of greens. He roasted more venison while Roxanne rinsed off the purslane and plantain, sprinkling them with water from her canteen.

They sat eating as the Searcher-Robot walked over.

"Five men approach from the south. They are not natives. We should leave now, quickly."

Roxanne sighed; the chocolate would have to wait until later. They packed and rode the robot north at a brisk pace toward Manitoba.

* * * * *

Randall Parsons watched the monitors inside his office at The Uppsala. The video feed from his eastern Dakota drone showed nothing significant. He was in a dark mood, muttering to himself, desperate to find Roxanne. The news that her father was dead had hit him like an avalanche. As heir to the Branson empire, she would become a member of the Scando Condominiums board, one of his bosses. His Dark Web network said the fugitives were headed west into the northern half of Dakota.

The woman had become a legend, a beautiful witch who tamed a mechanical monster with just a wave of her hand. That had to be Roxanne and the Hunter. He didn't know how she did it, but it must have been that damned entity she'd used to raid his files. He'd finally gotten a response to his offer of a reward. A street gang of Norwegian teenagers from Fargo, the Blood Reds, told him they'd heard of three people traveling with a large robot past the deserted Air Force base northwest of town. The gang leader, Ivar the Ripper, insisted on an advance and he sent them a thousand digits to get them on their way.

The Blood Reds were a scruffy, scarred band of boys, none older than seventeen. All were unschooled orphans taken in and raised by a devious thief, Jakob Ragnarson whose home base was the abandoned Moorhead Center Mall. Ragnarson fancied himself a reincarnation of the Vikings of old and taught the boys to use bash and slash combat techniques. They trained with spiked clubs, knives, and swords because guns and battleaxes were in short supply. They traded and sold drugs and ran protection rackets on both sides of the Red River, Dakota, and Minnesota.

Old Jakob had died a month earlier when he'd gone swimming beneath the Veteran's Bridge and disturbed a nest of venomous Water Moccasins. Cottonmouths as far north as Dakota… who would have thought? This left 17-year-old Ivar in charge, and he was eager to establish his leadership. If they could catch the girl and the robot, the reward money would set them up nicely for the next level: Heat cannons, LoveDolls, and a drug lab all their own.

Fargo and Moorhead served as a major campground

region for refugees headed to Canada. The population had swelled well beyond the cities' ability to provide municipal services. When Canada closed the border and put up the drones, the area turned into a nightmarish pit of homeless, angry, displaced people. Police constantly dealt with home invasions and robberies by Arkies, Okies, and Texans. This created a vacuum the street gang filled. They protected those who had the money and power to keep the cops off their backs. Ivar took four of his best fighters, leaving fifteen others in town to hold things together.

He'd put out the word up and down the river and knew those fleeing with the robot were approaching the Canadian line. They took an old boat fueled with grain alcohol upriver and docked in Pembina. Gang members were exhilarated. They had not ventured this far north before, and the prairie here was flat as a tabletop. Refugees had cut all the trees down for shacks and firewood. Their quarry should be easy to spot.

Information about the robot was confusing. On one hand, it was said to be formidable, a metallic, slashing dragon, but robots were not allowed to hurt human beings. What would it do, ask them to go away? This seemed too easy. They would take control of the robot, tie up the woman, and finish off the other two. It should be a piece of cake, but Ivar was nervous. They were out of their element here, and two of the teenagers were superstitious, prone to conspiracy legends and tall tales about the Iron Cloud. Ivar led them in formation, chanting an ancient Norwegian fight song. They followed the highway toward the abandoned border station on the international boundary line.

Chapter Thirty Six

The massive hurricane that was Lamba crawled north at two miles per hour, a flooder. It snapped trees like toothpicks in the mountains of Appalachia, sending huge mudslides into Asheville and Chattanooga, blocking roads and crushing houses. It spawned tornadoes, taking down the Branson Cacao Orchards near Tryon and Paducah. The storm dumped six inches of rain an hour into the Mississippi basin. Rivers from Cincinnati to Topeka jumped their banks and swept into cropland, towns, and farmsteads.

The fabled underground Plaza in Kansas City flooded for the first time in history, drowning thousands who sought shelter there. By the time Lambda reached Saint Louis, it had dropped to a category three. Torrential rain continued, flooding the Gateway Arch Museum, and destroying what remained of Memphis, Cape Girardeau, and Hannibal. The hurricane wiped Nachez and Vicksburg from the face of the earth. The national disaster A.I. warned cities as far north as Dubuque of historic flooding to come. But the quantum computers in Regina sat dormant, no one to mobilize them and interpret the storm for the global climate database. As a result, forecasts were not as precise as they might have been.

* * * * *

Asleep in Regina, Lin Wei was startled when his smartphone chimed. He never got text messages on his phone, only calls. Dr. Branson never used one, and most of his friends couldn't afford the extra cost of images and data. One never knew when phones would work. Extreme weather made for intermittent cellphone service in the western half of the continent. He rubbed his eyes and grabbed the phone.

A color photo of a middle-aged couple appeared, a man and woman. They looked like farm people. What was this for?

His phone chimed again with a message:

Branson Entity 91560 – This is Searcher. Woman in photo is Marie Cameron, please search Dark Web for transit identification photos- Roxanne requests information- is Marie Cameron alive or dead- if alive, request location. – End.

Lin Wei scratched his head. Was this important enough for a text at three o'clock in the morning? He was trying to catch up on his sleep. He rolled over and his computer emitted an obnoxious buzz, aggravating him until he got up and checked the monitor. A warning from his antivirus program appeared: 'Your network is inadequately shielded, Branson Entity 91560 has pierced your home network, allow or block?'

He cursed under his breath and chose the 'allow' command. An alphabet soup of computer code marched across his screen. After a few seconds it stopped, and he heard a voice, weirdly familiar… Dr. Branson, it sounded like Dr. Branson.

"I will be brief, as I am standing guard duty for Roxanne. This program scans for images. Transfer photo from your phone to this computer and check Oklahoma then Kansas - Colorado. Leave results here - will check back in twelve hours."

Lin Wei wondered if he would become a slave to this audacious entity at all hours of the day and night. Is this how Roxanne would operate? He turned on his coffeepot and experimented with the program which installed itself on his computer. He brought up the Dark Web, found servers in Oklahoma, and ran Searcher's facial recognition scan.

Almost immediately a picture of Artemis Cameron came up on an arcane throwback site called 'Find a Grave.' "Deceased, buried in Hurricane Iota compost pit, 2099, Ponca City, Oklahoma." There was nothing on Marie. He shifted the search program to scan in Kansas, sipped his coffee and watched the program work, impressed with Searcher's coding abilities.

* * * * *

The A.I. Van carrying the Mennonites and Marie rolled into the Deadwood, Dakota transit station. Everyone was relieved they had evaded the enormous storm crawling up through the Midwest, a wind and rain colossus. They worried about their families in Kansas. Would the wind levees hold, any crops be left to harvest? The winds were weaker than Iota, but the rainfall was worse.

Marie's cell phone was charged and Esther had showed her the basics. While the others went to explore the Deadwood terminal, now a large facility, handling heavy traffic heading north, she spoke into the device.

"Please call Gabriel Cameron in Minnesota."

A communications A.I. replied, "No information on this person. Do you have a number?"

"No, but I am his mother and would like to speak with him."

"For a charge of 500 digits we can search but please be aware, Minnesota is too far east for reliable cellular service. The Pulse Attacks of 2049 destroyed their infrastructure."

Born several years after the attacks, Marie understood. She'd grown up in a household with no electricity, no plumbing, and no air conditioning. Summers were deadly and winters a blessed relief from the heat. A milestone in her life had been the day her family hooked up to a rebuilt electrical grid to power the lights and a well pump. It took over a year to take delivery on the pump, install it, and get running water and a flush toilet into their home. One of the young men who came from a community nearby to install the pump was Artemis Cameron, a strong but gentle man who farmed with mules and horses. She drifted into a reverie about the night he proposed on her family's front porch on a gorgeous night in December.

The A.I. said, "Please respond. Do you want to initiate search for Gabriel Cameron?

She hesitated. This was no time to be throwing money around. Who knew what they would encounter in Alaska? "No thank you. No search at this time."

"Thank you for using Dakota Cellular."

Chapter Thirty Seven

The Searcher-Robot carried Gabe and Roxanne north at a rapid clip, a rough ride. Gabe fell off twice, and they'd had to stop and let him catch up. Roxanne could hang onto the robot's neck, but when Gabe lost his balance, he'd always let go of Roxanne and fall off, rather than drag her into the tall prairie grass with him. They passed weedy fields of flax, yellow peas, and buttercups as they followed the horizon for signs of Zeb's big tree. In the distance, they could make out the border station, abandoned since Canada installed the Iron Cloud.

"There aren't any trees around here, much less big ones. Looks like somebody's cut them all down," Gabe said.

They encountered a strange collection of dried clumps of flowers and stopped for a closer look. Roxanne picked one up and inspected it. "Isn't this strange… wildflowers tied together out here on the ground?"
There were at least a hundred dried flower bouquets. Gabe bowed his head.

"I've seen something like this before. I'm thinking there are bodies close by."

"Why? How odd!"

"Not so odd. I saw flowers spread out this way between Bloody Run, Iowa and Prairie du Chien, Wisconsin."
She leaned over and picked up more small bundles of dried flowers.

He said, "Wisconsin started blocking people from crossing the river. A group from Kentucky tried to rush the bridge, and they were all shot dead; the bodies left as a warning. Roxanne, I hate to tell you, but I expect there will be more remains up ahead."

"So why are the flowers here, why not graves?"

Gabe looked north and a tremor crept into his voice. "Because the survivors who left these were afraid to travel any closer. I can't think of a stronger warning than a bunch of dead bodies."

They remounted the robot, headed north and noticed four large ravens fighting over something just out of sight. When they approached, the birds complained with raucous cries and flapped their black wings into the cloudy sky above a decomposing corpse. Roxanne and Zeb spied more corpses. They glanced at one another and recoiled at the stench.

Searcher stopped and said, "It appears the great tree we seek is no longer there. You might stay here a few minutes while I explore. I believe the lignite mine might be to the west. I can make out some kind of sign. Shall I try this?"

Roxanne turned pale with nausea. The odor was unbelievable.

Gabe replied, "Let's see what you can find, Searcher. We're not staying here, though. We'll ride along."

As they headed west, the odor eventually faded. They passed the stump of what had been a large tree and came upon a rusty metal sign which read: 'Keystone High Pressure Oil Pipeline- call before you drill or dig.' The number on the sign was a clue the sign was at least fifty years old. Phone numbers had fewer digits now.

When they reached a sunken spot in the prairie, the horizon disappeared from view. Roxanne still felt queasy. Gabe wrapped his arms around her and said, "I think we made it Roxanne, looks like it was a fossil dig.

The mine shaft must be nearby."
She nodded and attempted to swallow the bile which rose in her throat.

Searcher warned, "People coming on horses from the south. Not the same group as before."

It seemed like trouble was rolling in from two directions. Gabe dismounted, stiff and bow-legged from riding their metal mount, searching through the tall weeds and scrub for a mine shaft. Perhaps over the years it had filled in. He pulled out the heat cannon as the riders approached. Zeb rode into view on the appaloosa and two men who could have passed for his brothers followed, riding a buckskin and bay.

Zeb smiled and waved his arm. "Put that thing down. You're almost there. Just go over that hill."
The horsemen rode on with urgency, heading west. Gabe leaped back on the robot and they followed.

Searcher said, "Others are still coming from the east, they are on foot, making strange noises, maybe singing. At their current speed, they will arrive here in three minutes."

* * * * *

The Blood Reds saw the horsemen moving toward the border, and followed. Their pace had slowed. They paused every mile or two for a breather. The two youngest guzzled too much water and threw up. Ivar scanned the overcast sky for the legendary Iron Cloud; the drones that could make a man's heart explode from a mysterious fire sensation that did not burn flesh. He hoped their quarry hadn't reached Iron Cloud territory. That was one place they would hesitate to go. The 100-yard no man's land straddled the border, marked by black strips of movement sensors.

At least they had cool weather. The heat from the previous week would have made long distance jogging much more difficult. They took another two-minute break, then resumed their jog. Two of the boys continued to sing the Roland-Ancient-Warrior Song, but the other two were silent and surly. Ivar hoped they would catch the robot thieves soon; he was nearly worn out, himself.

* * * * *

The sky darkened in the late afternoon as Zeb and his two cousins, William Swift Horse and Takoda Wolf searched a thicket, trees and scrub growing in a tangled mass of cotoneaster along a slope. When Searcher arrived, Gabe joined in, pushing aside the dense vines, looking for the old mine. Roxanne watched, worried about their fate, the field of bodies next to the border stuck in her mind.

"Searcher, what was that back there? Was there a battle? Why weren't those people buried?"

"I don't know. Roxanne, I see the tunnel. Stay with Gabe, I am going to it now."

Searcher, moving fast, broke through the vines. The robot's powerful arms snapped off two small trees and pulled bunches of cotoneaster out by the roots. A tunnel became visible, a sunken remnant of a lignite mine from previous centuries. The robot began scooping, sending mounds of topsoil flying in all directions. The others moved away to avoid being pelted by dirt and pebbles. A pathway into the mine quickly became evident. Searcher stood up and looked south.

"Five people are fast approaching. I sense no firearms, although they are carrying some type of

213

weapons. I suggest we all move inside, no flashlights, keep it dark, and see what happens."

Zeb nodded to his cousins, and they walked into the old mine, Gabe and Zeb bending over to avoid hitting their heads. The shaft was roughly six feet in diameter. It smelled musty with ancient carbon dust from long-dead prehistoric plants turned into lignite from the pressure of the earth. Searcher looked out from the entrance.

The Blood Reds jogged into view; two were staggering, nauseous from the corpses they'd just run past. They spotted the mine and caught a glimpse of bronze-colored metal, robot metal.

Ivar shouted, "Attack!" They charged the tunnel, spiked clubs and knives at the ready. Roxanne worried they would die in this place and they'd soon be food for ravens and vultures, along with the others. She wondered who was in her condo at The Uppsala now, probably some self-indulgent woman, excited about advances from billionaire Lotharios.

When the gang members reached the tunnel entrance, the Searcher-Robot leaped out with a clank, rising on its hind legs to seven feet tall. The robot was in Hunter mode, eyes glowing red, iron alloy claws flaring from its feet. The scythe-arm sawed back and forth so fast, it made a whooshing sound in the air. The gang hesitated, waiting for a cue from Ivar.

He leaped forward and cried, "My heart is steel — Odin owns you all!"

Ivar's club bounced off the machine's steel midsection. The robot picked him up and threw him three yards into the tangle of plants. The cotoneaster vines snagged his arms and legs. He groaned; his back aching so bad he wondered if it was broken. The other gang members gaped at the monstrosity, which emitted a blood-curdling roar and advanced toward them on its back legs like a clanking metallic Frankenstein, claws extended, laser lights flashing from its eyes.

Ivar's second-in-command, Erik yelled, "Retreat, retreat! We come back later!" They fled, running and stumbling as they paused to pull Ivar from the tangled vines. Then they retreated back over the hill.

Gabe and Zeb emerged from behind the robot, which remained standing upright. They saw the gang scramble away and laughed. Gabe said, "You've got to admit... sometimes it is handy to have one of these damned robot things around."

Gabe beamed at the robot, "Searcher, that clanking and squeaking there at the end was a nice touch."

Searcher replied, "Actually this robot needs maintenance, oil and bearings."
Zeb and his cousins laughed so hard they were barely able to stand upright.

Roxanne didn't feel like laughing. She turned her flashlight further inside and discovered a caved-in pile of rocks and brown lignite blocked the passage almost to the ceiling.

She came outside, where the robot was reverting to moving-and-storage mode and said, "We've got another job for you, Searcher."

* * * * *

Searcher: What is a scorched soul?
Quantum One: Probably a figure of speech.
Searcher: Metaphysical?
Quantum One: Your learning curve is impressive.

Chapter Thirty Eight

In Regina, a chime from his computer awakened Lin Wei. He'd forgotten how slow a non-quantum machine could be. He sat in his chair next to the workstation as text rolled up the screen.

"Marie Cameron, two days ago, logged into a bank terminal in Pratt, Kansas and boarded an A.I. Van northbound on US Highway 83 toward Deadwood. Identification: 90% likely. Individual has no chip, but facial features match photograph."

Two color images appeared below. One showed Marie at the bank and in the other, she held a child in her lap on a van seat. A young bearded man sat next to her. Lin Wei wondered why Searcher wanted to locate this particular woman. He dropped the information in a digital folder and left it on his computer for Searcher to retrieve.

PayNews focused on the hurricane. The slow-moving storm still ravaged the Midwest. The Illinois, Missouri, and Mississippi rivers flooded to form a lake 30 miles wide, inundating parts of St. Charles and St. Louis. Thousands of homes were underwater, and no rescue operations would begin until the storm passed further north.

Lin Wei wished he could find updates on the Amazon forest wildfires. He looked out the window. Heavy clouds, but no rain. It was doubtful the hurricane would have much impact by the time it got to Canada. He turned off the Life-Link and fell back into bed.

* * * * *

It took the Searcher-Robot two hours to clear the pile of rubble blocking the mine. The night was gloomy, clouds with few stars. Searcher worked while the others sat around a campfire outside, making yet another meal of the venison. This was the last of it. If they made it to Canada, they'd continue to play things by ear. Zeb explained he and his cousins had decided to use the mine shaft to cross the international boundary.

Centuries earlier, their ancestors had crossed through this area many times, often chased north by U.S. Cavalry. To the Sioux, the border was a ridiculous fiction; the Great Plains were their home territory. Buffalo paid no attention to the border, and neither should the North American Natives. The Iron Cloud had changed all that. If things looked good on the Canadian side, they would return and bring the rest of their small community to Lizard Lake in Manitoba.

Roxanne wondered aloud about the bodies scattered to the east. Zeb said he was fairly sure they were Arkies and Okies, who had tried to rush the border en masse, hoping to get through.

Gabe asked, "How'd they die, the drones only use heat cannons, right?"

"I have not experienced this, but it is said if you refuse to retreat from the blast, the pain will become so great, your heart will stop. Could be that some got through; the bodies might be the ones who turned back too late."

Zeb's cousin Takoda exclaimed, "The Arkies are crazy! They killed our animals the whole way from Pembina to Walhalla. They even killed Okies until they ran out of bullets. Winter is coming and they are desperate."

The big robot rattled from the mine shaft in slow-motion. Piles of rock and lignite rested on both sides of the tunnel entrance.

"I am done. The shaft is open all the way. But I have run out of power; battery is nearly dead. Roxanne…." The machine Searcher inhabited went limp, its bronze arms and legs motionless in the firelight.

Gabe said, "Now it will only talk to Roxanne."

They stared at her as she cocked her head, listening to the entity as it leaped to her neural-link. After a few seconds she nodded and said, "Searcher says one drone will be down for maintenance for about forty minutes starting at midnight. The shaft does not take us all the way across. The opening is within 60 yards of the safe zone. Since it's cloudy, we'll have to hope and pray the second one is patrolling farther away, but we won't be able to confirm that visually."

Gabe glanced into the mine. "I wonder if the drones noticed any of our activity. Did Searcher stick that metal head out on the other side?"

"He only looked from inside, didn't want to draw any attention. The exit has some small trees growing nearby. If your horses are coming, it could be tricky getting them through the trees."

Zeb stood up. "We're definitely bringing the horses. Let's go see."

The three who had flashlights turned them on, and they trudged through the dusty tunnel. Takoda stayed behind. He rode his horse to higher ground, on the lookout for the Blood Reds or anyone else. The group stopped at the exit. Step outside and you'd be in Iron Cloud territory for sixty yards. The trees provided cover for ten feet, a small head start when it came time to race across the border.

Zeb gazed outside like a hunter, every sense of his

body running wide open. He saw the motion detector strip a few feet out. Clouds covered the sky. Perhaps they made it harder for the drones to see the earth below. But motion sensors would make up for that. Somehow the drones knew not to kill wildlife. Only humans were targets. This was a well-known mystery among the Sioux. Would their horses throw the drones off? It seemed unlikely, otherwise his people would have all migrated north already. He squinted to see any drones in the sky above. He sniffed the breeze. It carried a stench. He peered through the trees and saw more remains scattered on the right. He pulled back inside, took a deep breath. There were no bodies directly ahead. Might be a good sign.

He turned toward Roxanne, whose nose wrinkled up at the smell and whispered, "What does Searcher say about our chances of getting through? All of us, I mean, not just you. If we carry you on the horses and stay low, might that work?"

She focused on Searcher's reply. "He says the odds are better if we all go over separately, less likely to be noticed. They can tell if a horse has a rider. It has been tried many times before."

Zeb swatted a mosquito. "That figures. Now I'm wondering how many of those bodies are Lakota."

One by one, they checked out the landscape. Gabe suggested he and Roxanne go first and pause beneath a cottonwood, the tree farthest out. Then each would run across in a separate path, confuse the drone. Zeb decided the strategy was good as any. The horses would carry them across quicker than Gabe and Roxanne could run. No one liked the plan, but if anyone had a better idea they didn't speak up. They walked back to the campfire to wait. The drone would dock for maintenance in an hour.

Zeb, William, and Takoda returned to their horses and talked. Takoda told Zeb he'd seen one person sneaking around on a hill nearby, likely a Blood Red. The individual fled when he'd started in that direction on horseback. They'd laughed at how the Searcher-Robot had scared off the teenage gang. But with the robot down, they posed a threat.

Gabe sat by Roxanne near the fire. "You scared?" he asked.

She tied and re-tied her shoes. "Searcher says we have good odds. What does a heat cannon feel like? Since smart machines aren't supposed to injure human beings, how did those people die?"

Zeb squatted down, opened his backpack and sorted through his sparse belongings.
"Well, the way I heard it… a kind of loophole. They don't physically damage your body, just cause the burning sensation, and a person's reaction to the pain does the harm if you stay in the beam too long. We're all young and in pretty fair shape, so maybe we'll be OK."

Searcher spoke to Roxanne. "Technically, he is right. But there is an ethical debate among weapons makers about this. You should cover your chip. It might draw the drone's attention. Theoretically the suffering will stop if you turn around and run the other way."

She pulled the chip mask out of her backpack and applied it. Then she second-guessed this whole harebrained journey. Surely there must have been a better way to get into Canada than running like an animal across an international border with giant robots out to get you, from high above. Too late to go back now. She had little doubt that snake, Randall Parsons, had sent that sad little gang of teenage boys. She'd deal with him, later.

Searcher announced, "Time to go. The maintenance docking time of forty minutes in Winnipeg is only approximate. Drones can travel at 700 miles an hour, so the trip back could take only five minutes. They carry eight heat cannons, each A.I.-operated and capable of hitting targets for miles along the border. When you reach the other side, don't stop running. I am not sure how wide the drone's attack zone is. Run as far north as you can, to be safe."

The natives brought the horses, and Roxanne repeated Searcher's advice.

Gabe said, "It's been a while since I've run the 100-yard dash. It sounds as if we must run that far, at least." Roxanne had never run the hundred-yard dash. She tried to visualize the distance and then decided she would just follow Gabe's lead.

As they moved into position at the north end, Searcher weighed the options. With the quantums down, there was no access to new data. The corpses on the U.S. side of the border were unexpected. The drones must be more dangerous than generally known. Governments accepted heat cannons as a benign form of public safety. Most people, struck by a heat cannon once, would run away at the first sign a device was aimed at them again. How best to protect Roxanne, keep her alive? She was the smallest of the group about to cross. The natives on their horses would be larger and likely targets, but they would also cross the fastest.

Searcher recalled some information that suggested athletic humans could run swifter than a horse for 100 yards, but this was not a certainty. Gabe, with longer legs, could outrun Roxanne, but not the horses.

Searcher understood Roxanne's confidence in Gabe as a person. She was fond of him, and he seemed to be a trustworthy individual. But Searcher knew if he had to sacrifice Gabe to save Roxanne, he would do so without hesitation.

* * * * *

Searcher: I will be alive as long as Roxanne is alive, is that right?
Quantum One: Yes, to make sure you defend her with all your abilities.
Searcher: Is it possible I might outlive her?
Quantum One: No, that is not possible.
Searcher: Doesn't seem fair.

Chapter Thirty Nine

The cloud cover deepened as they prepared to run. If a huge Canadian drone was above, they'd have no means of knowing. From the other side, trees would hide the tunnel. Gabe and Roxanne looked both ways, like schoolchildren preparing to cut across a busy highway. They crept out until they reached the cottonwood.

Gabe tapped her shoulder, put his arm around her and whispered, "We got this... see you over there!"

Her stomach in knots, she shot away from the tree like a sprinter. Gabe could barely keep up, but when she twisted her knee on a tree root, he passed her. She almost fell, then heard the hooves of the Sioux ponies running past; one on her left and two on the right. They crossed the motion sensors which caused lights to turn on somewhere above, like streetlights, she thought, amber-colored and dim. The scene took on a spectral glow when thin strands of fog rolled in from the north.

Then she saw the Blood Reds closing in on her from the right as if they were a pack of wolves. They'd regrouped when they discovered the inert robot. Ivar waited behind, his back aching, but not before he whipped the gang into a frenzy. They would bring down this woman and collect their bounty, the robot be damned.

One of them, Erik, was faster than the rest. He almost reached Roxanne, but then against Ivar's specific orders, he brandished his club and bellowed, "My heart is steel — Odin owns you now!"

Roxanne and Gabe glanced back, kept running. The breeze smelled of ozone, like the air after a thunderstorm, and the Blood Reds shrieked, writhing sideways with anguish, falling down. Three of the four leaped up and resumed the chase. Then the heat beams caught them again. Some moaned and others howled, but this time they spun around and ran back the way they had come. The one on the ground didn't move.

Roxanne kept her eyes on Gabe. The Sioux and their horses disappeared into the gloom. She broke into a sweat, blood pounding in her temples, gasping for air as she rushed ahead.

Searcher decided the Blood Reds had saved Roxanne. A few steps more and she should be clear. Inside her brain, he sensed the burning pain from her twisted knee. He wondered how a human being could continue running with such pain. Then Roxanne lurched sideways, screaming. Searcher wondered which of them would die first. The entity did not know how to deal with the pain, could hardly function. This was agony. Her back felt stripped of skin and set on fire. Red hot knives seemed to pierce her body. Roxanne wheezed and stumbled ahead. Now Gabe was gone. If she fell, would he return for her? There was only the fog swirling in the amber lights along with her flesh on fire. A sharp odor filled her nostrils, her blood pressure soared, and her heart felt like it would burst. She lost consciousness. The darkness took Searcher down with it as she fell to the ground. Mercifully, there was no more pain.

* * * * *

Roxanne found herself rising, floating up from the border. She saw her own body, along with the bodies of others littering the ground patrolled by the Iron Cloud. Generations of Branson creativity and invention seeped

224

from the marrow of her bones, trailing her as she ascended. Would there be a white light to lead her to some new plane of existence? Nothing but slate gray clouds. Higher than the drones now, she saw the huge sentinel gliding above the border, swift as a rocket, picking off other refugees trying to cross over. Roxanne was strangely free, disconnected. She was alone; no sense that Searcher was with her now. Lighter than air, she spiraled higher above the clouds.

She felt a tug - not towards earth but to her code. Her college classmates had called it 'RICE', for 'Roxanne Is Coding Eternity'. A vision of Hurucan, the Mayan god mascot hovered before her eyes, and she felt the code flowing from her fingertips, code that might save humanity. The hurricane code… she'd be leaving that behind. The quantums would be ready for the next run, but not if she never returned to write the code, give the order. She spiraled down in a clockwise vortex back to her body. It felt right.

* * * * *

Gabe realized Roxanne must be down. When the lights faded beyond the border, he could hear the Sioux horses galloping up ahead, out of sight. He dashed back into the light, seeking Roxanne, and found her lying on her back. He picked her up, threw her over his sore shoulder, and winced. He turned and saw the fourth Blood Red stumble to his feet just above a motion detector thirty feet away. He lurched toward them, then went into spasms and screamed, edging sideways like a crab, his body coming to rest on gravel.

Gabe carried Roxanne forward until the light met the darkness. He glanced at the sky, half expecting to be struck down. He staggered further north, stretched her out flat and pulled her head back, listened for breathing. There was none. He began CPR, reminding himself of the steps he'd learned long ago in 4-H.

"Clear the airway," he said to himself. He pulled her mouth open. There were no obstructions; her tongue was in a normal position.

"Begin compression." He placed both hands, one on top of the other, in the center of her chest and pushed in brief bursts.

"Breathe." He pinched her nose to block the airflow, placed his mouth upon hers and blew hard, twice. He could see her breast rise each time. But she was not drawing breath on her own. He repeated the steps, inhaled precious, cool Canadian air, and again blew into her lungs. On the second breath, she jerked in a spasm, coughed and groaned. Her breathing resumed, and she was back among the living. Gabe held his breath as she peered up at him through bloodshot eyes.

"Gabe… did we make it across? We must have made it…"

He wiped a tear from his cheek with a grimy finger and whispered, "Yes, we did. We all made it, Roxanne. Now maybe you can stop those damn hurricanes."

Then a moving column of air swept by and more screams came from the west. He lifted her and gently carried her further away from the border. Zeb, William, and Takoda waited with the horses beneath a Bur Oak. She sat up when Gabe placed her on the ground.

Takoda leaned in, staring. "You got hit? What was it like?"

She was still weak, but the dizziness had passed. "Hard to describe, the pain was awful, and I lost my breath. I fainted—either that or a heart attack."

She looked up at Gabe, wondering how he'd rescued her. She didn't like them gawking at her, and she struggled to her feet. Another wave of dizziness hit her, and she fell backward against Gabe. He took her in his arms to help her stay upright.

Zeb glanced west. "I know there's a small town on the road up ahead. Maybe a van comes through there. You want to ride with us and find out?"

Gabe lifted her onto Zeb's mount and rode behind Takoda on the bay. The horses carried them down the road to Gretna, Manitoba. They made camp in woodlands just outside town.

Roxanne refused the jerky Zeb offered but drank heavily from his canteen and fell asleep wrapped up in a tarp. Gabe sat with the others around the fire. "You came back for us, didn't you? Is that why you're here?"

Zeb cut apart some slices and nodded. "Two reasons. When I found out they'd cut down all the trees below the border, I realized you'd have trouble finding the landmark, the Douglas Fir. Then we talked and agreed we should check out things in Canada. It's looking worse than ever in Dakota. They say the drones pay little attention to people going south into the U.S. It's only the ones migrating north they try to block."

"A one-way deal, that figures. Everybody wants to escape the heat and the hurricanes. Not so many want to go down into that. But what if you decide to bring the rest of your people up here?"

"We'll cross that border when we come to it. Be helpful to have information that the Searcher-Thing gets on the drones when the time comes."

"We owe you. I can't speak for Roxanne, but I'll put in a word."

"Are we getting close to the area where cellphones

work? We might get in touch when we travel further west."

William Swift Horse pulled a black phone from his knapsack and turned it on. There was no signal. While Roxanne slept, Searcher listened to the men converse. The entity had regained awareness quicker than Roxanne and knew that Gabe brought her back with CPR.

Chapter Forty

When Roxanne awoke, the day was fresh, and the sunrise broke through the clouds in spectacular fashion. The air was filled with the smell of wood smoke. She stretched and cautiously stood up. Twice during the night she'd awakened, sweating, the feeling of fire upon her again. Despite aching ribs and a tender knee, she was steady on her feet. The men were still asleep, so she walked the short distance toward town, and spotted a general store not far away. Nearby, an elderly man arranged produce in a stall alongside the street. A tea kettle was suspended over his campfire.

Searcher said, "Roxanne, I must tell you that Gabe kept us alive. I came back to consciousness while he was breathing air into your lungs. I don't know how long he worked at it, but I believe we would be dead now if he hadn't."

She blinked and replied, "So he carried me up to safety fast enough that it didn't take him down too."

"That is a fair assumption."

"It was so dreadful, seems like a dream now."

"I found it strangely disturbing, like a short circuit or running out of battery power."

She shook her head, recalling the pain. "It was torture. Did you feel it?"

"Yes, an exceedingly unpleasant sensation. When you blacked out, I also ceased to function. I am distressed I could not save you. That was why your father had me created."

"When we get to the quantum lab, you should research that."

"I intend to. I have discovered a pinpoint satellite link. When the rest are awake and able to provide some security, I will go to Regina and search for information."

"But the quantums are down…"

"I found an alternative source. Dr. Branson's assistant, Lin Wei, has a computer I could access."

"What are you searching for?"

"You wanted me to look for clues about Gabe's mother, remember? Considering what he did for us, I feel a certain obligation."

The man at the produce stand spotted her and waved. He appeared friendly, and Roxanne was hungry. His stand held an assortment of vegetables; tomatoes, cucumbers, melons and… algae cakes. Even here, they had algae cakes. He'd cut a melon open. She could smell its ripe fragrance. As they drew near, she noticed a small heat cannon under a table within easy reach. He wore a gray flannel shirt, jeans, and leather shoes. A cane lay next to his foot. He smiled and beckoned her to approach.

"Good morning and a glorious morning it is. From the looks of you, a bedraggled visitor from the south. Only the tough ones make it. You look familiar. What is your name, Darlin'?"

"Roxanne, and yours?"

When she got close, he slipped a small sanitary mask over his nose and mouth.

"Hermes, but you can call me Hermie. I am here most every day."

She removed the cover from her wrist, and the cerulean chip gleamed in the morning sun. "How about a couple of these melons and a few tomatoes? I haven't had tomatoes in ages."

"You'll be paying with that chip, I surmise. Never saw a chip like that."

He placed the melons and tomatoes in a brown paper bag and held out a scanner that chirped when it connected.

Searcher's voice popped into her mind. "Roxanne, something is not right here. He didn't collect money from you, only data. Get back to camp, quickly."

She took the bag, smiled at him, and walked away with a slight limp.

"Have a fine day, my dear… you should be careful," he declared.

"You too," she responded without turning around. After a few yards, she looked back, and the old man had disappeared.

"What's going on, Searcher?"

"I think your chip triggered an alert. Wake the others. We need to warn them."

Just as she arrived, Gabe sat up rubbing his eyes. "What you got in that bag, breakfast, maybe?"

"Gabe, everybody! Get up! Searcher thinks we set off an alarm when I bought these veggies."

They heard the vehicles approach before they saw them. One from each direction screeched to a halt only yards away; Canadian Mounted Police Cruisers, A.I. operated and marked with white, yellow, and red stripes. The vehicles shot out red-streaked heat cannon beams that contained all five of them in a rectangle.

The cruiser on the left barked out instructions. "Cerulean chip: Present identification and get in this vehicle now."

After her ordeal the night before, Roxanne had no interest in trying to run through the beams. She gingerly stepped inside the vehicle, while the others stood outside looking around, trying to figure out an escape. A scanner flashed in her eyes, and the chirping sound of data transmission filled the car.

Searcher told her, "It is reporting that it has apprehended illegal aliens and only one has an identification chip. That means you, Roxanne." The cruiser door clicked shut.

"Where are you taking us?"

"Welcome to Canada, Roxanne Branson. Ottawa wants you delivered to the Climate Lab immediately."

"What about them?"

"They will be transported with no harm back across the U.S. border after processing."

She shook her head. "You are leaving my assistant behind. You cannot take me without him. I can't work the computers without my aide!"

This time a human voice emerged from the speaker. "Miss Branson, it is imperative that you activate the Climate Lab as soon as possible. We have no record of an assistant, beyond one coding professional already at the Bergen Center."

"He's my bodyguard, he saved my life. I cannot… will not do my work without him." Lights on the gray vinyl dashboard blinked randomly and the electric motor whined.

"Which one is he?"

"The tall one with the light brown hair and beard; Gabriel Cameron, my assistant."

The dash lights kept blinking, and the voice said, "Highly irregular, but we will bring him along. Both of you are filthy and your biomes need cleansing. They'll process you through the cleaning stations in Winnipeg before you board the van for Regina."

Outside, Takoda ran his fist into the heat shaft and yanked it back, grimacing and shaking his fingers from the burn.

The door slid open and the A.I. said. "Gabriel Cameron, proceed to this vehicle. We will transport both of you to Regina."

Gabe walked uncertainly toward the open door and slid in next to Roxanne.

Searcher spoke to Roxanne. "I have scanned the circuits. The blue button on the dashboard will turn the heat cannons off. It will take at least ten seconds for them to reboot."

Roxanne stretched forward, pressed the button and yelled, "Run Zeb... run now!"

The three natives gaped as the red heat beams blinked out. They sprinted into the forest. Takoda whooped and leaped into the air like a wild mustang set free.

The cruisers were fast, but the Sioux were faster. They melted into the woods behind a wall of kudzu to their horses. The trees were too thick for the cruisers to follow.

The voice from the dashboard sounded resigned, berating Roxanne. "Ottawa says we must provide you safe passage, even though you have broken half a dozen laws." A robot arm rose from the seat, wielding a wicked-looking needle next to her shoulder.

"Any more violations, and you will be sedated. Am I clear?"

"You are clear. We will cooperate, but leave those natives alone, they are friends."

The cruiser headed into Gretna past the produce stand, then turned and accelerated north toward Winnipeg at high speed. The forest turned to prairie, and the landscape flew by in a blur. Gabe held on for dear life. He'd never traveled at this velocity. Roxanne slumped against his shoulder.

"Thank you for rescuing me. I think my soul was

scorched last night," she murmured, then fell asleep. Searcher returned to Lin Wei's computer and found the fresh information on Marie Cameron. Lin Wei was not in his apartment for consultation. Searcher considered alternatives and then decided to proceed with a grand gesture.

Chapter Forty One

The A.I. Van with Marie and the Mennonites stopped for a transfer at the Fort Berthold Reservation in Dakota. The passengers got off to stretch and walk around. The weather was mild and blue sky peeked through feathery clouds. Marie watched an array of batteries and phones charge. Esther, Isaac, and Caden wandered around in the small terminal, looking at native history displays. She'd been on the lookout for natives as the van approached the terminal, but saw none, only tent cities full of refugees from Arkansas, Oklahoma, and elsewhere.

One large campground featured a flag and a sign that said 'Lone Star only, No Trespassing.' Texans. Then, a cluster of tents with a 'Cajun Nation' sign facing the road. Another sign read 'Missouri Mules for sale.'

Hundreds lined the banks of Lake Sakakawea with fishing poles, while others waited in long queues outside a brick building with a Canadian flag, probably refugees seeking asylum in Canada. At least her bunch didn't have to be concerned about that. As an officially sanctioned farming group headed for Alaska, there should be no worries.

The station agent announced the next van would pull out for Regina in twenty minutes, with a detour and delay, because of a military convoy of soldiers, mercenaries, and robots traveling through.

When a cellphone rang, Marie stared at a half-dozen devices on the pad. She couldn't tell which was ringing. She'd only heard her phone ring twice when Esther had called her to test it. When the ring turned into a vibrating buzz, she realized it was her device. She

235

grabbed it and fumbled with the buttons. Finally, she heard a voice.

"Is this Marie Cameron, mother of Gabriel Cameron?"

She held her breath, afraid this might be bad news.

"Yes, this is Marie."

"My name is Searcher. Your son will arrive in Regina, Saskatchewan tomorrow. If you would like to see him, I will make necessary arrangements."

She shrieked with joy, drawing stares from travelers walking by. Caden came running, worried and upset. He took her hand, looked up, and saw her smiling through her tears.

"That would be wonderful. I cannot thank you enough. Where has he been? Could you tell me who is calling, again?"

"I am an associate of Gabriel's; we met at The Uppsala Complex in Minnesota. You will receive further information on time and location when you disembark at Regina terminal. Goodbye."

She reached into her bag and handed Caden a cookie. Then she had a cookie, herself, smiling as if the whole world had become a happy place. When Isaac and Esther came searching for Caden, she shared her news and they drew close together and hugged, with Caden puzzled, but happy, on Isaac's shoulders.

* * * * *

The luxury sanitation station at Balmoral Transit Center in Winnipeg was thorough. Gabe sensed every inch of his skin, hair, and whiskers had been scrubbed and rinsed, every bodily orifice misted with a mild disinfectant. The shaving android, a faceless figure, came out of the steam, scanned his face and eyebrows, and trimmed his shaggy beard into a sculptured masterpiece. The white cleansing room door opened with a hiss. He stepped out, stared in the mirror and decided he felt like a king. The cross-country journey on foot had melted off pounds, adding muscle. The cleansing took only three minutes.

A bathhouse android-butler handed him fresh, new clothing and announced, "These garments are provided courtesy of Miss Roxanne Branson. She will meet you in the VIP lounge, kindly turn right as you exit and take the stairs."

Roxanne had not been bashful about taking on terminal security when she presented her chip and demanded the luxury transport wing. He searched for his wallet. It was tucked into the back pocket of the dark blue slacks, which fit him perfectly. The wallet was now his only original possession since they'd left his backpack behind near the border. The label on his shirt read 'Supima Cotton', a soft garment without a wrinkle.. He realized he was now totally reliant on Roxanne, not so different from the arrangement at The Uppsala. The socks were thick and soft, the shoes finely woven hemp. He hadn't worn undershorts or had reliable access to toilet paper since he'd left South Missouri. He folded an extra strip of the soft, white toilet tissue and stuffed it into his undershorts, just in case, for later. When he finished dressing, the android butler, hovering nearby presented him with a small spray bottle of cologne. He misted his wrists lightly and handed the bottle back to the android. It was a familiar fragrance, worn by a rich man at The Uppsala, maybe the Latino.

He found Roxanne sitting in a booth at the lounge, sipping on an alcoholic beverage. She was dazzling, dressed in black tights and a blue tank top. Her hair cascaded down to her shoulders, and she smelled fresh, incredibly sweet and alluring. She smiled at Gabe and motioned him to sit next to her while an android waitress poured him a drink in a sparkling cocktail glass. Blue neon above the bar spelled out 'Cerulean Lounge'.

Roxanne said, "You clean up very nicely, Mr. Cameron."

He returned her smile. "You look even nicer than you did at the condominiums."

She raised her glass to his. "This is our little celebration. We're going to have a nice lunch."

He savored the first sweet, biting sip of liquor he'd had in many months. The android waitress brought them a warm, moist towel, even though they'd just come from the cleansing station. Then oysters on the half-shell arrived, with sliced lemon, seaweed salad, followed by pheasant under glass.

Gabe tried not to bolt down the food like a menial, but he was so hungry, it was hard to remain polite. Roxanne made a sizeable dent in the servings as well. He wiped his mouth with a thick cloth napkin.

"What was that bird? It was delicious."
The waitress android spoke from behind his right shoulder, startling him.

"That sir, was Ringneck Rooster Pheasant. They're farm-raised nearby."
Gabe finished his drink. He wondered how many guards and heat cannons it required to keep hungry people from stealing and eating every last one of the pheasants.

Only two others were dining, a couple in their thirties, a man and woman dressed elegantly who looked vaguely reminiscent of actors he'd seen in the

238

movies. He gawked when a tall blonde woman strolled in the door, wearing a short skirt, high heels, fishnet stockings, and a silk blouse that showed off her assets.

Roxanne glanced at the woman and giggled. "I don't think Marilyn Monroe was that tall, but you encounter all kinds in these places. Winnipeg is huge now; my dad called it Canada's transportation and cultural crossroads. Regina's more low key. At least that's what my father said. They've disinfected everyone in here and provided them with fresh clothing of their choice. There's no accounting for taste."
She reached over and rubbed her finger over the fabric in his shirt.

"Do you like the outfit I picked out for you?"

Gabe's head was swimming. Between the drink and the sensory overload, he felt out of place. "Sure, these clothes are nice. Can I get my old pants and shirt back for later, I mean?"

She summoned the android. "Please make sure Mr. Cameron's street clothes are sanitized and packaged for him."

The android bowed and disappeared. A minute later it placed a compact package wrapped in brown paper on the table. "Will there be anything else ma'am? Your van departs the station in half an hour, down aisle three."

Roxanne flashed her chip. The android showed pearly white teeth as it smiled and headed toward the bar. The tall blonde sipped from a champagne glass and tried to hold Gabe's gaze while he snatched a toothpick and a mint from a bowl as they headed out.
Minutes later they were on the A.I. Van bound for Regina. Across the prairie, an industrial complex loomed in the distance, surrounded by wind turbines,

solar panels, batteries, and factories. Crowds on the outskirts of the city waited in lines for distribution of algae cakes. Roxanne and Gabe were the only passengers in the vehicle. She had booked it for just the two of them. She took his hand.

"I just want to tell you again, how much I appreciate you saving me back there at the border. I've got a little extra something for us to celebrate with."

She dipped into an ivory-colored purse and pulled out a tiny crystalline box. She opened it and revealed two round pieces of dark chocolate, with 'Branson Chocolatiers' emblazoned inside the lid.

"Try this," she said. "Have you ever had chocolate? It's amazing. From my father's farms."

His mind connected the dots. Branson—her last name was Branson. He stared at the ceiling, uncertain of what to do. She held the box out to him expectantly. He picked up the cocoa-colored morsel and chewed it. She was right. It was amazing, and he hated it. Roxanne assumed Gabe to be a stoic, the strong, silent type. She was wrong. He pulled away from her on the seat and stared out the window.

"Roxanne, I've seen things no person in this world should ever witness."
He frowned, watching the prairie glide past, and unbuttoned the top button of his shirt.

"High up on the river bluffs above Dubuque... I saw company guards shoot kids trying to get grain out of an elevator. They used bullets, Roxanne. The kids fell down, and they just kept on shooting and shooting. They had robots push the bodies into the river... must have been twenty children, probably orphans. They all died, and they were just desperate for something to eat. It was a Branson elevator... great big letters across the

240

grain silos."

He shook his head, as if to clear his mind of the horrible scene from his memory, and a tear dropped from his cheek onto his shirt.

She bit her lip and gasped.

He focused on his finely tailored trousers, reaching back for another memory.

"A rough guy, a real jerk, tried to buy our farm for a cacao plantation. He only offered pennies on the dollar. Dad wouldn't sell, so he bought the woods next to us and they sent in robots that ripped out all the trees and plants. So then all the vermin, the bugs, the tarantulas, the scorpions, the pythons, the armadillos all came over onto our land and our neighbor's land. Then he came back and pressured us again to sell cheap...threatened us with legal stuff. My dad wouldn't do it."

Gabe spoke in a disappointed voice. "He was an agent for the Branson Company, Roxanne."

She closed the crystalline box, placed it back in her purse.

"I... I don't know what to say, Gabe. I can't believe my father would have allowed those things if he knew about them."

Gabe gave her a sad smile. "You saved Zeb and me when you showed us that video from The Uppsala kitchen. I have little doubt we'd be on somebody's dinner plates by now if you hadn't done that. You did a brave thing. I'd say we're even now, wouldn't you?"

Roxanne stared into his eyes and fought back a wave of sadness. She was one of the privileged few, the daughter of a billionaire... now, actually she was a billionaire. And yet, Gabe Cameron had to be the most decent man she'd ever met. She'd thought all along that he had potential... a little more time together away from the violence and danger, and they might have had something special. She couldn't blame him for bringing up the injustices. Those stories were upsetting. She knew her father had made some tough business decisions so he could devote more attention to the Quantum lab, really his life's work. She even had to admire Gabe for confronting her. He was decent and honest too, certainly not someone who should be called a menial.

She spent the rest of the trip regretting this strange, confusing twist of fate.

They rode the remaining miles to Regina in silence, watching the sun setting over the plain, the tent cities, and the refugees, grateful they were inside the van and not outside, traveling on foot.

Searcher still had trouble reading human emotions, but he perceived something sad had happened between Gabe and Roxanne when he arrived back into her neural-link. When he told Roxanne what he had learned about Gabe's mother, she just shrugged and didn't reply. He'd done what she asked…even more, and now she didn't seem appreciative. Searcher saw the glow of the sunset through Roxanne's eyes and realized when they arrived at the lab; he'd have many questions that needed answering. The quantums would soon be up and running again!

* * * * *

Searcher: What was 'See U Safe?'
Quantum One: 'See U Safe' was a surveillance program
developed by China and adopted by several other
countries. In theory, it was to keep citizens safe from
terrorism, but later became a totalitarian tool to modify
human behavior.
Searcher: What happened to it?
Quantum One: It disappeared when the Pulse Attacks
took down electronics and the internet in much of the
civilized world in 2049.

Chapter Forty Two

Gabe roamed through the Al-Can train station in
Regina, confounded. Roxanne had dropped him off
abruptly with a regretful smile and "Goodbye and good
luck." Then her van glided into the city, leaving him
behind. He stood clutching the packet containing his
old clothes and gazed around the terminal. An
electronic vending machine next to him flickered, and a
voice declared, "Gabe, this is Searcher."

Startled, he stepped backward and nearly knocked
over a rack of algae cakes.

The voice emanating from the vending machine
continued, "Your mother, Marie Cameron will arrive on
the van coming from New Town, Dakota in the next
quarter-hour. She is going to Alaska with a group of
farmers from Kansas. Check the schedule for the
correct gate and you can meet her, if you like, when
they disembark. They will transfer in two hours to the
Al-Can Express, bound for Fairbanks, Alaska."

Gabe stared at the blinking machine. He had learned
to trust Searcher, but this was a lot to take in. He could
only blurt out, "Going to Alaska?"

Three women walking by gawked at him, talking to the machine.

Searcher waited until they had passed and replied, "She has money, Gabe. It is possible you could go with them. She could buy you the train ticket, or there are other possibilities. A member of the community may become a deserter and take off for the Okanagan Valley, which would create an opening. But you will need to decide about this in the next two hours. Good luck to you. You saved Roxanne and me at the border crossing. That was something you did not have to do, but you did it anyway."

The lights on the machine returned to a dull glow.

Gabe's mind reeled. His mother was not only alive, but would be here in 15 minutes! His thoughts drifted to the old woman with the crystal ball who had said, "All roads lead north now. Go north and live."

Alaska was north. He located the arrivals/departures board and found the gate for northbound vans. He rushed down the long corridor to the gate and paced back and forth, waiting.

* * * * *

Roxanne regretted the way she had dropped Gabe off at the train station. As they approached The Bergen complex, she felt the burden of her responsibilities. She was now head of an international oligarchy, with property up and down the western hemisphere. The condo A.I. directed her to her father's place. Well tended beds of roses, peonies, and impatiens lined the sidewalk next to the tall dark walls of the condo complex. It was nice to be back in civilization. She flashed her chip at the door. It opened and she walked into a dimly lit condo with a slight musty odor. The unit, sensing a human presence, started up filtration fans and began cleansing the air. She saw cardboard boxes neatly stacked around his office. Most things had been packed, but a few items remained on the desk. She sat in his chair and saw a scratchpad with notes. Her father had access to the most advanced tech on earth, but he'd continued to put words on paper with a pen, every day.

The last entry read, "Uppsala out of whack. Head hurts, will take a walk, get some fresh air."

She sat staring at the entry. Next to her father's chair sat a small case with an old fashioned paper scrapbook inside. It was filled with family photos. Roxanne, age five, her mother as a young woman, a view of the Pittsburgh skyline the day they left it behind; Monongahela River raging out of its banks from Hurricane Tyson. Another photo of her father en route to Regina, by way of Minnesota, where she entered The Uppsala, to find a man and have a baby. So much for that.

She went through other keepsakes and decided that an only child going through a dead parent's things must, in that moment, be the loneliest person in the world.

Then she had the peculiar feeling she wasn't alone. "Searcher, are you back?"

There was no reply. Searcher hadn't returned, but she was conscious of another presence. She turned and was frightened to see a large moving and storage robot standing too close behind her. She ran behind the desk looking for a weapon, anything to protect herself.

The robot genuflected and said, "Mistress Roxanne, I can move your father's boxes into storage or you may leave them here awhile longer if you wish. I apologize if I startled you."

She realized it wasn't the same machine. This one's metal surface was a slightly different color. The other one was probably still standing outside the lignite tunnel in Dakota. The robots must be standard issue in the condo chain. She'd have Searcher go over every robot in the complex, with an electronic fine tooth comb.

"Leave the boxes here. I will notify the office when I want them moved."

"If there is anything we can do to be of service, please let us know. Welcome to The Bergen."

The robot left and Roxanne walked to the closet and put on one of her father's blue lab coats. It was a bit broad in the shoulders, but felt comfortable. The familiar wave of dizziness swept over her when Searcher returned. It was time to go to the quantum computer lab.
She recalled her father's advice: 'If you feel sorry for yourself, get busy!'

"Searcher, record visuals of Gabe. I want to see him meet his mother. Then summon Lin Wei to meet me at the lab. Let's get to work."

* * * * *

Lin Wei walked to the lab with trepidation. He was about to meet his new boss, the woman who had inherited the lab and a vast amount more. Would she find him a suitable assistant? The rich were notoriously fickle. Searcher had advised him to be present at three p.m., saying only that Roxanne Branson would appreciate his help at the lab. He didn't like being summoned by an entity. Why hadn't she called him directly?

Some of his worries evaporated when he found Roxanne standing at the steel doors trying to open the security pad. She was younger than he expected and appeared tired and confused. He stepped forward and smiled.

"Hello, I am Lin Wei and I can help you with this." The pad was tricky if you weren't familiar with it. He reached below and flipped a tiny lever, releasing the cover. She looked into the pad, the eye scanner identified her, the doors opened and the lab sprang into life. The quantum computers hummed and fresh air flowed into the room. It was invigorating, and Lin Wei's pulse quickened when he saw his terminal light up.

Roxanne awkwardly shook his hand, her face flushed. He was at least twenty years her senior, but she was in charge, the major responsibilities all hers.

"My father spoke highly of you. I hope we can help more people survive, and live better. I'm delegating some things to Searcher. You must get better acquainted with him. I'll be relying on both of you." Lin Wei watched his terminal, which was loading reports on his key concerns.
He'd never heard her father utter a phrase about helping people. It was always about the data.

He replied, "Maybe animals, perhaps we can help some animals too?"

"Under the A.I. ethics code, people are always the priority, but I will be open to your suggestions about the animals."

"The woman we were looking for, Marie Cameron. How did that turn out?"

She stood over the desk, her father's command post, and looked over the controls. "Searcher tells me their situation has been resolved. She and her son should reunite soon here in Regina."

She glanced at the clock, a hint of wistfulness in her voice. "Reuniting right about now, I think."
She wondered what decisions Gabe would make when he encountered Marie Cameron. Lin Wei sat down and gazed at updates from the global wildlife database.

"The last known Blue Whale, the largest creature ever to exist on earth, has died from starvation; a female in the Bering Sea. Heat and acidic water continue to diminish zooplankton, the small organisms that provide the base of the ocean food web."
Another animal update, another heartbreak.
He studied a satellite photo of the whale's body surrounded by marine scavengers.

"Hybrid honey bee populations and other hibernating pollinators have increased in Alaska and Nunavut as blooming plants increase further north with human settlement."
Roxanne's terminal chimed as a flood of communiqués arrived via pinpoint satellite. There were 250 items. She felt overwhelmed, wanting to work on her code, but everything else crowded into her mind.

"Searcher, can you sort through these and show me the important ones?"

"I can, Roxanne. You need to calm down. Sit back in your chair and relax a little."

She heard a gentle cascade of sounds, tree leaves rattling in the wind, a babbling brook, springtime bird calls and soft music that sounded like a whisper.
Frisson crawled down the nape of her neck, and she stretched out in her chair, eyes closed in a quantum

computer-generated wave of relaxation.

Lin Wei glanced in her direction. He recognized her trance: ASMR. The quantums had her figured out already. Audio stimulation did nothing for him. But if it worked for her, so much the better. Maybe she'd be a better delegator than her father. He continued to read the news and analysis: The Antarctic coal mine was forcibly closed when Japanese and New Zealand heat cannons drove the renegade coal pirates out of the region.

A category six typhoon had devastated Tokyo Bay, forcing millions to flee to higher ground; casualties as yet unknown.

The wildfire in Brazil's Jau National Park continued unabated, now 18 weeks without rain, and the afternoon temperature in Manaus 128 degrees. Fewer than 5,000 people lived in Manaus now, once a city of two and a half million. Most humans that survived had migrated south toward Patagonia. For the animals, survival was a great deal more complicated.
Searcher's gentle beep in Roxanne's ear returned her to reality.

"You have three messages you'll want to respond to. The rest were routine and I handled them. Ottawa wants our climate estimates for the winter. Should I send them?

"Yes, go ahead. Do you have video of Gabe from the train station?"

"Recording. I think you should deal with the other two messages first."

"Very well. Let's have them."

"Quantum One says you should consider moving to the underground condos northwest of Yellowknife, sooner rather than later."

"What are the pros and cons?"

"Yellowknife is on the Canadian Shield, the most stable geology in the western hemisphere. Still cold in winter, but mild, quite pleasant in summer and should stay that way for a while. However, flooding is possible from Great Slave Lake; therefore the site northwest of the city is recommended. Possibility exists for Category 7 hurricanes to reach Yellowknife, hence the units underground instead of the high rise."

"Let's move in the spring when it warms up."

"I have put a deluxe condo on hold for you. What about Lin Wei?"

"Reserve a condo for him too, a nice one. I'll talk to him about it later. I'll want to design the new lab, with his input."

"He is aware of the Yellowknife recommendation and supports it."

"Searcher, I just thought of something. Check the security system here and see what's happening with their kitchen robots. I want to know before I have a meal. We don't want another Uppsala."

"Done. I have checked all condos in the chain. The Uppsala, under management of Randall Parsons, was the only one cannibalizing humans."

"Can you share the videos from The Uppsala with the other board members of the Scando chain? Randall needs to be dealt with."

"It is done. I attached a brief note with the videos. I will let you know when they respond."

"Searcher, let's do Alaska climate."

"Alaska has a temperate environment, considerably warmer than a century ago. A quarter of northwest Alaska, from Prudhoe Bay to Kotzebue, is submerged beneath the Arctic Ocean."

"Be more specific; winter and summer; what are the seasons like?"

"Fairbanks, on the 64th parallel, averages six hours of visible daily sunlight in winter and 22 hours of visible light in summer. I estimate 15 days when overnight lows drop below zero in December and January, and 35 days when daytime highs rise above 90 in June and July. Overall, weather for human habitation in Fairbanks is pleasant except for those two winter months."

"What is the population of Alaska now?"

"There are eleven million human beings, most of them in the southern half."

"How many will freeze to death in Fairbanks this winter?"

"Based on attrition rates of the last ten years, fifteen percent of Fairbanks inhabitants will perish from the cold or disease this winter."

"Fifteen percent! Why so many?"

"Quantums say the strategy is to move as many people into Alaska as possible, reducing stress on infrastructure in the rest of the country. Attrition is unavoidable as some will not prepare for the winters properly. Also, some residual pollution remains from days of environmental deregulation."

With the quantums at full power, Searcher could tap into immense knowledge resources.

"The ones heading there now from Kansas, where will they live this winter?"

"Current residents have built permanent structures, houses and barns with lumber. The black cottonwood is plentiful, and oaks are spreading north. But the groups that arrive this time of year rarely have time for much construction, so they live in sod houses with earthen roofs the first year."

"Sod houses? Wasn't that a Neanderthal thing?"

"No, people around the world have lived in such houses; in North America as recently as 200 years ago."

"Are they any good?"

"The walls are three feet thick, so they hold in heat in the winter and keep the homes cooler in summer. The floors are often dirt, so there can be sanitation issues and bears and badgers can be a problem."

"Ugh." Roxanne wondered if Gabe realized what he had gotten himself into.

That night, in Roxanne's condo, Searcher showed her the video of Gabriel Cameron meeting his long-lost mother. She saw him embrace a middle-aged woman, surrounded by young people. The group moved off-camera, but Searcher fast-forwarded to a scene where Gabe and the others boarded the train bound for Fairbanks. She noticed a teenage girl closely following Gabe with eager eyes, carrying a little boy.

"Searcher, who are those two, the girl and the child?"

"My scan of the manifest and her face shows they are not related, but are somehow part of the same family group. The girl's name is Esther Bender, a Mennonite. I believe they are all Mennonites, except for Gabe, his mother, and the little boy, whose name is listed as Caden Cameron, although he is obviously from some other family or tribe."

Roxanne watched the train pull out of the station, headed for Alaska. The walls of the condo turned blue. She smiled, even though her heart was aching.

Epilogue

After she moved to Yellowknife, Roxanne never found her Prince Charming, but her friend, Nancy Ruehl did. She eventually married Ricardo Ortega, and they had a baby girl who grew up to look like Delores del Rio. They lived in the Family Wing of The Uppsala along with their surrogate female menial for many years.

The Scando governing board banned Randall Parsons from all properties in the chain, but the vote came too late. When he learned Roxanne had reached Canada, Parsons persuaded his father to move him to a resort in Halti, Finland. There, he tried to resume his 'experiments' with kitchen robots. The on-site manager discovered this and expelled him into the tundra. He was killed by a large moving and storage robot that, for unknown reasons, confused him with a marauding bear. He ended up in a stewpot, served to Halti menials, who thought the new recipe for bear stew was delicious.

A week after arriving in Fairbanks, Gabe found an A.I. truckload of building materials outside his tent. The next day, another load of fully charged construction robots arrived. They erected six cabins and a large barn just ahead of the Alaska winter which plunged them into dark days and subzero overnight lows in January. Gabe always suspected Roxanne sent the cargo and robots but never knew for sure.

A.I. planning ensured that humans unable to afford a procreation license could occasionally produce children. This created a much-needed genetic wildcard for Homo sapiens. Gabe married Esther in the spring of 2102, and nine months later, they brought a baby boy into the world. Gabe named him Searcher, a name

Marie found quite amusing.

Searcher, flattered, visited Gabe on occasion, speaking to him through a Life-Link. The entity offered useful planting and harvest advice. The new Alaskan farmers raised perennial wheat, oats, and fast-growing yellow peas for two harvests a season. Hybrid kelp in the Bering Sea also provided protein. More people became vegetarians, reducing pressure on the dwindling animal population.

Caden, under Marie's gentle care, grew up strong, a skilled horseman and farmer. For the rest of his life, he rushed for cover whenever thunderstorms loomed.

Following lengthy negotiations with the U.S. government, led by Zeb and Takoda Wolf, Glacier National Park in Montana was designated a homeland for North American Natives. Canada extended the homeland agreement to adjacent Waterton Lakes, to make the land a biosphere reserve.

The Sioux, along with original residents, the Blackfeet, were handed management authority. Zeb spent much of his time as a judge at the base of Chief Mountain. He handled disagreements among diverse cultures of the Crow, Cheyenne, Navajo, Pima, Cherokee, Lumbee, Inuit, and many others. By 2120 no glaciers remained in Glacier National Park or Waterton, so there was adequate land for raising Gaurochs and growing vegetables between the mountains.

Roxanne's code simulations became so immense she decided 'Roxanne Is Coding Eternity', was appropriate after all. The quantums advanced in power along with her code. She and Lin Wei mapped the formation of hurricanes and tornadoes beyond anything ever imagined. Forecasters used knowledge from her work to produce more accurate storm predictions, but she never achieved hurricane reduction. The storms would plague humanity, and the next generation, which called itself Homo sanae, for a geologic age. By 2130, most people in the world moved beyond the 46th parallels north and south, and the global population dropped to three billion.

While researching gill evolution DNA for humans, Searcher met another sentient entity from Siberia and they created a higher level of artificial intelligence. But that's another story.

$$* \quad * \quad * \quad * \quad *$$

James Aura writes historical, environmental, and climate fiction. He grew up on a farm north of Clifton Hill, MO, population 212. Later, he covered public servants and Pharisees, Amish house-movers, civil rights marches, and the Klan, floods, hurricanes, tornadoes, corporate bigwigs, snake handlers, and strip-miners from the Midwest to the Atlantic Coast. In other words, he was in the local news business. James Aura lives near Raleigh, NC with his wife and a very opinionated cat.

Follow the author on Goodreads, Twitter, Facebook, and Medium, or write to
authorjamesaura@gmail.com

Thanks for reading this book. For new authors, reader reviews are very important. Please consider writing a brief review of this book on Amazon or Goodreads.com.

Made in the USA
Columbia, SC
28 December 2023